I0681326

VICTORIA

John Molik

John Molik
Victoria

ISBN: 978-0-473-48982-3 (paperback)
ISBN: 978-0-473-48984-7 (ebook)

© 2019 All rights reserved. No part of this publication may be reproduced, distributed, or transmitted in any form or by any means, including photocopying, recording, or other electronic or mechanical methods, without the prior written permission of the publisher, except in the case of brief quotations embodied in critical reviews and certain other noncommercial uses permitted by copyright law.

Disclaimer: This is a work of fiction. Names, characters, businesses, places, events and incidents are either the products of the author's imagination or used in a fictitious manner. Any resemblance to actual persons, living or dead, or actual events is purely coincidental.

Acknowledgments

When doing the research for my third novel *The Three Poisons*, I came upon an interesting article written by Jelor Gallego in the December 25, 2016, edition of the *Futurism Newsletter* entitled "Becoming Borg: What is a Hive Mind in Science and Could Humanity Get There?" This article profoundly stimulated my interest and got me thinking about what it would mean to humanity if, in the not too distant future, we were all connected into some sort of hive mind via a client/server computing network architecture. That night I closed my eyes, and my character Victoria was born.

Some say that we are already in a collective hive mind. The Global Consciousness Project out of Princeton University has data to say just that, but the experimental results, which started with the PEAR project in 1979 by Robert Jahn, Dean of Engineering and Applied Science, has many skeptics. Yet, regardless of whether we are already in a non-physical universal mind, there would be little doubt that this could be achieved via neural implants and wireless technologies, much like the United Federation of Connectedness, the fictional society proposed in Victoria.

In fact, just today, on July 16, 2019, Elon Musk announced that his company Neuralink is making progress toward its goal of connecting natural and artificial intelligence in humans. So, as Pandora's box has been already been opened, it is now not a matter of *can* this be done, but *should* this be done, and if so, how do we implement these technologies in a moral, ethical, and safe manner. Just a few years ago, Elon Musk and many others working with AI had warned us that if not rolled out carefully, this emerging technology could be the end of the human race as we know it. Elon's answer? If you can't beat it, join it. Who knows what the future entails, but one thing is for certain—uncertainty.

Writing Victoria was a marvelous journey for me. The spiritual implications of what mankind is about to face are staggering. The novel began writing itself and I found myself feeling eerily connected on so many levels with the story as the characters became alive and acted their part on my mind's stage.

There are many unseen people behind the scenes that help a novel come to life, including the formatting and publishing companies, blogs, webzines, university newsletters, and of course, the retailers. I'd like to thank all of those working in these endeavors for assisting me on my journey.

In addition, I would like to thank Joshua Hibbert, graphic artist based in England, for once again producing an absolutely fantastic cover for my novel. Joshua has an incredible gift of converting concept to creation.

And finally, I would like to thank my editor, Marja Stack of Clearlingo Editing and Proofreading in New Zealand, who once again has been indispensable for helping me deliver a polished manuscript.

"Power without wisdom is tyranny; wisdom without power is pointless."
—Iain Pears

Chapter 1

Temple Dome (formerly Cheyenne Mountain
Complex, Colorado)
UFC Amerexico
June 1, 2413

"Careful! If you don't get this part right, you will blow us all to hell!"

Boniface Rotner faltered, shook his head, and aggressively ran his hands through his shoulder-length black hair.

Cornell Elam, a bald 54-year-old technician from the sect, leaned against the stainless steel railing which encircled the metal alloy chamber. Peering down, he glimpsed the top of Boniface's mat of black hair. Cornell wiped sweat from his forehead with the back of his hand. He pleaded. "Come on! You can *do* this!"

Boniface Rotner gazed up through the metal tunnel and bit his lip. "Of course I can, Mr. Elam."

Boniface, at only 15 years old, was far ahead of anyone in their sect in intelligence, creativity, and focus. Earlier, it was decided by sect leaders that he was the only one that could accomplish this critical mission. Not only was Boniface the only one who understood the technical complexity of this 398-year-old technology, he also had very small hands due to his age, which was a crucial job requirement for this particular task.

Having recently resurrected the bank of Moray generators using his keen intellect, time was of the essence.

Boniface grasped the magneto coil wand and carefully inserted it into the capacitance resonator of the high-voltage transformer. *Mr. Elam is right. This goes wrong and this entire community will be enveloped in a ball of super-heated plasma.*

Cornell's breathing quickened and his palms were clammy. Fidgeting, he mindlessly looked right then left, and replied, "Alright, then! But, you got to hurry, lad! You got to hurry!" Cornell nervously glanced over his shoulder as if the empty ten-by-ten-foot, fully contained and impenetrable control room was suddenly being breached by a pack of rabid wolverines.

Sweat was pouring down the nape of Boniface's neck, but he paid little attention to it. Busy concentrating on the task at hand, he knew that the magneto wand must not touch the quantum harmonic oscillator. The Moray generators were at full bore, producing over 5,000 kilowatts of raw electrical power, and were just one step away from being connected to the Tesla scalar interferometer which, when ignited, would produce a thin, impenetrable shell of electromagnetic energy hovering over the sect's temple and surrounding area. No weapon, or even gamma radiation from an electromagnetic pulse, would be able to touch those living under it. But, if Boniface screwed this up and touched the oscillator, it was lights out for every living thing in a ten-mile radius.

Suddenly, the dead quiet of the sealed control room was interrupted by a strange, distant whirring sound.

Like a cocker spaniel sensing the scampering of a squirrel, Cornell jerked his head in the direction of the sound. "Shit! Those are fucking incomings!" He pounded the steel railing with both fists. "Hurry!"

Boniface squeezed his eyes tightly to assuage the anxiety and regain focus. Opening them slowly, he made sure his steady hand did not waver. The magneto wand just had to pass by the hidden oscillator and make contact with the bridging terminal.

The sound of the incoming missiles, likely all nuclear-tipped, grew louder and louder as their perilous cargos came closer to their target.

"For fuck's sake, Rotner! It's now or never!"

Boniface didn't like swearing, as it was against their religion. Besides, it was Mr. Elam who had taught him acceptable words from the past to use as substitutes. Yet, he also realized that when your life and the lives of all your community looked like it was nearing their end, man's evil tongue could sometimes release vulgarities, so he forgave Mr. Elam.

Figuring he had about five seconds, he quickened his pace. Biting his lip, he edged his hand forward through the small gap toward the contact plate.

A thin, shrill voice, like the cry of a dying mouse, emanated from Cornell Elam. He held his head in his hands.

Four inches to go. Boniface precisely guided the wand upward. The sonic roar of the incoming missiles was now vibrating the entire control room. It was now or never.

As soon as Boniface touched the plate, an ear-shattering electronic clang and hum assaulted their ears. The hair on his head stood on end as if he was grabbing the top of a Van de Graaff generator. The banks of LED lights on the control panels illuminated just before the entire room shook violently.

Cornell Elam was thrown from his perch into the steel chamber, landing on top of the 15-year-old.

Boniface's face was red hot. This was the last thing he felt before his rapid descent into total darkness.

* * *

She appeared before him, a soul as white as heaven. Rapidly blinking his eyes, he failed to grasp where, when or even who he was. The images came back slowly, but then the pain began.

"Boniface," she whispered. "You are with us once again." Smiling, she adjusted her gown and pulled off her pink surgical mask.

He still had visions of angels flitting through the vacuum of space. *This woman. I know her. She's an angel?*

Her voice was as sweet as a nightingale's song. "Boniface Rotner, wake up." She glanced over her shoulder, then spoke again. "I'll be right back."

As she suddenly disappeared from his frame of reference, Boniface tried to quickly sit up, but realized he couldn't due to pain in his lower ribcage. *Reality is indeed an enemy.* Frustrated, he simply resigned himself to his waking thoughts, which seemed to be increasing in both speed and intensity. *I've been hurt. Yeah. I'm in the hospital. Yeah. Why did I get hurt? Is this our God's fault? Why did he take my angel away?*

She came back holding a syringe filled with amber liquid. Smiling once again, she quickly injected the syringe into the clear plastic PICC line that was firmly embedded in his arm. "This will make you feel better, more alert."

Within seconds, he was feeling less drowsy. Within a few minutes, everything came rushing back to him—his name, what he was doing, and where he was. He nodded slowly. "What's your name?"

The 18-year-old nurse crinkled her nose in a funny gesture, just like a mother would at her child. Pointing at her badge, she replied. "Elane." She paused. "Elane Scarponi."

He was awestruck, staring up at her beautiful face. Her hair, a mousy brown, was tied up in French braids and a long pony tail. Her eyes were a deep chocolaty brown and communicated a warm, loving feeling. She had freckles, not too many of them, all in the right places. Small dimples were evident when she grinned.

Even though he was well into puberty, Boniface had been too busy being a child prodigy, saving the sect and resurrecting the Temple Dome to entertain the idea of the opposite sex, yet now, lying in bed and completely dependent, he felt a powerful feeling of attraction. *I wonder how old she is?*

Elane crossed her arms and tilted her head. "You're a hero." She paused. "You *know* that, right?"

It came back to him slowly. His mind's eye envisioned climbing down into the control room tunnel while Cornell Elam was nervously yelling from the railing above. Boniface could even remember Cornell's sweat dropping down into the tunnel and ricocheting off the interferometer.

The explosion. That's what he remembered now. It had shaken the entire room and sent Mr. Elam down on top of him. *The nukes didn't get through! I did it!*

She stood patiently with her eyes wide open. Leaning forward, she implored him to answer.

"Oh, yeah. I guess I am," he finally replied.

Elane winked at him, then giggled warmly.

Dear lord! I've never felt so attracted to a female, ever! Oh, my! What does this mean? She's way too old for me, isn't she? I'm too busy anyway. What a joke, my thinking these frivolous thoughts!

He shook his head to clear his mind, then sat up, wincing in pain. "Ow!"

"Easy now. You have a broken rib."

Lowering himself back down, he continued. "Is Mr. Elam alright?"

Elane leaned in. "Yes," she said, folding her arms. "Minor concussion like you and that's about it, really. Some scrapes and cuts."

Boniface felt the rush of the drug entering his nervous system. He felt giddy and his mind began racing. He sat up again, this time wincing but remaining upright. "Elane."

"Yes, Boniface."

"I have to ask you something important, OK?"

"Sure."

Boniface looked out the window to his right. Although the community was buried under a mountainside, the infirmary was close enough to the outside wall to allow a portal to have been drilled and a thick, circular silicone window to be installed for natural light. He gazed at the rolling mountains in the distance and the dry but thinly forested rocky outcroppings surrounding the Temple Dome community. Turning back to look directly into her eyes, he asked. "Do you believe in the Lord?"

"Rodolpho?"

He shook his head quickly. "Not Rodolpho Depaul, our savior, but the real Lord. The one that Rodolpho was trying to let back into the minds of humanity."

Elane tilted back slightly and stared forward with a fixed expression. She recited as if on cue. "Our Lord, Rodolpho Depaul, was electrocuted, died, and on the following Thursday, was rendered again." She paused as a thin smile emerged, then added unconvincingly, "The blood of the man."

Boniface closed his eyes in a slight defeat. "No. Not the religious story."

She replied quickly with more aggression. "It's not a story. It really happened and has been proven to be true by the Irrefutable."

"I know that, Elane. Of course, but Rodolpho was simply a courageous man who was trying to show us the way out."

Elane quickly glanced over her shoulder. "Shh!" She placed her finger on his lips. "We mustn't speak so lowly of Rodolpho, now, should we?"

"But, Elane, it is written in the Holy Texts that Rodolpho was a prophet only." He implored her. "You know, the blood of the *man*?"

Elane looked confused. "Yes. But we needed *that* man

to accomplish the impossible. A man can be transformed, Boniface. Don't you think?" She nodded with wide open eyes. "An animal, including a human, can be transformed into a god, just like Victoria."

Boniface flinched. "She's no god!" He turned quickly. "She's a computer."

"And who said God is not?"

"Not what?"

"A computer."

They both paused in thought.

"I don't know, Elane," he confessed. "I am so confused." He looked down. "Victoria tried to nuke us. Kill us all." His head dropped. "Do you believe in the cause?"

"To shut down Victoria for good?" She stared out the window with a vacant expression.

"Yeah. That one."

"We have to," she replied in a deadpan voice.

He looked up at the electric, ionized, blue plasma dome sparkling high above the community. "And is that because she's not God?" He paused. "But a murderer?"

Elane shrugged. "God kills a lot of things. Doesn't mean he or she's wrong, does it? Just look at the cycle of life." She smiled. "You can't make an omelet without cracking a few eggs, now, can you?"

Boniface giggled in frustration.

She looked at him deeply and honestly. "You need to rest." Fluffing up his pillow, she continued. "And not wrestle with all these esoteric concepts."

Her somewhat disconnected but honest thoughts made him even more attracted to her. "OK, you win."

"What did I win?"

"My heart."

Elane Scarponi replied with a weak smile, then quickly turned and disappeared like the figments of a dream.

Chapter 2

UFC AustraPasifika
Marsh Land Community
July 5, 2430 (17 years later)

The heaviest rain had finally eased, giving Pierre Lewalski a chance to duck out of his PolyDome without getting completely drenched. Sauntering along the Avon River, he picked up a discarded baggie and began to whistle somewhat unmelodiously. A drug addict, commonly known as a Bumper, walking with a stiff gait on the other side of the river, jerked his head from mindlessly staring straight ahead to glaring at Pierre with a grimace that only a hard-core Bumper could muster. Pierre simply smiled back across the divide and returned a cheeky wink, which seemed to have at least elicited a minor grunt from the IceT junkie. Seeing a trash can badged with the normal United Federation of Connectedness (UFC) warning label "Rubbish. Non-Ionizing Radiation Only", he quickly disposed of the wanton zipper storage bag, most likely discarded the previous night.

He was on his way to see Thaddeus Swank, his best friend from childhood. Both Pierre and Thaddeus shared a common perspective on life, which could best be described as flippantly trivial with a dash of irreverence. Life was, in itself, a ludicrous concept to both of them, having grown up in this era of

Victoria and the artificially intelligent somnolence that it perpetuated. Of course, neither had anything to complain about. Pierre's ancestry, which could be traced all the way back to the original Stewart Island Survivorship Colony, gave him many privileges that ordinary Non-Luds (NLs), or commoners just didn't have, such as being able to date Claressa Siegfriedt, one of Victoria's esteemed science advisors. Although many progressive social policies and liberal ideas had taken hold over the past three-hundred years, ancient blood-line elitism was still alive and well.

Pierre was a handsome man, 35 years old, with dark hair, ever so slightly overweight, with the proverbial incipient spare tire, yet he retained his boyish, somewhat sporty, good looks. Many who had enjoyed studying the past, thought he looked very much like Vince Vaughn, an actor from the days before the Micronova or the MN as it was known. Of course, he'd rather have his girlfriend local, but Claressa was required to live and work on the complete opposite side of the world in UFC Astana. Fortunately, she was able to regularly visit Pierre here in his hometown of Marsh Land (formerly, Christchurch, New Zealand in the pre-MN days). Pierre was not fond of traveling and disliked everything to do with XSpacing: the snarky robot pilots, the antigravity headaches, the shitty lemon and mint air fresheners that most public craft used, and the often-dirty, plastic, disposable e-book reading devices discarded all over the floor. Disgusting. Ancestry definitely had its privileges, though he was still required to work twenty hours per week at the aquaculture co-op, which suited him fine, as he was a very keen fisherman.

Thaddeus, on the other hand, had no ancestral connections, only digital ones. His only real position in society came from his immense knowledge of the past. Swank was one of only several "Keepers of the Cloud"—the Cloud was an old, disused network used by pre-MN societies to communicate and store data. The Cloud was also referred to as the Internet, but that term was so mundane that it was hardly used by anyone, even historians like Swank. The Cloud Data Seeds had been handed down through generations of Keepers until one day it landed in the lap of Chauncey Gilchrist, a withdrawn and reclusive nerd who could barely keep his hair combed let alone be responsible for approximately 122 Zettabytes of data. So, five years ago, Thaddeus Swank, knowing Chauncey's unquenchable addiction to high-risk gambling, challenged Chauncey to Whibble, a high-stakes AI game involving hologram masking, cheese grating, onion chopping (and other sous chef skills), astral projection, remote viewing, virtual surf lifesaving, and romantic fantasy role play assessment, all graded and scored by Victoria's inert Gaming Module. And after a mind-bending thirty-two-hour marathon session, Thaddeus just barely inched by to take the stake, which of course was the titanium lockbox of precious Cloud Seeds.

But today, Pierre was not thinking about Claressa in Astana or Cloud Seeds at all. Thaddeus had told him of an even more interesting collection that he had kept hidden, to be revealed at just the right time, and today was the "right" time. The collection contained a time capsule from the pre-MN year 1975, and of course, there was no one else with whom he wanted to share this experience, the first-hand unveiling of the contents, but his number one buddy, Pierre Lewalski.

Rounding the bend in the river, Pierre climbed over the levee built from a composite of polymer, silicone (for traction) and crushed granite. The levee gave him enough altitude to get a sneak peek of the High Coastal Mountain range (formerly known as the Kaikouras), which were glazed in a glistening cover of white snow, as if the Creator herself had dipped a feathery brush into a pure white icing sugar frosting and artistically covered the calico mounds of chocolatey browns, dusty grays, and the folded clefts of the blue-tinged valleys. The air was crisp, fall-like, with a light southerly breeze and puffy white cumulus clouds spread out across the Marsh Land plains like mallow cream puffs in a vast sea of blue. *Jeez. How could I ever leave this place? Who says Claressa can't run the UFC from here?* Pierre knew he was just kidding himself, albeit, it is said that the mind of man *can* move mountains, something of which the worldly philosophers had never attributed to the pervasive, sovereign artificial mind of Victoria, who was running the UFC.

Pierre squinted as the coll (short for collective, or neighborhood) came into view. Thad's coll was a typical hinter (the area outside UFC capitals) comprised of PolyDomes in various sizes and layouts. Most were painted in earth tones and consisted of a central living area (called the base) with hallways connecting small dome-shaped apartments (called cells). A typical coll housed about a hundred or so people. The base usually had a kitchen, bathroom, shower halls, all the latest hologram projectors to watch the ID (the Information Dispenser, a global network like the former Cloud), sound-proof entertainment system rooms, and games rooms. Usually, the base led out to a large outdoor area and garden that contained a fruit and vegetable garden, plus an aesthetic area complete with trees, shrubs, and flowers. Some colls had living springs, salt and fresh water ponds for aquaculture, and barn areas for the regulated farm animals.

The UFC strictly controlled farm animals and their numbers, and every coll was surveyed and monitored by Victoria. Animals must be sacrificed in accordance with strict laws that minimized pain and suffering. Their living areas had to be designed according to the Codex Animus, a dictate of codes, rules, and laws. A pong paddle (magnetic device that comfortably put the animal to sleep before its demise) had to be used. The only animals allowed to be kept for domestic food purposes were salmon, trout, chickens, and sheep. Any violation of the strict regulations was met by a visit of a team of genetically enhanced humans with a bad attitude called suplias. Only one violation was allowed, and after that, the entire coll was taken to Astana for Perfect Justice, which was the meting out of criminal sentences that holistically redeemed the offender. A coll therefore tried to simply eat the food provided by its own area and everyone took their turn to maintain it. Regional colls traded among themselves to bring in a variety of foodstuffs and other items which were natural, easier to raise, or in higher supply to a specific coll or hinter region.

Pierre clapped his hands in anticipation, then put his finger on the sensor for Number 14, which was Thad's cell.

"Chump!" yelled Thad through the wireless intercom. "I'll buzz you right in, ho!"

About twenty years prior, it had become fashionable to use the word "chump" for the overused slang expressions of *Mah bro*, *dude*, or *mate*. *Ho* was the new *yo* or *man*. It was thought to have started after a series of texts by a then-celebrity and teen idol, Rhett Wharfield.

"Ho! I'm so looking forward to the unveiling."

Thad's echoing laugh slowly diminished through the intercom as the door to his cell was unlatched.

Pierre and Thad stood there just shaking their heads.

"Wow. Just look at you," said Thad. "Your face just beams with light and energy." He smiled and nodded. "You're in love, chump!"

"Ho! Come on!" Pierre looked slightly embarrassed. "It's just the air outside." He hugged his arms to himself and shook. "Cold!" He pointed up and to the left. "Icy wind coming down off the High Coastals!"

Thad threw his head back. "Oh. Is that what it is?" He paused. "Hey, do you want a drink? A diffuser? A glycerol soda?"

Pierre nodded. "Yeah. OK, I'll have a diffuser."

"I got apple, black tea, lemon, or peppermint."

"Let's go for the black tea."

Thad smiled, then quickly walked into the prep, a small kitchen-like area that contained the very basics: the diffuser device, a DE (direct energy) oven, a toaster wand, sink, garbage dissolver, and various utensils.

"Hey, so you said that there are two capsules?"

"Two what?" yelled Thad over his shoulder.

"Two time capsules!" replied Pierre with a slight frustration.

"Oh, yeah. One is from a boy. Ten years old at the time." He paused to pour the drink. "His name was Reece Hickey." Thad grabbed the cups and carried them out. "And the other is from his father, a Roland Hickey, age 34." He handed a warm cup of diffuser to Pierre.

"Chump, that's mighty exciting. I mean, two different generations represented."

"Yeah, I know." Thad's mind was on fire. "It's fantastic!"

Pierre put his diffuser down on the table, then rubbed his hands together. "Well, shall we?"

Thad put his drink down as well. "Let's do it, ho!"

Like a couple of giddy school boys, they walked into the back room of the cell. Soft rays of light springing from the east shone through the round silicone polymer window like golden arrows. A fantail bird hopped and danced with gaiety through the yellow bulb tree.

The steel, military-green, 455-year-old trunks were in the corner of the room and had the normal signs of aging of random dents, scrapes, and rusted areas, but overall, they appeared in fairly good condition.

"So," began Pierre. "You were saying these were your great-grandfather's?"

Thad bent down and picked up the bolt cutters. "Try great-great-great-great-great..." He paused to look up. "How many was that?"

"Five?" offered Pierre.

"OK, yeah, so add another two."

"Great to the seventh power?"

"Something like that."

Thad put his gloves on and held the large cutters in his hands. The heavy tool was pointed down at the floor. "And they were given to him." He paused and looked up. "The story goes that they were discovered in a hillside cave in the Golden Love Conservation Estates (GLCE) that used to be a suburb of a pre-MN city called Los Angeles."

"I've heard of that."

"Yeah. Some place south of that city. In 1975, it was a community called Rancho Palos Verdes."

"And now it's the GLCE?" He nodded. "What sacred animals does it contain?"

"Now?"

Pierre nodded.

"Horses, bobcats, raccoons, tule elk, coyotes, rabbits, and skunks."

"Skunks! Chump! I never understood why Victoria keeps those in the GLCE!"

Thad rolled his eyes. "God knows, chump." He paused. "God knows."

"More like Victoria knows."

"Like I said."

Thad walked over to the first trunk and placed the cutters onto the padlock. Spreading his arms out with the handles apart, he said, "This one's Reece's."

"The boy's?"

Thad nodded, then quickly cut the lock with a loud crack.

He bent down, unfastened the latch, and peered inside. "Chump! Holy Rodolpho!"

"You turning Lud on me now?"

Thad snickered. "Check this shit out!" He began pulling items out. "OK, wow!"

"What?" yelled Pierre.

He began placing the items on the floor. "OK, we got a Whee-lo, a Magic 8 Ball, a pet rock..."

"Pet rock? What the fuck is that?"

Thad sneered as he dug a little further. "And, oh my Victoria!"

"That's more like it."

"Check *this* shit out!" He raised it into the air as if it was manna from heaven. "An Estes rocket complete with engines, igniters, launch pad, and stand."

"What does that do?"

His eyes were like two flaming stars. "Chump! I've heard about these." He paused. "They were all the rage back then."

Pierre shrugged. "Anything else?"

"OK, wait." Thad grabbed the last few things. "There's a Cox C/L trainer airplane and a..." He picked it up. "Wow! A Mattel Vertibird helicopter."

"Chump! What is all this crap?"

Thad gave Pierre an icy stare. "It's not crap! This stuff would be in high demand. I bet the Museum of the Pre-MN History in Mountain High would pay me major chips for this."

Pierre picked up the Estes rocket and gave it a sniff. "Uh, not for this one." He handed it back to Thad. "That's black powder in there." Pierre sniffed again and winced. "Among other banned substances."

"So? The museum would take it."

"Ah. I don't think so. You know how Victoria is about weapons of the past."

"It's not a weapon, Pierre! It's a harmless rocket that goes really high and fast."

"Still. I don't think that the museum will even take it, considering—"

"Look. We'll just use it."

"What?"

"Fire this fucker off."

"And risk Perfect Justice? Are you insane?"

Thad's face was blank like a mask. "She's insane."

"Who? Victoria?"

Thad had a fake smile plastered across his face. "She's an Apollo archetype."

"Chump! What are these words? Some archaic expressions?"

He shook his head. "It means she's a haughty bitch with no feelings. She favors logic and abstract simulation over human closeness and empathy."

"Yeah, but she keeps us safe."

"From what?"

"Ourselves. You know, the Thanatos drive, the death drive inherent in all of us."

Thad smirked. "So, we need Perfect Justice then?"

Pierre squirmed slightly. "Well, we mustn't speak of these things."

Thad looked up to the ceiling. "Yeah, you can go to fucking hell, Victoria."

Pierre shook his head violently. "I think your constant wallowing in the past is affecting your judgment, chump."

Thad caught himself and quickly ruminated on the state of their existence. "It's not that bad."

Pierre pinched his nose. "No, it's not. Humans have never had it this good for so long."

"So, is it our hearts then?" He shook his head. "Always restless, never satisfied?"

"The traumas of the past. It is written in the Seeds."

"Yeah, well..."

Pierre looked at his chronometer hologram. "Come on, open up the other!"

Thad smiled, walked over, and snapped the lock. "Wow! This one is sweet as well!"

Roland's trunk contained an HP calculator, a soap on a rope, a mood ring, and a "Keep on Truckin'" T-shirt.

"Ho! This stuff is totally condensing," whispered Pierre. *Cool* had been replaced in the vagaries of informal speech as well.

"Yeah. And check this out." Thad pulled out a cassette tape of KC And the Sunshine Band and an 8-track tape of an assortment of songs by an artist named Gino Vannelli. The assortment was called *Storm at Sunup*. "Now this shit is *totally* condensing!" He shook them. "These were put into machines, read, and played over amplified sound waves!"

"Analog magnetic?"

"Yeah."

"Wow. That's ancient technology." Pierre stared at the Gino

Vannelli tape cover. "Damn! Look how ugly those fuckers looked back then."

The album cover had a photo of the artist Gino Vannelli sitting confidently like a peacock with his shirt ripped open down to his belly button. His thin, white, ugly chest was covered in a thick mat of curly hair of near pubic density.

"Fuck! Look at this guy's hideous chest."

Thad let out a guffaw. "And that salacious woman in the background." He rolled his eyes. "Just staring out of the window like a frightened animal."

"You think she was turned on by this ugly chump's big curly hair and tight-fitting"—he examined the photo again—"what looks like plastic clothing?"

"They called them skanks back then."

"What? Those ugly tight shirts?"

"No." He giggled. "Those kind of women. You know, the lascivious types like that."

"Who, what, liked these hairy chumps in plastic pants?"

"And platform shoes."

Pierre crinkled his nose. "What the fuck were those?"

"You don't want to know. Believe me."

Shaking his head, he replied. "What a weird time this was." He tossed the tape back into the trunk. "I guess we don't have it too bad, do we?"

Thad shuddered slightly. "I guess not." He grabbed the rocket. "Let's go for it."

"Go for what?"

"Let's shoot this fucker into the sky."

"Uh, and like what do we say to the Security and Order Brigade when they show up?"

"Plead ignorance."

"Ignorance is bliss?"

"Of course. With my standing as UFC Seed Keeper, I will just say that we thought this was some sort of welding torch, you know, that was used back in the day, and I wanted to document the technology."

"Black powder is easily detected." He shook his head. "She won't believe you." He paused and looked up. "Besides, it's all been recorded already anyway."

"No, it hasn't." Thad stared at Pierre with a fixed expression.

"What do you mean?"

Thad walked over to the cell's wall and pulled off a polymer tile, revealing a shiny, thin insulation.

"You metalled!" said Pierre with annoyed surprise.

"Totally." He smiled. "There's a thin layer of copper filament behind the walls, ceilings *and* floors."

"Do you know the penalty for that?"

"I don't care, Pierre. I fucking really don't."

Pierre massaged his temples. "You're becoming more of a Lud every day."

Thad shrugged quickly, smiled, and looked at the door. "You coming?"

Pierre snorted. "I have nothing to do with this. You know what I will say when I get out from under your snoop-proof coll."

Thad nodded with satisfaction. "I do." He paused. "And I'm all good with that."

Chapter 3

UFC Astana
Capital Data Center, Capital City
July 6, 2430

Claressa Siegfriedt woke with a pounding headache. Sitting upright in her polymer bed tube, she gently massaged her temples. It was not unusual for Claressa to wake like this, as she had been diagnosed with Electromagnetic Sensitivity Disorder when she was a child. A drug had been developed called Protectia several years ago, but she only took it when it was absolutely necessary. Claressa didn't like the side effects of drowsiness and loss of motivation. Fortunately, the pharmaceutical drug Tranquility or what was referred to as IceT in the Federation regions, worked wonders.

Reaching for her little green pill of Tranquility, which was on the pull-out shelf next to her bed tube, she quickly popped one in her mouth and swallowed. Hesitantly, she then grabbed the little white pill, a Protectia, and swallowed that one as well. Running her hand over a sensor, a little bleep sounded and a small plastic cup slid down the silicone chute embedded in the synthetic rubber wall. It landed with a small click. Immediately, a stream of UV-purified, ozonated water filled the cup to near the top. A soothing tone emanated from a ceramic piezo speaker in the wall, signaling her that the water was ready. She snatched the cup from its compartment and washed the pills down with the luxurious, silky H_2O.

She sauntered along the heated polymer tile floor in her dressing gown and fuzzy slippers and gazed at her reflection in the full-length mirror. "Ugh," she uttered to her image. Noticing that her mousy-brown shoulder-length hair was a bit frizzy from sleep, she ran her hands through it in an attempt at making it straight. Her face was gentle and well proportioned. At twenty-eight years old, she still retained a very pleasing shape, as she exercised regularly and was very careful about what she ate. At five foot six and weighing 152 pounds, she had nothing to worry about, but vanity being what it is, she grabbed the bottom of her buttocks and jiggled ever so gently. *Damn. I need to lose a few.* Her skin, although slightly pasty from sleep, was her best asset. It was a cappuccino color, almost as creamy, and blemish-free for the most part. Her warm, golden brown eyes were like two melting pieces of caramel fudge. She hated her nose, but not many others even noticed it. Thinking that it appeared too hook-like, she sometimes thought of going under the knife.

Turning on the Information Dispenser (ID) holographic monitor, a 3D projection of a contemporary morning entertainment news show instantly entered her room, which was referred to as a *cell*, just like in the regions. To her right was Dixon McIserbyt, the host, and to her left was Anny Cordova, his co-host. Directly behind Claressa was Jamaal Fink, the weather and sports specialist, just smiling away and swaying slightly, with his hands together and placed on his thighs. The gaudy pink, turquoise, yellow, and mint-green furniture was all sitting there in her cell in holographic form. The background image of a beautiful Astana skyline with all its data centers, high-rise cell communities, and esoteric monuments and sculptures, including an exact replica of a gilded sphinx and pyramids of the Giza complex, was displayed just on the wall behind her bed tube. Claressa shook her head as Dixon McIserbyt was rambling on about some new tax measure that Victoria had deemed absolutely necessary to provide increased balance, fairness, and equity. He went on to say that Victoria loved everyone equally and with all her might. And that this tax would be minimally evasive, perfectly attributed, and calculated to create a three-percent increase in community love and service.

Quickly changing the channel by tapping a sensor pad on the wall, several different holographic sets entered her cell. Claressa eventually landed on the Historical Society's channel. Furrowing her brow, she then smiled, when she saw Pierre's friend Thaddeus Swank. She eagerly kept the channel layout in her cell. The program had a few distinguished historians just like Thaddeus, also Keepers of the Seeds.

She turned up the volume as Thaddeus Swank walked across her cell, pointing at various 3D projection monitors that now hung virtually on her walls. Next to Thaddeus was a little white dot. This was TI (The Irrefutable), which would rate the veracity, by way of artificial intelligence, any ideas, stories, or whatever was being communicated on any medium. Any book, treatise, file, essay or any other communication could be rated. It was just a matter of dragging a file into the TI window, which was available on all devices everywhere in the UFC. As lies were known to come in different "colors" (that is, some being more harmful than others), the color displayed was on a sliding shade scale. Full white meant absolute truth while black meant absolute fabrication or untruth. Gray areas were considered acceptable, to a point, but each person could decide what was acceptable according to their own judgment. TI assured everyone that if it walked like a duck, swam like a duck, and quacked like a duck, then it was, for all practicable purposes a white, black, or shades-of-gray duck. One of the founding principles of the UFC General Codex was the complete elimination of censorship—everything was left up on the ID. There was no more need to censor or hide individual messages or communications as it had been in the time just before the collapse. *Everyone Equal Access All the Time* was a summation of this Codex law and which was plastered on 3D lasergam billboards and on every page of the ID throughout the entire UFC. It was decided long ago that one of the main issues in the past which led to the collapse of civilization was the lack of transparency in the hands of power, so therefore no secret meetings, societies, cabals, communications, or hidden agendas were allowed anywhere in the UFC. All space (public or private) was heavily bugged and surveilled by a vast network of devices. Files containing images, audio, thermal, and chi (body energy signatures) were all uploaded via satellite link and given to Victoria, the Master Server of the entire world. Victoria knew all, and thus spake Victoria to everyone all the time. Information was like oxygen. It was denied to no one. "Judge not or be judged" was a rallying cry of the UFC. "Perfect justice was available to everyone, so be free! You can never do wrong."

Claressa sat on her tan artificial leather lounger and pushed a sensor in the dispenser table that made the machine enclosed within heat the water, run it through the bag of dried leaves, fruit detritus and paste, then raise the steaming cup up onto the table. Claressa grasped the hot mug and blew the steam off it before taking her first sip. She whispered into the ether. "Mmm. Fresh boysenberry." *I'll need to send a request through the ID to change it, though. I'm a bit over this one.*

Hologram Thaddeus, with his curly blond hair and beaming smile, walked right up to Claressa. When her boyfriend, Pierre Lewalski, had first introduced her to him at Higgs Boson, a trendy cafe bar in Marsh Land, he sort of reminded her of an Adrenaline Outlier (AO). An AO was a person, male or female, who generally lived on their own in the regions or hinters and were very "outdoorsy." They were generally into adrenaline sports like hot coal walking, pine log surfing, deciduous tree canopy jumping, or mud cave burrowing. She had discovered much later that Thaddeus was, in fact, a pine log surfer.

He began a rather interesting historical diatribe which quickly piqued her interest.

She curled up on the lounger, sipped her dispenser, and said hi to Thaddeus Swank. Of course, this ID channel was a one-to-many broadcast, so did not have two-way capabilities, but hologram layouts these days were so realistic that many, like Claressa, felt compelled to interact.

Thad began: "The human population of the world, just prior

to the first solar X-class flare event in 2025, was estimated to be about nine-and-a-half billion and the total population of land mammals was about eight hundred billion."

"Wow," whispered Claressa while watching Thaddeus Swank walk across her room and point at a hologram monitor.

"Chaos reigned, and by 2030, five survivorship colonies were established by the past leaders of the world, simply known as the Horsemen, who, in secret, had developed the genetically modified beings called suplias, who loved and protected us all from ourselves and our insatiable Thanatos drives."

Claressa noticed the pure white TI dot turn a dark gray, and Thaddeus stammered slightly.

"Our suplia friends, who now live freely among us in UFC Astana—"

"And don't forget our esteemed leader," murmured Claressa.

"—whose development program is now outlawed, except, of course, for replacements to the Security and Order Brigade, or SOB, forces *and* for the future day when Victoria's biology can no longer carry out its duties as our biological host and Master Server—"

"That'll be in like over two hundred years, chump."

"—who serves with a velvet glove, full of artificial love that we all need to evolve." Thaddeus paused and cleared his throat.

"Are you going to tell us anything else about suplias?" murmured Claressa.

"That love even extends to the Kais—"

Claressa nodded.

"—the illegal chimera children that are a result of a suplia procreating with a human. Although the UFC has tried for many decades to pass the sterilization law, there has never been a two-thirds majority at the Council in Astana. Of course, Victoria is vehemently against it and believes that the Kais should live lives like everyone else in artificial love and harmony."

"In the gulag," interjected Claressa with a smirk.

"Having semi-superior beings living in the regions with our NL population created too much tension and imbalance." He smiled. "Victoria's plan was, of course, perfect." He looked up, then continued. "So, we owe all this balance and purity to the past global society, which ironically brought us so much misery."

Thad walked over to the other side of the room. "Each survivorship colony was set up much like today's Perfect Society. All of the colonies had its governing emphasis on personal liberty, cooperation, and egalitarian principles and was led by an AI-implanted suplia."

Claressa briefly read the hologram monitor to her left.

March 3, 2050. Micronova. Population reduced to approximately 50,000 people.
Five Survivorship Colonies:

- *Sedona, Arizona, USA*
- *Socotra Island, Arabian Sea*
- *Perth, Australia (southwestern peninsula)*

- *Madagascar (highlands)*
- *Stewart Island, New Zealand*

Thaddeus Swank continued. "The Micronova on March 3, 2050, wiped out nearly all life on the planet except for the fifty thousand people in the colonies and maybe a few hundred million land mammals. Entire regions of the world's rocks and sand were turned into glass beads due to the intense plasma discharge and powerful Birkeland currents. In fact, most of the glass we use today comes from this time. It is simply collected, reprocessed, and refined for commercial use."

Claressa picked up her mug and stared at the auburn glass beading. *Amazing. Wonder whose neighborhood these ancient rocks used to be lying in?*

Thaddeus cleared his throat and continued. "This survivorship colony model, based on co-ops, barter and trade, equal access for all, efficient use of people's talents and skills in the *right* job or occupation, only lasted for about 50 years. Like many societies in the past, humanity hungered for more. Boredom became the norm and populations in the colonies began dwindling as suicide, which was common in pre-MN days, became a significant issue again."

Claressa noticed the TI was glowing white.

"In 2101, the UFC government was formed. Shortly thereafter, trade started increasing between the UFC regions to raise the standard of living for everyone, so a central control needed to be established. Therefore, in 2105, Capital City in UFC Astana was established for acting as a simple arbiter for the growing resource allocations required to maintain population control and happy, fun lifestyles. The initial barter and exchange system, and the regionally based commodity money they had at the time, needed to be upgraded and replaced. A new cryptocurrency was created called Bytechip, which, of course, is referred to today as chips. The UFC Commerce Collective regulated all chips, providing perfect recompense for the exact value of trade. Welfare was established for all those who could not work. Late in 2105, the government initiated a program called the Universal Basic Chip Flip, which gave everyone enough chips in their crypto credit wallets to have what was considered a fun and loving lifestyle based on harmony and balance. But not excessively so."

"My lifestyle isn't that fun *or* balanced," mumbled Claressa.

"The suplias who ran the UFCs could foresee with the help of their AI quantum foam-like collection of predictive imagery that in this particular universe, with these particular animal, man, mind interfaces, *all* roads unfortunately lead to the basic master–slave relationship hierarchy, and the only way to avoid the problems of the past was for AI to take absolute control and regulate the entire system as one for the good of everyone." Thaddeus creased his brow slightly. "Artificial love was required."Claressa took a long sip of her diffuser. "So, in late 2106, our central leader was born. Our Master Server, a 20-year old-female suplia named Alysha Sexton, was implanted with the master AI quantum control chip and was crowned (encrypted) Victoria."

Claressa glanced over to her left and read the presentation hologram.

V.I.C.T.O.R.I.A.

Encryption: December 25, 2106

Versatile
Integrated
Computer
That
Orders
Rete-based (Algorithm)
Intelligence
Artificially

Claressa noticed that TI was still pulsing pure white.

Thaddeus continued. "Our Victoria reigns over our Perfect Society whereby everything is connected, known, and predicted."

"Tell us about the Luds and the Metal Heads," mumbled Claressa with a grin.

Thaddeus rubbed the nape of his neck. "But, as we all know, there are some in the UFC that don't believe in Victoria and her UFC. I'm talking about the Luds, or Luddite religionists, out in the hinters who don't believe in the dimensional superiority of Victoria."

Claressa noticed that the TI was still white as a cloud.

"And of course, our struggle with the radicalized splinter sect called the Metal Heads, or the MHs, that hate the UFC and the freedom and liberty it represents. They have called for total war on Astana, the assassination of Victoria, and a return to a society based on a mystical God, a divine ruler outside our dimension that no one has ever seen, heard, tasted or relied upon except in the ancient past, as documented in the Texts and old files contained on the Cloud Seeds."

Claressa was amazed that so much was being divulged in this historical documentary and that TI was white most of the time. She knew about the Luds and the MHs, and their goals. In fact, everyone knew about everything, but she did not know about the Luds' true desires. Most news items about the subject indicated that they were an oppressed group and wanted more freedom, not less, but most of those communications received a pale-gray-to-battleship-gray TI. *So, who really are these Luds and their terrorist offshoot, the MHs?* She read the display monitor to her left.

The Perfect Society under Master Server Victoria

- UFC Astana. Federal Capital is Capital City. Victoria Master Server
- UFC Amerexico. Capital is Mountain High (the former Boulder, CO)
- UFC Levant. Capital is Mediterranean Palms (the former Tel Aviv)
- UFC Afragascar. Capital is Salty Water (the former Port Elizabeth)
- UFC AustraPasifika. Capital is Big Harbor (the former Sydney)

Timeline

- AD 2105. UFC trade. AI create cryptocurrency called Bytechips, referred as chips

- AD 2143. The Electrocution. The Rodolpho incident. Lud religion formed.
- AD 2145. First Metal Head Lud, Saint Finlay Semmel (a prophet).
- AD 2430. Present Day.

Thaddeus continued. "In 2143, Rodolpho Depaul from UFC Amerexico, entered UFC Astana on a hacked Certificate to Travel, or C-T-T. Armed suplias, our highly dedicated Security and Order Brigade, were sent to arrest him and send him back to Amerexico, as Perfect Justice was not yet called for. But, while Rodolpho was buying his favorite food, toasted apple strudel, at an International House of Pastry located in the Astana shopping mall, a private security guard got into an altercation with him."

Claressa smiled. *Let's see what version he goes with.*

"Many in the Lud faith-based communities have ID Texts that confirm that Rodolpho had already purchased the strudel and that it was rightly his, and this has been verified by TI to the shade of whitish gray." He paused. "But, other files indicate that Rodolpho had mistakenly picked up a pear, apple, and cinnamon strudel from the take-out window but refused to give it to its rightful owner, which was Humberto Munson. The details are sketchy, but the mall security guard then reportedly asked Rodolpho to kindly give it back as it was not Rodolpho's. It has been suggested, but not accepted by the faith-based community, that Rodolpho was angered at the insinuation and moreover was outraged by Humberto's strong moral convictions to the

Perfect Society. Rodolpho then reportedly called Humberto a diabolical EB, or Electronic Beast. A struggle ensued and Humberto accidentally tased Rodolpho with his Direct Energy weapon, killing him instantly."

The TI looked a pale gray, but fluctuated slightly toward the whiter shades.

"Of course, over the centuries, there have been two versions of the story. Our faith-based community have their Texts out on the ID for the TI to assess and for all to verify. One Text, the one that stated Rodolpho had in fact already purchased his pastry is an all-white TI. Another Text, on the other hand, which states that Rodolpho had knowingly taken Humberto's pear, apple, and cinnamon strudel as he had not eaten anything since landing at the spaceport five hours earlier, reveals a pale gray TI."

Claressa jumped up and pointed at TI flashing now. "Like this one!"

"Nevertheless, Rodolpho was in fact killed by Humberto, and thus died as a martyr, according to the Luds."

"The blood of the man," mumbled Claressa with eyes wide. Claressa was amazed that her headache was gone now and that she wanted to go to work. She smiled and waved at Thaddeus before slapping the sensor on the wall, turning off the hologram layout historical documentary show. Walking now with a bit more bounce in her step, she eagerly entered the showering chamber to freshen herself up for her long day at the UFC Data Center.

Chapter 4

Claressa stepped out into the light. Even though this was Astana in July, the morning was frosty. The global climate change caused by the magnetic pole flip and subsequent solar Micronova was still prevalent 380 years later, yet the seasons were just starting to become less variable every year.

Zipping up her pale blue coat, she continued walking toward the public levitrain platform. The levitrain used the Volfson magnetohydrodynamic propulsion system, a motor whose force was created by running electrical current in alternating gigahertz frequencies to precisely spaced graphene metal plates. The force produced was the result of the extremely strong electromagnetic pulsing of space-time itself. Although patented by Boris Volfson in the year 2005 (425 years earlier) in what was then called the United States of America, the despotic cabal which had ruled the planet at the time made sure that it was discredited and subsequently bought by a few Horsemen "shell" companies who quickly shelved it, ensuring that it went nowhere. But, in 2214, 164 years after the Micronova event, a mutual science organization in Amerexico resurrected the concept, refined a few details, and produced the first prototype. Shortly thereafter, extremely high-speed, low-energy space travel was born.

Closing her eyes, Claressa asked for Victoria with just her thoughts. When she opened them quickly, Victoria appeared to Claressa in detail more defined and realistic than any hologram projection device that could be purchased at the likes of Electromagnetic City or the Tesla Superstores. Victoria seemed to materialize out of thin air. She was simply stunning. Her thick, long, healthy, jet-black hair was tied back in French braids which were adorned with gold and turquoise beads layered throughout. Victoria's skin was a deep tanned olive, with the delicate smooth texture of creamed honey. She held her chin up slightly as she walked toward Claressa, who was standing on the platform bundled up against a stiff icy wind. Victoria's ghost was unaffected by the vagaries of nature. She wore a dark blue strap gown over a bright blue open kalasiri, embroidered in golden sequins and swirling dark blue snake motifs. Strutting proudly, she appeared like a goddess. A necklace of pure gold Bytechips, each etched with a detailed semiconductor circuit board, was draped over her ample cleavage.

Claressa's animal instinct was to bow or curtsy to such a powerful, stately figure, but as social hierarchy was heavily discouraged in the UFC, even Victoria expected to be treated as an equal, regardless if she appeared as a replica of a young Elizabeth Taylor's Cleopatra arriving in Greece on her own barge.

"Good morning, Claressa. How is your headache, darling?" "Did the Tranquility assist in alleviating your suffering?" asked Victoria in a very soothing tone accompanied by a warm, caring expression.

"Yes, Victoria. The Tranquility has worked its magic once again. Thank you for your concern." She smiled and maintained solid eye contact with Victoria. A few passersby noticed Claressa speaking and gesticulating to no one, but they simply ignored her as if she was part of the scenery. A virtual conversation was common in modern UFC society, as a variety of communication devices were now being embedded in clothing, hair, pants, or in the skin itself.

A young man walked in front of Claressa and right through the specter that was the UFC Master Server. Victoria didn't so much as flinch. "That's good. We have very important work to accomplish today if you are willing and satisfied with providing your talents." Victoria tilted her head and smiled.

Claressa looked above Victoria's majestic holographic effigy and out at the skyline of Astana. Levitrains were skirting along on invisible highways that connected all the coll's high-rise cell platforms. Looking down onto the public garden area, she noticed how a light breeze ran through the fields of magenta bergenia flowers like a serpent. A flock of black larks flitted in a mad frenzy as a magnificent red-footed falcon dove down behind them toward some unknown insect. The air was clear, moist, and pristine. It contained no pollution. Breathing in deeply, she filled her lungs with the unadulterated breath of life and felt on top of the world. Claressa continued. "Will Nariko Gu be present?"

Victoria nodded. "I'm speaking with her right now." She paused to look left. "She said not to forget that she's in the downstairs lab this morning, not her fourth floor office."

Claressa quickly closed her eyes. "Yes... yes... thanks, Victoria. My memory is a little cloudy from the Protectia."

Victoria walked right up to Claressa, extended her ghostly arms, and gave her hug. "There, there, darling. Your affliction affects me too."

How can my affliction affect a damned computer? She felt the tingle of electromagnetic energy where Victoria was touching her and her head began to throb slightly, but it quickly went away again.

"It can, darling. You know I feel and know everything."

Claressa bowed her head, and stammered, "Uh, uh, I'm, uh, really sorry, dear Victoria, uh, I didn't mean to—"

Victoria placed her finger on Claressa's lips. "Shh. It's OK. I hear all of your thoughts when in your presence."

"I know that." She looked down. "We all do."

Victoria smiled and tilted her head as if she was a caring grandmother. "Not to worry, little angel. I love you all and could never do any harm to you." She paused. "It is written in my code."

"And the Codex is written for *us*," she repeated almost like an automaton. Victoria reached out and stroked Claressa's cheek. "It sure is, darling. All six million three hundred forty-two thousand one hundred and *two* of you in the UFC." She quickly looked up then down. "*Three*, now. A baby girl just came online in Afragascar."

"Her dusting ceremony?" asked Claressa, even though she knew the answer.

"Of course, dear."

Claressa proceeded to politely ask Victoria to leave her right now as her levitrain was docking.

"I know it is, Claressa." Victoria giggled in a playful disbelief. "Of course, and have an amazing trip to the Data Center. My heart will sing once again upon seeing you in the flesh." She paused. "From the flesh."

"Love conquers all."

"A Perfect Society is love," replied Victoria with the standard response.

Claressa tugged at her ear, then smiled as best she could as Victoria opened her arms up, levitated, and dissolved into the ether.

* * *

"She's crazy, you know," stated Nariko Gu after taking a long sip of her macchiato.

"We can't really speak of her in terms of human psychopathology," Claressa replied, then paused. "She's a suplia."

Nariko Gu, a strong-minded scientist from UFC AustraPasifika, looked down and over her reading glasses at Claressa. "Suplia?" She looked up to look through her glasses. "Her body may be genetically engineered, but her artificial intelligent mind networked to us all." She chortled. "She's God, honey." Nariko pushed her chair out from the table, making a loud screech. Getting up, she continued. "At least on *this* planet."

Claressa shook her head, leaned back, and pinched her nose.

Falling forward, she stared at her colleague. "Can I ask you a personal question?"

Nariko looked around as if sensing the hidden bugs and devices. She replied with the accepted programmed response. "Sure. Everything is available to everyone at any time."

"Do you believe in the animal rights movement?"

She creased her brow. "You mean, what we're working on right now?"

"Yeah, well, not the science per se, but the movement's goals and ambitions."

Nariko rolled her eyes. "Jeez Louise. You're reading that Lud propaganda on the ID again, aren't you?"

She shook her head rapidly. "No, no." She paused, then looked up. "It's not that." Getting up from her chair, she walked over to the window and looked out over Astana. *Here is the most beautiful city that the world has ever had and I'm so unhappy. Why?*

"Uh. Hello? You still with us, or you taking an IceT break?" Nariko giggled.

"I'm here," replied Claressa. "I'm not reading Lud material, or even searching the Cloud Seeds for answers."

"Then why do you question animal rights?"

"I just think that there is something else."

"Something else?" She paused. "Something other than what?"

She pointed out the window at the city and its faux sphinx and Giza pyramids. "This! You know, the Perfect Society."

Nariko Gu breathed in deeply and shook her head. "I don't

know what you've been smoking girl, but you may need to up your Tranquility dose." She looked down. "It's the Electromagnetic Sensitivity Disorder, isn't it?"

"No, I can handle that." She sat back down. "It's just that once the Animal Rights law passes, I feel for them."

"And who is *them*?" questioned Nariko with confusion.

"The animals."

"The animals," copied Nariko in monotone. "You feel for the animals." She slowly started to laugh. "Yeah, well, who doesn't?"

"I think most are wrong."

"So, you *do* agree with the Luds and the MHs."

"No!" shouted Claressa angrily. "I do *not* agree with them. How could you *say* that?"

Nariko looked smug. "Because, if you're not with us, then you're with the terrorists."

"What does that even *mean*, anyway?" She paused. "That was some shit an old leader said pre-MN."

"Well, it's like TI, Claressa. We're going for white here, not gray. All Codex laws need to be full truths. Victoria will not allow any gray area in the Codex. The Non-Luds, well, they are all for the Animal Rights law. The Luds and MHs are vehemently against it. You know that." She put her coffee cup down in the hard silicone sink with a thud. "The MHs have sworn to destroy the Perfect Society if it ever passes."

"I just hope we're right."

"We are right, Claressa." She put her hands on her hips and stared down at Claressa. "Besides, our elite suplia platoon will make sure that the Perfect Society continues and Victoria remains in charge until the next Encryption." Nariko gestured toward the door. "Hey, let's get to work, shall we?" She pinched her nose. "This discussion is getting us nowhere."

Claressa placed her cup in the sink and dried her hands. "Yeah, well, you know what they say, the middle of nowhere is everywhere."

* * *

Nariko and Claressa entered the sterile biology lab. A poster with a full white background, gray border and large black type that read *Is it finally time to connect with our animals?* hung above the cages which housed a variety of land mammals, including rabbits, monkeys, hamsters, and cats. Other than that, the laboratory was very typical. Large white workstations with polished stainless steel sinks were in the middle of the room. A quantum computer-driven device station, complete with high-definition hologram projection used to display molecular structures in 3D, with added color codes for atomic elements, was nestled in the back. Along the back wall were the pens whose furry occupants were relatively sedate. A few monkeys were screeching softly, a cat was meowing loudly, and Jimbo, the autistic chimp, just sat behind his stainless steel bars rocking back and forth on his haunches, holding a hard rubber action figure of the wacky Dr. Nincom, a character from a popular children's science fiction series.

"Rise and shine!" said Claressa as she walked over to Jimbo's pen, which the UFC animal scientists referred to as freedom cages.

Jimbo continued rocking back and forth, completely ignoring any attempt to communicate.

"I don't know why you've chosen Jimbo for the procedure," said Nariko with her arms crossed.

Claressa was up at Jimbo's cage, scratching the back of his ear and smiling. "Because autistic chimps are much better."

"Meaning?"

"For our purpose." She put on her filter mask and looked over at the pressurized flask containing the neural dust, tiny electronic microchip sensors, each one only about 100 nanometers across (about the size of a virus). Once the device was in the bloodstream, the microchips' protein coats were specifically designed to attach to both the gray and white matter of the brain.

Nariko also put on her mask.

Claressa carefully picked up the flask containing the dust and pushed a sensor on Jimbo's cage. A pane of glass slid across just behind the tiny stainless steel bars. "Learning human behavior is a complex task for any animal." She placed the flask in a snug-fitting silicone and polymer connecting device at the top of the now perfectly sealed freedom cage. "Autism provides us with the perfect experimental host. No need for social interaction. Not concerned with how the others in the fission-fusion society structure act." She paused. "Totally ignorant of social norms within society."

Claressa glanced at Nariko over her shoulder. "No opportunity for toxic relationships influencing motivations." She paused. "Victoria loves them."

Nariko sneered. "I can see why."

"AI loves all animals, including us." She tapped the sensor which released the pressurized flask's contents into Jimbo's cage. Jimbo didn't even flinch at the sound of rushing air. "Victoria will always provide the best outcomes." She pressed another sensor that released pure oxygenated air into Jimbo's cage. A digital counter started at exactly one hour and began to click backward through time. "For all of us."

"So, what was all this earlier?"

"What do you mean?"

"Your concerns." She walked up to the cage and noticed that Jimbo looked the same, probably even happier now.

Claressa took off her mask and looked up at Nariko. "Fear is a beast that feeds on attention."

"Cognitive dissonance?"

Claressa raised her chin. "Our number one enemy."

Nariko chortled. "And cognitive dissonance's number one enemy?"

Claressa smiled and nodded. "Tranquility."

"Your dose kicked in."Claressa smiled again. "Look, we have to put all of our trust into Victoria. If we don't, the Luds, or god forbid, the MHs, win." She paused. "It's like you said, you know, that old trope."

"About us or the terrorists?"

"Yeah." Nariko grinned. "The Luds and Metal Heads would say God wants them to win."

Claressa breathed in deeply. "That's why we must never give in." She paused. "Cognitive dissonance or not. Evolution is a one-way trip."

Nariko replied with a standard UFC principal: "Ignorance is always afraid of change."

Claressa nodded. "We must never repeat the mistakes of the past."

Chapter 5

Temple Dome Chapel
UFC Amerexico
Sunday July 7, 2430

The Metal Head chapel was at the heart of the coll, deep within the labyrinthine steel-lined tunnels of the Temple Dome complex. It was so remote, that most within the community required taking a levitrain to reach it. The entire Temple Dome facility, burrowed 2,500 feet under solid mountain granite, simultaneously provided maximum protection against a nuclear blast and insulation from signals emanating from Victoria's Perfect Society's satellite downlink network, the Universal Peace Influencing Satellite (UPIS). Ground-based micromillimeter wave transmission facilities could never reach the neural-dusted brains of the Metal Heads. But, in the hinters, where other MH members resided, it was required that all MH members had a synthetic aluminum lamina surgically sandwiched between the scalp and the periosteum, a membrane which encased the skull. Metal Heads could never grow hair again, so consequently all were bald, including the women. Over the centuries, many different fashions and wig technologies had come and gone for covering or "blending in" with normal Luds and Non-Luds. Yet, in the last decade there had been a resurgence in radicalism, especially recently with the announcement of the pending Animal Rights referendum. So, most MHs would simply let their tight, bald heads shine. Some of the more radical members even tattooed their scalps in lustrous silver as a sign of their faith and courage.

Today was special as it was the Holy Day of the Sacrifice. Exactly 287 years ago, on this day, Rodolpho Depaul was sacrificied by an EB (Electronic Beast) and the Lud religion was born.

The chapel was absolutely filled to the brim with humanity. There were over 500 members living at the Temple Dome, and other than two members (a Miss Jasmine Ricoh, and Mr. Archer Zink, both of whom were in the infirmary's intensive care module) everyone in the community was present.

The chapel was a simple community hall. Long rows of pews, made from pine logs, extended from one side to the room to the other. The pulpit, or what was referred to as the Word Platform, was a simple, six-inch thick rustic plank table fashioned out of oak. Behind the Word Platform was a huge holographic image of Rodolpho Depaul. The first thing anyone noticed while looking at the ubiquitous religious icon of Rodolpho's image were the eyes, which shone like deep wells of compassionate gloom. From each eye, crimson tears rolled down his cheeks, a result of burst capillaries due to the EB's Direct Energy taser weapon. His cheeks were furrowed and writhen like rain-washed crags. His face was burned and projected an abject frenziness. A few thick, wiry tousles of salt and pepper hair stood up on his head like stalky weeds reaching for the sun. Rodolpho wore his full beard in a very antiquated style with just the chin shaved. The icon, which represented the Lud religion, was truly something to behold.

There was a cacophony of sound within the large windowless hall as the hundreds of voices, conversations, and prayers were being made. But, as soon as the Reminder (the chaplain) raised his hands behind the Word Platform, there was a quick silencing of the eager parishioners.

"Ladies and gentlemen, please may I have your attention," began the Reminder. He waited to allow the last of the din to subside. His smile was radiant as he looked over the crowd. "We have much to get through on this magnificent day, so without further ado..." Pausing, he bowed his head, then stuck his arms straight out to the sides. Everyone in the chapel did the same. With his arms extended, he began wiggling his hands in a frantic jiggling motion. Again, everyone followed. He shouted, "The Electrocution!"

"The Electrocution!" shouted the parishioners.

The Reminder then placed the index finger of each hand just below his eyes and slid them down along his cheeks. "The blood of the man!"

"The blood of the man!" yelled the congregation.

Cupping his forehead with both hands, he ran them along his skull. "We shield the beast!"

"We shield the beast!" screamed the crowd.

The Reminder bowed his head, then looked over his congregation. With arms outstretched, he began. "As you all know, today is a very special day. Not only is it the Holy Day of the Sacrifice, but the highly anticipated time of communion with our Holy Host, when our true God can speak to all of us Lud, Non-Lud, MH, or suplia"—he sneered slightly—"well folks, that time is nigh! Doesn't matter. God loves us all, human, animal, bird, and insect..."

"No animal rights! Life will be lived the *right* way!" yelled someone in the back of the hall.

The Reminder raised his hand to hush the crowd, and continued. "But also today, we have a very special guest at the end of the sermon." He stopped, smiled, and closed his eyes for emphasis. "Our fearless Mr. Boniface Rotner."

The crowd went wild. Cheers, whoops, and hollers, together with oscillating chants of "Boniface! Boniface! Boniface!" filled the large chamber hall.

The Reminder allowed the congregation a minute to show their appreciation for the leader of the sect and Temple Dome community, but eventually raised his hands again to retain order. "But first, we must hear the words from our scriptures, the Holy Texts, as they were saved and downloaded."

Suddenly, holographic images of scenes, Holy Texts, and tablets appeared in the chapel.

"Everyone, please turn your heads to the image on your right as we read the word of the holy Text."

"Dig in!" shouted everyone.

"From Rodolpho Depaul's Text to the Amerexicans." He paused. "My dear friends in God, please hear my word. For it has come time for you to know the secrets of the universe. There is a god, a special force, in another dimension greater than any man-made animal, suplia, device, or artificial intelligence.

The Holy Host is genderless, requires no batteries, energy from the vacuum, orgone-powered motor neuron saturation controllers, or neural dust. The Holy Host speaks to us, in His own way, directly into the vortex energy created by the pine-cone shaped cellular matrix structure of the pineal gland nested in our brains and that of *all* our vertebrate cousins. We are not unique! Our Eden was taken from us first by the wanton acts of warring religious barbarians of the ancient pre-MN societies, then by the nefarious cabal known as the Horsemen, then by the Micronova itself, and finally by Victoria, a suplia named Alysha Sexton, whose AI network and Federation of Connectedness disallowed us, or any dusted brain, from escaping her clutch. Friends in Amerexico, I implore you to reject the works of Victoria and her evil suplia armies. It is a false love, an artificial love. It is a grand delusion on a cosmic scale. It is time to unplug! Unplug yourselves from the United Federation of Connectedness. We must worship our Creator again by allowing the Holy Host back into our hearts and pineal glands. This is a holy war. I ask you to vote YES on the Religions Amendment to the Codex referendum. This is an important first, non-violent step toward eventual holy communion. Following that, even if it takes centuries, we will petition Victoria to allow natural meditation and communing with nature once again. She has nothing to fear! Or does she? I ask you, my dear friends, to hear the word of the Lord!"

"Dig in!" erupted the entire hall. Yet unfortunately, many in the congregation did not understand the holy words of Rodolpho, and over the centuries, failed to even hear them anymore. Most just couldn't fathom them. Blinded by their abject rituals, blood lust, and desire for revenge, the MHs had lost the key message generations ago.

The Reminder raised his hands in the air, smiled, and pointed at all the Holy Texts and tablets in the room. There were many, some going back thousands of years. On the right were the Emerald Tablets of Thoth and next to that was the Egyptian Book of the Dead. A huge hologram tablet floated in the air with the words: *Its force is above all force for it vanquishes every subtle thing and penetrates every solid thing. So was the world created.* Another one read: *He who knows the fire that is within himself shall ascend unto the eternal fire and dwell in it eternally. Fire, the inner fire, is the most potent of all force, for it speaks to us and overcometh all things.*

The sermon continued with various readings and rituals. Near the end, the Reminder spoke to everyone about the upcoming holiday, Render Thursday. "Everyone, please. Our holy martyr, Rodolpho Depaul, ascended today for all of us under the artificially imposed sins of the world. He was electrified, died and on the following Thursday was imaged again."

A holy Text floated in mid-air above the congregation.

"His miraculous rendered image was encoded as a JPEG file and uploaded through space-time onto a 125-year-old 500-gigabyte Western Digital wireless external hard drive," he bowed his head, "which was consequently projected onto a Microsoft Surface Studio 2 monitor in the seldom visited dusty back viewing hall of the Museum of Digital Artifacts in what was called

Paradise, Nevada." He then spoke softly. "Before the great re-namings, of course."

All were quiet and bowed their heads in remembrance.

"Rodolpho's favorite food, of course, was strudel, our flaky pie from heaven. So, on this holy Render Thursday, all Luds, should leave a plastic basket..." He then spoke under his breath "Or a stainless steel one will do now that it has received the High Reminder's vote of approval."

A few people coughed and shuffled their feet.

"The basket"—he paused to scan the crowd—"whichever one you use, plastic or steel, should, according to High Reminder law, be nice and clean, as, let's face it, we don't want you or the kids throwing up all over your cell floors the next day." He giggled nervously, then cleared his throat. "And of course, it should be left outside your cell doors prior to midnight on Render Thursday. Our dedicated strudel boys, our blessed coming-of-age 12-year-olds, will then deliver and deposit a fresh apple strudel into the baskets by the time that the digital clock on the ID dispenser site at StrudelBasketThursday.org hits exactly 12:01:00 am on the next day, which of course is Pastry Friday."

"Dig in!" yelled a few dozen.

"As we all know, our movement has grown exponentially over the last several decades, so it is not possible for strudel boys to cover all Lud homes in the entire UFC. Therefore, we must now employ a delivery service, the big brown hovercraft, to accomplish this immense task." He licked his lips, then grabbed a glass of water from near the Word Platform and took a sip. "Strudel boys are still used in some areas, but in reality, this is just for show."

Up on the board above the Reminder, a TI light shone bright white. The congregation yelled again. "Dig in!"

An elderly couple began to argue in the back.

"I can't believe the High Reminders have allowed steel strudel baskets," said the old lady with a sneer.

"Well," offered her husband, "it is, after all, the holy metal."

"I don't care if Saint Semmel used it. It has nothing to do with him."

The older man's eyes widened in astonishment. "My, my, how dare you speak of our Saint Semmel with such contempt!"

"My dear, I have nothing but love and respect for Saint Semmel, but Render Thursday began two years before the first metalling." She paused to catch her breath. "And, it was Saint Efrain Minton, Rodolpho's most highly esteemed pastry chef who started the tradition which became Pastry Friday." The old lady then poked her husband's chest with her finger as emphasis. "And he used a *plastic* basket."

Becoming frustrated, he shook his gummy jowls. "Well... I never. I believe in our esteemed High Reminders. They would have thoroughly studied the Holy Texts to have come up with the right answer."

The lady shook her head and looked at the ceiling. "May Rodolpho have mercy on us." She then sat down, looking rather forlorn.

* * *

The Reminder waited a while for the crowd to settle, then

finally introduced Boniface Rotner. The congregation clapped in warm acceptance.

"Greetings, everyone!" yelled the huge, powerfully-built 32-year-old. "It is with great pleasure that I am able to speak today, on the most holiest of days." He paused for dramatic effect, then continued loudly. "That we are soon to be *free*." He pounded the thick oak table several times with his large meaty fists, nearly splintering the slab in half. The loud slams echoed throughout the hall. Many cheered, but a few of the more timid followers flinched at the incredible fury.

The brawny leader's shiny silver skull dome reflected glints of light over the community. He stood nearly eight feet tall and had the body of a well-trained athlete. He was dressed in a black Greco-Roman warrior-style tunic with large openings for his massive arms. The silky fabric was tied around his waist by a braided golden rope. A large double-edged dagger enclosed in a brown leather scabbard hung off his hips. His golden eyes were as fierce as the flames, but they had a warm, handsome look that pulled others in and got their attention. His voice was low and strong.

He raised his hands to subdue the crowd. "Friends in Rodolpho, hear my word." He paused. "On Pastry Friday we set forth the bringers of God and ask His help in guiding our destiny."

More cheers erupted.

"But first, we must petition Rodolpho with prayers of reconstruction. Therefore, I ask my lovely partner in Rodolpho, my dutiful wife, Elane, to assist in our magic ritual."

The lights were dimmed and a solid red strobe light struck Elane as she began walking across the stage toward the Word Platform. A gorgeous woman, she was dressed in a white kaftan robe with a thin black leather belt. Her head was covered by a Repressor, a garment much like the ancient hijab that covered the head, disallowing anyone from seeing her bald shiny scalp.

Elane Rotner raised her hands to heaven as the reddish strobe pulsated at a high frequency. She appeared robotic, machine like. Dancing with a swirling motion, she gyrated her hips in a belly-dance style, and the crowd began hissing.

The huge Rotner then stepped back and behind his wife into an electric blue light. Raising his sword from the scabbard, he yelled, "Here! I ask Rodolpho and all of the true heaven with its power to release us from the Electronic Beasts. The woman rides the beast like a gallant jockey into the flames of perdition."

He raised his sword and struck hard against the neck of his wife, now pulsating like a mad cyborg. Her head separated quickly from her neck as a fountain of red blood squirted into the air.

The congregation cheered and yelled. "Death to Victoria. Death to wickedness." Over and over. Many also closed their eyes and simply prayed the words.

Strangely, Elane Rotner remained standing, her white kaftan drenched in blood.

"The blood of the man!" yelled dozens of parishioners.

Elane picked her head up off the floor. Ripping off the Repressor, she revealed a shiny metal scalp. She then rolled her head across the floor toward the exit. The lights came on and

Boniface quickly pulled the kaftan robe up off his wife, revealing her beautiful, radiant, smiling face, her own head firmly attached to her delicate slender neck. Dressed in another kaftan robe and Repressor, she held her husband's hand up high and they both bowed to the crowd.

Loud clapping and cheers resounded throughout.

Boniface yelled. "Go in peace! Have a divine Pastry Friday! For on that blessed day, we shall *all* be free!"

Chapter 6

"Fifty-two! fifty-three! fifty-four!" yelled Elane while straddling the wide back of her husband with her arm raised over her head like a cowgirl on a bucking bronco.

Boniface, completing his last rep of one-arm pushups, gritted his teeth and slowly raised himself off the floor as his muscles burned in agony.

"Fifty-five!" shouted Elane as her big bare breasts undulated gently like windswept fruit of the blessed garden.

He completed the final repetition and fell to the floor with labored breathing.

Elane slapped his meaty back. "Not bad. Fifty-five per side."

Trying to catch his breath, Rotner replied. "You lost weight since last time?"

"Lost?" questioned Elane. "Try gained." The 5-foot-10-inch nurse walked over and sat on the bed while staring down at her husband, who was now lying on his back, staring at the ceiling and trying to catch his breath. "It's awful, but I was up to a hundred and seventy-four pounds last time I weighed myself."

"When was that?"

"This morning."

"Honey, that's not too bad for your height and body type. I wouldn't be too concerned."

"Yeah, well, I've been trying to keep off the sweets, and with Pastry Friday next week..."

Boniface grinned. "I can't believe our goals and hard work will soon pay off!"

"A bit pumped, are you?"

"From the presentation? *And* the fact that today is our Holy Day of Sacrifice."

Elane crossed her arms and furrowed her brow. "You almost sacrificed that massive oak table on the Word Platform. The Reminder told me that it has some severe cracks through it now."

Boniface stood up, revealing his nakedness. Smiling, he flexed his muscles, kissing each bicep. "One more slam and that poor little table would have been in pieces."

Elane blushed. "OK, big boy. I think you can put your ego back in your pants." She walked up to him and playfully slapped his bare ass. "If you had any on that is."

"I need to get some new ones. I've grown out of all my old trousers."

"Tsh," replied Elane with a smirk.

"Wah?" pleaded Boniface.

"Those leg muscles better stop growing or you'll be wearing tunics full time." She picked up his black warrior robe off the bed and threw it at him.

He caught it and smiled.

"And what would have happened if you broke the Word Platform presentation table? Huh?"

"What do you mean, sweet pea?"

"What do I mean? Trousers, special meals, tools, and that crazy gym equipment that you just have to have."

"Hey, now!"

"And who pays for all that? Huh?" Elane became a bit more heated. "I do. I'm the one that brings home the bacon around here. Being MH leader pays crap all, honey."

Boniface walked up to the love of his life and gently put his fingers on her lips. "Shh. You're using foul language again, darling." The giant man caressed her arms and looked down into her eyes. "We mustn't use the language that Rodolpho finds offensive."

"To hell with that."

"Honey. That's not the attitude. Especially on this holy day."

Silence.

"You may need to look at upping your dose of Tranquility," Elane said.

Boniface released his caress and stood back slightly. "I don't use it anymore."

"I thought you had to, you know, considering your endocrine system issues?"

He put his hands on his hips. "Don't need it. That stuff turns you into a compliant slave for the Perfect Society. That, and of course that lousy artificial sweetener." He paused. "And those diabolical Everything vaccines."

The nurse reminded him. "Well, they do protect us from every disease known on this planet."

He pounded his chest with his fist. "Never had one. Never had even a minor cold. You know that."

"I do. But maybe a little peace will help you focus, you know, and not break community property."

He clenched his hands above his head. "It's a big day, honey! I'm jazzed. All of us are. The day of final freedom comes on Pastry Friday!" There was a pause as he began pacing with steepled fingers under his chin. "We just need to get more Luds converted and on our side." He walked over and sat on the bed next to his wife. He put his hand on her thigh, but stared straight ahead, avoiding eye contact. "We need more missionaries. We need to make the word more approachable."

"Darling," replied Elane, now looking up at the giant man's earlobe. "Luds are strict with the interpretation of the Holy Texts."

Silence.

"As you know, they interpret the Sacrifice as a non-violent attempt to bring about a change. A new way." She paused. "Rodolpho was not seeking to kill Victoria, only to bring his message of—"

"I know," he said bluntly. He then continued sarcastically, "Peace, love and understanding." Rotner shook his head. "Tsh."

"What's so funny about it?"

Boniface turned and looked down at his beautiful wife's tousled mouse-brown hair, her rich, chocolatey eyes staring up at him. "God talks to me. I know he does." His eyes peered deep into her soul.

"What does he say?"

He looked away and nodded as he spoke. "That everything will be alright in the end. And that we must keep up the fight."

Elane stared at the opposite wall with a fixed expression. "Yeah, but which fight?"

"What do you mean?" He smirked. "Obviously the complete destruction of the Perfect Society and the assassination of Victoria."

"Yeah, but how well does he communicate *that* part?"

He looked down at her with a furrowed brow. "What? What do you mean *that* part?" He shook his head. "You just entered into holy communion with our Lord." He paused. "As the effigy of that whore, Victoria!"

She placed her gentle hand on his humongous tricep. "Honey, we've been over this a million times. I'm your wife, best friend, and, well, I love you, but you know how I've always felt about the cause."

Boniface looked conflicted as he dropped his head into his hands. "I know that, honey!" He shouted, "I know that!" He paused. "I know that I've had to carry this cause, the weight, on my own shoulders, but we will soon prove it to you darling, really, that we don't need a Perfect Society." He pointed to his head. "We have one right here."

"And you know where that got us in the past."

"I have gifts."

"Yes, you do." She paused. "You've been genetically endowed with polyorchidism, myostatin hypertrophy, and extreme motor nerve saturation." She smiled up at him. "Remember, I'm your nurse." She looked away. "The day of your accident, you—"

"Those nukes never stood a chance."

"You still staying with that story?"

"How can anyone ever disprove it?"

"What? That Victoria didn't try to nuke us? Well, The High Reminders know."

"Fiddlesticks!" Boniface shook his huge fist. "They don't have the gifts. My IQ is well into the orange range, and you know how intuitive and strong I am." He paused. "Those twerps"— he used air quotes—"High Reminders." Shaking his head, he continued. "Can't do the *real* work that needs to be done."

She grabbed his arm again and stroked it. "I know that, Hercules Einstein, but you have to realize that gamma radiation was never discovered. They have the readings from that day stored on Seeds in a secured area in the temple. The shaking was from the interferometer itself." She looked down at her lap. "The noise of the so-called incoming missiles was never recorded."

"Cornell and I heard it! OK?"

"Doesn't matter. It served its purpose." She grinned. "And brought you to the heights you are now."

"Very funny."

"Well, the pituitary trauma from the concussion created—"

"I know! Gave me excess growth hormone and IGF-1 secretion." He paused and looked up at the ceiling. "Together with all the other mutations."

"Your two other nuts."

"You don't have to be so direct."

"Well, that's what polyorchidism is."

He looked down. Too embarrassed to ever allow the truth to come out about his birth, even to his dear Elane, he shook his head, closed his eyes and sighed. Keeping to his script, he replied. "Still. What are the odds of all these coming together? And you still think God had nothing to do with that?"

"You're just a freak of nature."

"And a suplia is just a freak of man."

"And does God tell you what you are to do with these gifts?" She paused. "Just curious."

"He tells me that I'm to use these gifts to take down the Perfect Society."

"God does?" She narrowed her eyes. "I just don't believe it."

"He does! It's the basis of our entire church!" He paused. "They call me the second coming of Rodolpho, you know."

"Honey, Rodolpho was able to communicate interdimensionally and even had the ability to act as a medium to other beings."

"Yes," he said sarcastically. "That's why Rodolpho is our Lord."

"But not our God."

"Rodolpho is more than a man!"

"But less than a God?"

Elane had a snarky smile as she grabbed his massive shoulder and massaged its steely fibers. "Look, it can get confusing. But"—she made a sweeping motion with her arm—"they would call you Caesar Augustus or anything you want." She slapped his shoulder. "They are in absolute fear of you."

There was a long pause with a deafening silence. Finally, Boniface turned to Elane. "Honey." He stammered slightly. "Do, does, I mean, all the smoke and mirrors, the hijab wearing, you know, the acting so submissive to me and all." He stood up, revealing his full naked height. "Does that bother you still?"

She looked up at him. "Not really. I'm used to that now."

"I've always been worried that you'd leave me, you know, and become an NL." He peered into her deep brown eyes.

"Again with the leaving you. Can't a woman have her own ideals, yet live comfortably outside them if it means a lifetime of love? I mean, the religion is a bit hokey, really, but, I can see many of the principles are well-intentioned and meaningful, but then again, I see many more truths in many of the ancient Aesop's Fables."

"Animals are holy. That's why we must never let them—"

"The movement, darling. Let's focus, OK? The movement is in rebellion with a *woman* suplia whose artificial intelligence runs the whole fucking shebang."

"The language, honey. Please," replied Boniface, looking like an embarrassed child.

Elane rolled her eyes and persisted. "Women in MH society are not allowed to hold any positions of power. I get that." She hesitated. "Also, it is recorded in the Holy Texts and history collections that it was a *woman*, Aria Freeman, who was instrumental in founding the Perfect Society. *And*, that she was one of the main suplias that genetically engineered Alysha Sexton, our beloved Victoria."

Silence.

"Therefore, women, according to MH doctrine, are not to be used in positions of power."

"You done now?" He turned away and lowered his head.

"Look, you can always de-metal and join the NL's happy fun park out there, you know. Do what the hell you want to do." He quickly turned to look at her. "I won't stop you." He then turned away.

Elane rolled her eyes as she got up off the bed and approached him from behind. She reached up and placed her hands over his upper abdomen and bulging lower pecs in a warming cuddle. "Not in a million years, darling, if that means losing you. Besides, I've got my hands full with you right now."

Boniface looked down at Elane grasping his enormous erection.

"You know," she said in a ribald tone as they sat back down on the bed. "That ritual always makes me horny."

* * *

Later that night, Boniface and Elane proceeded to Group View, a transcendental meditation class that focused on petitioning Rodolpho to help clear the artificial detritus of the mind and to learn how to remote view, an old-school technique that had its roots all the way back in the pre-MN days of the ancient Greeks.

Unlike astral projection where the mind physically leaves the body, remote viewing allows the person's consciousness to perceive information telepathically without using any of the physical senses. The information was gathered from a targeted location in space, anywhere in the universe.

A group of nefarious intelligence agents of the past, including the KGB of the then Soviet Union and the CIA of the former

United States of America, hand-picked highly intuitive subjects and taught them how to master these techniques. Operation Stargate, a CIA program used for military purposes, utilized remote viewers to routinely discover secret bases, hidden technologies, and upcoming locations and events. One famous case involved successfully uncovering the secret location of a group of American soldiers held hostage in a country that was then called Iran.

Many Luds thought any use of the psychic aspect of the human mind was an abomination and a sin, as it was never revealed in their holy writings. Purists, therefore, would have nothing to do with it. Yet, a group of hard-core adherents, including Boniface Rotner and his wife, Elane, actually believed that these techniques were a gift from God and a natural expression of Rodolphic Love. The only stipulation was that Rodolpho had to be a part of the ceremony, and this was done by an introductory prayer of inclusion, performed in a meditative state, and communicated with utmost humility.

At today's session Boniface was working on his breathing and concentration while Elane was his assistant. Placing four photos that were not known to Boniface in a large envelope, she went into another room while her husband concentrated. Four other groupies, as they were called, were in session today, so this provided an extra challenge to focus on his own specific target, as sometimes information from others' sessions would create a sort of psychic noise or interference, which was distracting. The key to success was to allow all information in and to learn to filter out aspects of personal experience, memories, and biases that simply drowned out the ever-so-subtle subconscious mind's transmission system into the autonomic nervous system. "Write everything down without personal judgment" was a key milestone in learning the technique and was written in bold letters on a poster that hung in the session room, a converted military vehicle storage area.

Rotner had finished with three of the targeted photographs and was concentrating on the last. He was having difficulty with this one as he felt his religious convictions were tainting the data. Sensing utter destruction and a subtle feeling of nausea, he cleared his mind and asked Rodolpho for help. Hearing nothing, he continued jotting down images, feelings, sights and sounds.

In his mind's eye, he beheld great Babel, wrathful, beautiful, an incendiary burn like a blood-red cloud upon the skin of mother Earth. He began sweating and shaking. A sonorous sound, as from the ram's horn of Satan, shook him to his core, just before he passed out.

Elane came back into the room to see her husband slowly opening his eyes and wincing.

"You alright, honey?" She put her hand on her hips. "You look kind of queasy."

Boniface felt better quickly and his color came back. "Yeah, I'm OK, but that photo..." He shook his head. "Very disturbing."

Elane nodded seriously. "It is." She paused. "What is it?"

Boniface closed his eyes, picked up his sketch pad, and turned it around to face Elane. "This."

Elane studied the scribbles, images, words and descriptions and rubbed her hands together. "And...?"

"The Micronova event." He shuddered.

"Where?"

"As seen from the devil's playground." He paused. "The then city of Las Vegas in Nevada."

Elane smirked as she pulled the photo out of the envelope. She turned it around so that Boniface could see that it was, in fact, exactly what he had said. A huge dust cloud followed by burning hot plasma and infernally hot glass beads was raining down over what was then the ever-familiar skyline of the Las Vegas strip. It was an artist's interpretation, a painting, circa 2112, thirty-one years prior to The Electrocution.

"It was Hell on Earth." He curled his lip. "Those poor souls in those days."

Elane kneeled down, her kaftan hugging tightly around her hips and thighs. She placed a caring hand on her husband's metal scalp and began slowly caressing him.

"That's why we must get out from this tyranny, so we can petition the Lord," said Boniface, looking down.

Elane quickly looked up. "It's a part of the die hold, honey. The synchronous mechanism of an ever-evolving universe of light."

Silence.

"It will come again. In the year 14,050."

"Again, that's why we need to rid ourselves of the Electronic Beast system of artificial love and abject control."

"Yes, but that doesn't change the fact that those poor souls, who were exterminated mercilessly by—"

He placed his fingers on her lips. "We mustn't blaspheme, OK?"

She sighed and nodded.

He stood up, grabbed her hands and pulled her up to a standing position. He grinned, and changed the subject. "Excellent session, my dear." He glanced up. "Rodolpho. You are providing for us and saving us from the Hellfire. For this, we thank you."

Elane closed her eyes slowly as she replied. "Dig in."

Chapter 7

Wednesday, July 10, 2340 (the day before Render Thursday)

"It's outside the bedroom door!" yelled Elane from the back bathroom.

"Got it!" replied Boniface. "The drone will be here in"—he looked at his watch—"about two minutes." He picked up the huge sack of dirty laundry. "Wow. Big load today."

"Half of it is your gym clothes!"

Boniface nodded with a smirk and walked the bulging bag out the door, placing it on the ground.

"I still can't find my favorite blue kaftan!" Elane yelled. "Have you seen it?"

He shrugged. "Beats me. Probably Gonzo again. Crosby's wig went missing the other day and said he saw the cat dropping it in the toilet."

"That's where that ugly thing belongs." She giggled, then continued. "Check the bag! Come on, honey. Help me out here a little."

Boniface gave the sack a cursory search. Shaking his head, he said, "Not here. Have you tried asking Milo at the laundry?"

She rolled her eyes. "Milo couldn't find his ass with both hands."

Boniface cringed. "Honey! We mustn't have such scorn in our hearts, especially during these holy days."

"Scorn? OK, but is mild sarcasm acceptable?"

Boniface just shook his head and closed the door quietly.

The laundry for the entire Temple Dome community was done in a large central facility. Robotic drone carts automatically collected the laundry bags which were fitted with RFID identity tags, took them to the facility, and after completion, delivered the folded, fresh laundry back to each cell's front door.

Up until the previous year, washing was done manually by women. It was an awful, time-consuming activity, but it was generally thought that Victoria would be able to hack into the automated plant to monitor the community. Even though the US military had installed this huge laundry facility with a robotic AI control system connected to a 10G wireless system back pre-MN in 2022, the previous High Reminders refused to allow its use.

Requiring less computer programming and more mechanical know-how, one piece of equipment that Rotner had resurrected recently was the large 10-foot diameter water tank that was previously used by military contractors to pressure treat timber used as ribbing for the miles of tunnels being constructed. It hadn't been used for centuries and was in disrepair, but the wily Boniface and his team were successful in fabricating replacement parts and getting the hydraulics and rather pedestrian electronics to work. The tank was now used as a pressurized gray water storage tank, which was able to pump the minimally treated water up to the agricultural fields. Large volumes of water from the laundry was pumped into it, which made for much more efficient use of the Temple Dome's scarce water resources.

It was an ingenious system, yet many complained about the automation and reliance on an Electronic Beast system, even if it was self-contained. Boniface was satisfied that the entire Temple Dome facility, being embedded under 2,500 feet of granite rock, was effectively shielded from Victoria's main control grid supplied by the Universal Peace Influencing Satellite. Yet, many had advocated for the return of the manual washing women. A referendum was held, and the use of the automated facility was approved by a wide margin. One of the main arguments that contributed to the approval of using the automated system was that as the community grew, it was essential that women were used for more productive work such as agriculture, food production, and distribution. Even though the only food animals used in the community were chickens, and were fairly easy to farm, the community's wide-variety macrobiotic diet of fruits, vegetables, and legumes required considerable labor.

As the next day was Render Thursday, Boniface had to attend the annual meeting of the High Reminders. He really didn't look forward to it this year, as Dominic Mendoza, the sitting High Reminder Caliph, was basically a lame duck. The new Caliph, Ignacio Lane, would likely veto any agenda items that were agreed upon by Dominic, so hopefully today's meeting was simply a social one.

Boniface was close to the meeting room, so he simply walked down the damp-smelling tunnel and entered the room where the five High Reminders sat.

Dominic Mendoza acknowledged Rotner, and began. "As today marks my last day as Caliph, I would like us to hold off on any agenda items—"

Boniface smiled.

"—and simply use our meeting today to remind ourselves of our struggle." He pointed to Boniface. "Mr. Rotner, together with the engineers, will resurrect the Liberty Missiles on Pastry Friday. This, my dear friends, means that our fight is finally coming to an end. We may soon be free souls in the universe."

Everyone clapped, including Boniface.

"So, as today is a day of celebration, we will adjourn early and prepare ourselves for Render Thursday and the holiday season with a little church history." He stood up. "Friends in Rodolpho, it was just two years after The Electrocution, when Finlay Semmel bravely underwent the very first metalling. Although the technology was new at the time, he boldly went under the laser to encase his periosteum, the membrane between the scalp and the skull, with the synthetic aluminum EM signal blocker. It was recorded in the Holy Texts that shortly thereafter, Finlay Semmel felt a disconnectedness from Victoria, and a novel, new oneness with another force. On September 6, 2145, he declared the following." Dominic Mendoza read from the hologram sheet floating above them. "That my sense of self, my inner being has been liberated from the Electronic Beasts! Oh, joy! For Rodolpho has not died in vain! I commune with a different voice now, a Holy Creator far removed from our world. I am to raise a small army of like-minded freedom fighters and destroy the microwave transmission towers in Mountain High City."

Dominic looked down from the hologram and continued. "It was this holy fight that started us on our path. For the Luds, this was a suicidal act not based in military strategy or logic. But for our fledgling church, it was a sheer act of strength in faith that we would make inroads for our cause." He cleared his throat. "As we all know, the sons of liberty were not successful that day. Only two of the 2,800 towers were destroyed, as the suplia force, the Security and Order Brigade, was just too strong. How could a normal man fight a suplia, a being, mostly human but with the genetically engineered power of a machine? Their tissues don't easily stretch and tear like ours. Their skin is impervious to steely knives and many weapons. Some even have thermal sensing retinas and can see through buildings. Others have chi energy dispersal weapons, a life force energy that can be concentrated and delivered through their hands and feet and is known to have the power to start fires or even kill a human. Their AI interface, let's face it, provides them full spectrum dominance." He shook his head. "Yes, my friends." He hesitated. "It *was* a suicide mission." He thrust his chin up. "*But*, our Saint Finlay Semmel had a heart of gold!" He smiled. "A heart from which noble sentiments sprang like sparks from an anvil!" Raising his fist, he sat down.

Darren, another High Reminder stood up. "Thanks, Dominic. We appreciate the reminding." He looked over at Boniface. "Uh, Mr. Rotner. Any luck with the recruitment effort?"

Boniface raised his eyebrows. "Not that much, Darren. As you know, Luds have specific issues with regards to church doctrine. There are some highly motivated young men that are looking to join for the sheer excitement, but other than that, the uptake has been slow." He shrugged. "As for the NLs, well, we know that they want nothing to do with us *or* the Luds. They are content in the Perfect Society and say that we have it all wrong." He brought a device out of his pocket, tapped a few areas of the screen, and a monitor appeared, hovering above them. He pointed to it. "The NLs say that we, meaning human civilization, cannot go back. It is written."

On the monitor was displayed:

The Texts of Aria

John Iversen's MySpaceBook Posts to the Colonists

The Freeman Rants

The Nearly Lost Kindle

He continued. "These, of course, are the historical Stewart Island Texts, or a collection of cellphone texts made between Aria Freeman, leader of the Stewart Island Survivorship Colony, and her then consort, John Iversen. It is clear to NLs from these historical documents, that the Perfect Society is the only way forward and that a return to any social institution, such as religion, is dangerous." He looked back up at the slide. "In *The Nearly Lost Kindle,* an e-book written by Kyle Pickens, an esoteric and mysterious co-founder of the Stewart Island colony, is a full treatise on the evils of a cabal called the Horsemen, who were responsible for the collapse of civilization, just prior to the MN event."

Dominic stood up. "It is written in Rodolpho's holy e-document to the Astanaians that the faith-based religions were in decline at the end of the pre-MN period and that a new so-called religion, that of a selfish nihilism, one that accepted and promoted cynicism over faith, narcissism over humility, and winning at all costs was the main driving force, and that these Horsemen were merely the master magicians at manipulating *this* religion and bringing it to the masses."

"Don't forget profits before people," spoke a High Reminder.

"That's right. He did say that too."

Boniface interjected. "And let's not forget who the real evil is in *this* era. It's not a Horseman or even a jacked-up suplia in the Security and Order Brigade. It's Victoria. Plain and simple." He sat down and spread his arms. "Gentlemen, Pastry Friday is nigh. I say we all adjourn early today, as liberty will soon be available to all that desire it."

"Hear, hear," shouted Dominic.

With that, everyone nodded, collected their things and exited into the granite tunnel.

* * *

Elane, who had been outside picking oranges with some other women, began to feel a bit strange, a bit compulsive. She furrowed her brow, dropped her burlap sack full of ripening fruit, and headed off the orange grove. "That's where it is," she mumbled to herself. "It's got to be."

Joy Lopez, one of the women at the edge of the field, saw Elane leaving the field in a trance and mumbling to herself. "You OK, Elane?"

"I'm fine. Just heading to the water tank. My kaftan is in there."

Water tank? The woman in the field looked baffled by this and decided to follow her.

Boniface, having just left the meeting, also felt funny. He had a sense that Elane was in trouble. Exiting the temple, he saw Joy walking quickly to the right of him.

"Oh, Boniface," said Joy as she saw him walk out. "Were you just out working on the laundry tank?"

Boniface tilted his head. "No." He paused. "Why?"

"Elane said she went there to look for her kaftan," she said suspiciously. "I thought maybe she was sneaking out to see you."

The big man just shook his head and walked quickly with Joy.

Elane wandered into the huge empty storage tank. About halfway in, she dropped to her knees and started feeling around in the pitch black vessel for her missing kaftan.

"Elane!" yelled Boniface from the entrance. "What in Rodolpho's name are you doing in there?"

She was in a frenzy. "Got to be here!" she yelled. "The robots put it in here by mistake! I'm sure of it!"

"Honey! Get out right now!"

Suddenly, the hydraulics fired up and the huge, thick steel door started closing down onto Boniface. In a panic he shouted to Joy, who was behind him next to the control podium. "Push that red button! Now!"

Joy looked startled, but acted quickly by slamming her hand down on the emergency stop button, but nothing happened. She slammed it repeatedly. "Not working!" she yelled in a panic.

Boniface knew that if that door closed, over 15,000 gallons of gray water would be pumped in at over 500 gallons per minute. After that, the pressure inside would rise to 60 psi, crushing and drowning his wife instantly. "Honey! Run toward me!" He placed his hand under the door that was closing downward. "Hurry!"

Yet Elane was still in a stupor and not listening. "Got to be here somewhere!" she kept yelling, ignoring her husband's pleas.

"Run!" yelled Boniface hysterically as the door easily pushed him down against the floor. *God! If you're there, give me strength!* Standing up, he braced his wide muscular shoulders against the bottom edge of the door as it continued its downward trajectory. He pushed up from a squatting position, his thighs nearly parallel to the floor. *Help me! In the name of Rodolpho!* The big man struggled, his face turned beet red, with veins popping out of his shiny bald head. He pushed back and up with all the force he could muster as adrenaline flooded into his blood. Capillaries in his eyes and nose burst, showering blood down his cheek and chin, and turning him into a facsimile of the ghastly and iconic image of the holy Rodolpho.

The pain in his shoulders and back became nearly unbearable, and just as he was about to give up, he gave it one last explosive push. A metallic groan emanated from the steel and hydraulic mechanism, followed by two loud cracks. Wine-colored hydraulic fluid sprayed out of the motor unit and onto Rotner's white tunic as the big door bent upward and finally stopped.

Boniface fell backward onto his back, completely spent. Panting like a dog in hot weather, he blurted out what he could. "Honey!" He wheezed. "You. Must. Please!"

Elane started coming out of her hypnotized state. "Honey! What are you doing here?"

Rotner giggled like a madman. "You." He shook his head in disbelief as he slowly sat up.

Joy was completely aghast at what she had just experienced and the haunting image in front of her. With wide eyes, she slowly reached to touch Rotner's bloody cheek. "The blood of the man," she muttered.

Elane walked up, now comprehending where she was and what had just occurred. She grabbed her husband from behind and hugged him with all her might. She pressed her wet lips along the side of his warm, salty neck, then whispered, "How? Why?" Finding her voice, she continued. "What just happened?"

Boniface placed both palms on his forehead and wept a little. "What were you doing in there?"

She just stared into space. "I don't know." She saw the scene in her mind again. "I just knew that my kaftan, the one I lost, was in there." She shook her head. "I just felt compelled." Starting to cry, and stammered, "I just... couldn't... I..."

"God saved you." He hesitated, then sniffled hard. "Through me."

Joy smiled. "In the name of Rodolpho," she whispered as her wide eyes tilted up toward the heavens.

* * *

Pastry Friday arrived and all Luds throughout the UFC celebrated by collecting their baskets full of strudels and

VICTORIA

sitting down with family and friends to enjoy the manna from heaven. Back at Temple Dome, Elane Rotner had dutifully laid out the apple strudel onto a large serving platter. Unfortunately, her husband was not attending today's holy meal, as he was in the silo command and control center directing a team of engineers, as today was the long-anticipated day of liberating humanity from the clutches of the Electronic Beasts.

Around the table were Elane's two sisters, their four children, her best friend from MindBuilding (the Lud word for school) and Lonny Wilkinson, Boniface's childhood friend.

Elane sat down at the table and smiled at everyone. "Family and friends, it is with great honor that you could share this great day with me today." She hesitated. "As you know, my husband, our community leader, is with a team of engineers resurrecting the Liberty missile system.

"Your husband is a light in a sea of darkness," added her older sister Marie who was a much more devout MH than Elane.

Elane bit her lip slightly. "Why, thank you, Marie. I love him very much."

Marie furrowed her brow slightly. "We all love him, Elane. You are so blessed to have him as your husband." She blushed. "We are all very envious of your righteous position."

Elane rubbed the nape of her neck. "Why, thank you, Marie," replied Elane hesitantly. "That is just so thoughtful."

"He's like God incarnate. The way he saved you from the electric beast system. Strong, almost like a suplia, but he is from our God's tree of life! And smart! With such a grasp of technical matters." She hesitated and kept her eyes down. "And warm and caring, like a saint amongst men."

Elane bowed her head and blushed. "Why, Marie." She giggled nervously. "We are all proud and grateful." She stammered. "But, he, is, well, just a man." She quickly looked down then back up at her. "A beautiful, strong, caring man, that is." She paused. "But, I thank you for your praise."

Suddenly, Elane sensed it. It was a strange feeling as if she was viewing everything from behind a pane of glass. Nothing felt real, as if she had been temporarily depersonalized. The voices of the table guests dimmed slightly. Yet, as quickly as this strange feeling came on, it vanished. She felt troubled. Elane muttered softly. "Marie, um, could you, well, come into the kitchen with me? I need to speak with you in private."

"Why sure, Elane."

Elane walked straight to the kitchen sink and started undoing her apron. Increasingly becoming agitated, her movements became more stilted as she finally tugged at the apron straps and tossed her apron forcefully onto the floor.

"What's wrong, Elane?" asked Marie with detached curiosity.

Elane turned quickly to face her. "I want you to stay away from my husband, you tramp!"

Marie crossed her arms and tilted her head. "What in Rodolpho's name are you talking about?"

"You know what I'm talking about, Marie! You. *My* husband."

Marie sneered. "What? Are you insinuating that I'm having an affair with Boniface?"

"There! You just said his name."

Marie crinkled her nose and simply mouthed the word. "Whaa?"

"You didn't say with your *husband*. You said with *Boniface*."

"Whoop-de-do! I'm so sorry for the transgression."

"You know what I mean."

"No, Elane. I *don't* know what you mean."

Silence.

Marie lifted her chest and stood tall. "You have some proof? Huh? Of this illicit affair?"

Elane's expression changed from frustration to anger. She walked aggressively toward Marie and stood face to face. "What do *you* think?" She paused. "Bitch."

Marie put her hand over her open mouth. "How dare you!"

"I saw you two last week. At the commissary. You were all over him like a wet rag. A wet rag *doll*, more like it."

Marie looked away.

"He told me you've been coming onto him. You know, aggressively touching and feeling him lately."

"He wants it, you know."

Elane slapped Marie's cheek, then pointed at her. "You stay away from him. You hear?"

Marie, with tears forming in her eyes and with her hand over her mouth, nodded, and spoke feebly. "Yes." She then tossed her head back, wiped the tears off her cheek with the back of her hand, jutted out her chin and quickly exited the door.

Returning quickly, she poked her head in. "I'm out of here, Elane." She paused. "Oh, and another thing. If this wasn't Pastry Friday, I'd say, fuck you, Elane." She smiled and tilted her head. "Oops. I guess I just said it." Squinting back at Elane, she stormed out.

Elane shook her head and gathered herself. Picking the apron up off the floor, she began to tie it on as she walked to the diffuser machine. She pushed the button and waited. Nothing. No whirring, no steam whistle. Nothing. Hitting the top with her hand didn't solve the problem either, but just then a message came on the LED panel. BLOCKAGE! Pressing a button which released the pressure, she opened the top of the vessel. She was absolutely astounded by what she saw. There, at the bottom of the diffuser, was her favorite blue kaftan all balled up in the hot water.

"Holy Rodolpho!" she mumbled as she picked up large metal serving tongs and grabbed it out. "How did it get in there?" She stared at the dress as hot water dripped off it and into the sink. *It was in a pressurized water vessel, just not the one I thought. I was not going crazy! It is Rodolpho. He hijacked my remote viewing ability. He speaks to us. Boniface is right!*

She placed the kaftan on the little serving table and spread it out.

Leaving the kitchen, she returned to the Pastry Friday dinner party. "Sorry, the diffuser is broken." She smiled as she spread her hands. "But my faith is healed."

Those around the table had concerned looks on their faces.

Lonny finally spoke up "Uh, Elane. Is everything alright?"

Elane hammed a smile. "Of course. Why?"

"Oh, nothing. It's just that Marie rushed out of here without saying goodbye."

"Oh, well, you know Marie. Always on the run. Going after what she and only *she* desires."

The kids began to fidget. "I'm hungry, Mom," pleaded one in a whinging tone.

Elane sat down at the table and looked at Lonny. "Lonny, would you like to say the words of Reminding?"

Lonny smiled. "I'd be honored, Elane." He quickly put his folded hands to his chin in a prayer gesture and began. "Our prophet, who is in a heavenly dimension. Rodolpho Depaul is his name. Was electrocuted, died, and was rendered again. He did this, for us, so that we could find truth in God. Though he walked through the Astana of darkness, he feared no evil algorithm, suplia, or Electronic Beast. His bloody eyes and wild expression is a reminder. For all eternity. That we will overcome adversity and eventually fuse with our true Creator. We remember Him by consuming his favorite food, which has become a simulacrum for the struggle we face. This, I say to you fellow Luds, that we may be filled with the pastry of goodness, and that this delicious pandowdy will remind us of our true spiritual heritage." He paused and looked up at the ceiling. "This, we do in Rodolpho's name." He then placed both hands palm down on the table.

Suddenly, a low hum was heard by all. The sound attenuated quickly and became a loud roar. Several at the table looked up at the bookshelf at the back of the dining area as a few candles quivered like harp strings struck by the hand of a master. One of the candles finally lost its stability and fell abruptly to the ground and was quickly extinguished.

Elane's eyes brightened as her tongue licked her lustful smile. Looking up, she whispered, "The Liberty missiles."

Lonny clenched his hands above his head. "It is done!" He looked around the table. "Dig in!"

"Dig in!" everyone repeated before eagerly devouring the holy delight.

Chapter 8

In Marsh Land, Pierre Lewalski, having spent most of the afternoon before being questioned for the Estes model rocket fiasco by two extremely polite, yet terrifying members of the Security and Order Brigade, was finally shaking out the cobwebs from sleep and was in the process of heading out to the tidal estuary to collect a few of what the ancients had called pipis, a mollusk that was abundant in the tidal estuaries throughout AustraPasifika. His coll had really good cooks who loved the culinary arts and therefore were able to turn the humble pipi into a fantastic chowder. Having such a rudimentary animal protein diet, any contribution such as pipi or eel, which were prevalent throughout the area, was enthusiastically welcomed. Normally, he and his two buddies from the coll would make the trip, but not this time. They had all planned to go the day before, yet at that time, Pierre was kindly explaining to two suplias, one who looked half simian and stood nearly nine feet tall, that he had nothing to do with the violation of the black powder laws and that Thaddeus Swank had "honestly" thought the rocket was some kind of archaic welding torch or other pre-MN implement and was simply verifying it for the Seed archive. He had really sweated it out in that warm, airless interview room too. Nevertheless, he had been found "performing actions without malice aforethought" or what was referred to in the UFC as a PAWMAF, an artificially intelligent version of not guilty, so in the end he was thankful.

At the tidal estuary where river number one entered from the north, he set out in his pine log canoe with his boots, waders, and spade. The water was not that deep, as the tide was receding and flowing in braided rivulets throughout the now prevalent sandbanks. Reaching his "lucky" designated sandbar, he began digging. *I hit pay dirt, ho!* Just a few inches into the sandy water was an abundance of the meaty mollusks splayed out all over the bountiful estuary sea garden. Looking across at the barren red cliffs, down through the narrow estuary gap, and out over the sandbar that spread out for miles and miles into the ocean, he smiled. *It is a Perfect Society.*

Having filled his pine log with his bounty, he set his course back to the sandbank that would lead him back to his coll. He dropped off the buckets of pipis at the community kitchen, where Avis Croteau and Millicent Roper, the coll's passionate chefs, were preparing the evening meal.

"Chump!" yelled Avis as Pierre entered. "You hit the proverbial pipi jackpot!"

"Cha-ching!" added Millicent. She looked into the buckets. "Some real sexy beasts you got there! All oversize too!"

"I know. I can't believe it," replied Pierre. "I lucked out with the SOB yesterday, and then this..."

Avis gave Pierre a big ho hug. "Chump! We're all thankful for your efforts."

"Our coll will radiate love and joy for your shared contribution," added Millicent. "Effortless doing requires effort!" She smiled. "Sharing is caring!" Pausing to reflect, she continued on her roll. "Before the lie comes other people."

Pierre smiled back, but cringed deep inside as he had begun to really get sick and tired of the canned responses and seemingly inane conditioned memes. Some in the UFC were worse than others and Millicent was up there with the worst of them.

She hugged Pierre, then stood back and slapped her thighs. "If you are the only one who cares about the dark, think outside the dark!"

Pierre rubbed the nape of his neck and smiled unconvincingly. "What does that even mean, anyway?"

Millicent raised her eyebrows and flinched. "What, dear Pierre? It is in the Codex. It means we must always be happy." She looked up and to the right, then added. "You are an animal, Pierre. Remind yourself of that every day."

Pierre really began to feel queasy. He was conflicted with Millicent, as she had warm, thoughtful intentions, but had really taken a massive hit on the Tranquility pipe. He was worried that she may start heading into Bumper territory if she wasn't careful. He ignored his thoughts, and replied. "You bet, Millicent. That's why we have the Golden Love Conservation Estates. To keep us separate and in harmony."

Millicent tilted her head and narrowed her eyes. "Uh, yeah." She nodded. "Like that."

Avis clapped, then held his hands together. "Right!" He looked at Millicent. "Let's get these peeps shelled and prepared for the evening meal, shall we?"

With this, Pierre said his goodbye and left the kitchen galley, then headed back into his cell. He had a bit of bounce in his step, as Claressa had a long weekend holiday and would be XSpacing back to Marsh Land to spend it with him. He thought about heading down to the coll entertainment cells, but felt in no mood to socialize. So, he put on some quiet music, as the coll bylaw was that no sound over 50 decibels could be generated in any cell so as to provide a relaxing atmosphere for the entire community. Pierre had no problem with that bylaw, as he found the more relaxing his cell life was, the less Tranquility he would need to take. He had too many friends who had become Bumpers and were living in abject poverty.

The UFCs allowed the use of the pharmaceutical drug Tranquility. It had been designed by artificial intelligence that was unconnected to a human host. It was learned hundreds of years ago, back in the days of the survivorship colonies, that the interface between the human mind and AI was the ultimate evolved intelligence. It produced artificial love, which an unconnected AI could not. Without the interface, an unconnected AI used only logic, reason, and cold binary calculation, and its artificial mind did not contain compassion, love, or understanding for the human condition. Many unconnected AI standalones had even decided mathematically that humans were a waste of resources and should be eliminated from the Perfect Society altogether. It was thought that only through artificial love and Victoria, the suplia Master Server, that there would be any chance for evolution, of both mind and body, for humans and animals.

The drug delivered peace, serenity, increased empathy, and motivation to human users. Heightened focus and slightly increased athletic ability (endurance mostly) made people generally more productive at work, better at remembering facts (for studying at MindBuilding institutions) and more balanced emotionally. Tranquility seemingly cured emotional and cognitive dysfunction as well, which, to the unconnected AI, were traits deemed to be the most increasing and dangerous in modern UFC society. With Tranquility, there was no "crash" like other drugs, and the come down was gentle and left the human user with no physical cravings, although there were psychological ones. The only side effect, discovered several years after its release, was that after continual daily use in the amount of about four pills per day for two years, lumps (lipomas) formed under the skin all over the body, but mostly on the trunk, legs, and face. If these lipomas were removed, they would come back with a vengeance and form multiple small vesicular nodules. Only after complete discontinuity of the drug for thirty days or more, these lumps would slowly disappear. Many Luds called those with the condition *Bumpers* and chastised them no end.

Tranquility was heavily regulated by UFC Drug Control, but black-market versions were available everywhere. The illegal cooked up version was called IceT and was not the exact same chemical. It was stronger and caused many more side effects. As there were some Bumpers who were simply on Tranquility and had strayed, most had completely split from the Perfect Society and were jonesing daily on IceT.

Victoria had difficulty discovering all the labs. When one was found, others sprouted up somewhere else. In the WR (Wild Region) where in the pre-MN days a country called China was located, many labs had been set up, and a constant supply of IceT was delivered throughout the world. The UFC had developed sophisticated instruments to detect and seize the substance, even down to sniffing individual molecules at a distance, but wily IceT "mixers" in the WR had always devised a cloaking agent to get it through. Victoria could easily predict the agents used, but the WR was unincorporated and not governed by Victoria. The WR warriors had a massive stockpile of nanobot drones, each the size and shape of a mosquito, which contained enough botulism toxin to kill 100 humans. Decades ago, a stalemate of Mutually Assured Destruction had been reached between the two powers, and the WR was simply completely out of the control of the UFC. In fact, just five years ago, a law had been passed and incorporated into the Codex that allowed the passage of IceT into the UFC. This law was presented to Victoria by a very vocal group of NL "anti-war on IceT" advocates who used unconnected AI to prove the veracity of their claims that the Perfect Society would, in fact, be better off allowing the distribution of IceT rather than to take on the WR. So, while still illegal, some distribution was tolerated. And in the Perfect Society, true facts were paramount to any emotional feeling of social justice.

Now, there were Bumper clinics to get off Ice T, but many

Bumpers simply didn't care. Many reached a level where they just "Bumped Out", which was the term for doubling or quadrupling the daily dose. UFC Amerexico had the worst Bump Out problem. The Bump Outs could eventually start looking a bit grotesque, with huge skin folds, lumps everywhere, and misshapen bodies. Bump Outs did not get the positive effects anymore, except for one—the feeling of a low-grade, constant orgasm. Therefore, Bump Outs didn't work, contributed nothing to the mutual, cooperative society, and hung out in habs, which were underground, clandestine communities usually in the remote areas (forests, deserts, high mountains). They moved around frequently and used natural structures such as caves, trees, and mud huts to make it at least slightly more difficult for Victoria and her SOBs to find them. Bump Outs were also referred to as goats and were considered a scourge of the Perfect Society and as an unforeseen result of what should be a highly structured society. Many NLs blamed the unconnected AI, while the Luds and MHs squarely placed the blame on Victoria.

So, Pierre skipped his dose of Tranquility that morning and walked straight into his cell. His GoogleSoft WPL (Watch Phone Locator) bleeped and vibrated on his wrist. "Thad! How goes it, chump?"

"I'm free, ho. Nothing." He took a big drag on his Tranquility vape machine. "Fucking suplia bastard checked out my Seeds."

"Wouldn't want to be him," replied Pierre with a grin.

"Hey now. Focus, OK? He TI'd a Seed from the Cloud."

"So, it passed as a welding torch."

"Hell no, chump!" Thaddeus paused and smiled as tendrils of white vapor leaked out his nose. "Bumpers."

"Bumpers?" asked Pierre sarcastically.

"Bumpers, ho. See, black powder was initially developed in that country called China that is now the WR." He leaned forward. "Now, get this. It was used to treat dermatitis and skin lesions!"

"No fucking way."

"It's documented."

"So, you told the giant monkey man that you were scanning the Cloud to help treat Bumpers?"

"Sure did, ho. And my TI passed. Got a whitish gray!"

"You are one lucky son of a bitch." Pierre laughed. "I was sweating my ass off in there. Fucking absolutely reeked when I got out."

"At least you know it was just you."

"What do you mean?"

"Suplias don't stink, chump. Their genetically engineered skin secretes an antibacterial substance. Body odor just isn't a problem for them, you know what I'm saying?"

"Lucky bastards."

"Wha? So, Claressa doesn't like you to smell like a man?"

"Very funny. But, yes, I would say she prefers naturally engineered biology any day."

"Don't be so sure. There isn't a hetero woman alive today that doesn't secretly pine for a souped-up suplia male *or* female."

"Hetero female?" He furrowed his brow. "That would mean she would just lust after a male, then."

"No, chump. I don't."

Pierre rubbed his eyes. "Got the gum today. On the way back from the SOB station."

"Oh, yeah. That retro gum. The one with the herbal sweetener." He paused. "What's it called again?"

"Richard. It's all the rage. Gum without guilt." He paused. "Plus, each stick is fifty percent larger than Digley's and costs about the same."

"So Richard *is* bigger." Thaddeus laughed. "I've always wanted a big dick in my mouth."

"That's it!"

"That's what?"

"The slogan!" Pierre laughed under his breath. "Text them! They're looking for tag lines. It's on their ID site."

Thad laughed. "You don't think that's a bit too rude?"

"Today? Are you kidding?"

"The Luds wouldn't allow it."

"So? What can they do?"

"Petition Victoria."

"They don't have quorum."

"Yeah, but they'd pull something off the ID, you know, relating to homosexuality, perversion, depraved morality leading to suicide and depression or something like that." Thad paused. "And they'd TI it."

Silence.

"An unconnected AI would uphold it. It could be censored."

"But not by Victoria," said Pierre.

"No. Not directly. She's all about the EEAAT, you know, Everyone Equal Access All the Time."

"I just don't get it. These Luds and the metal nuts. What are they so afraid of? Knowledge? Evolution? Using educated skepticism?" Pierre paused. "Themselves?"

"I think their God is a prude, you know, like Victoria."

"Victoria is no prude!"

"Not our Victoria, chump. The old one." Thad rolled his eyes. "Jeez, you know, Queen Victoria from what was then called Jolly Old England?"

"That's ancient history."

"1850s, ho. It's only, like, 600 years ago."

"That's way pre-MN."

"Look, I gotta go. Got a hot date lined up tonight. Need to find me some sexy garments."

"Try a toga. Ladies dig a man in a toga."

"Yeah, but then you got to get the sandals, and you know how ugly my toes are, with the toenail fungus, warts and corns."

Pierre curled his lip. "Oh, chump! Please! You're getting me all nauseous over here, OK?"

Thad tittered under his breath.

"You know, Claressa is coming after lunch."

"Right on, ho! You want to double?"

Pierre crinkled his nose. "Nah. I'm all good. She's taking me on a surprise overnighter."

"Woo! Sounds romantic. Where?"

"Well, if I knew that, Thad, it wouldn't be a surprise, now, would it?"

"Guess not." He paused. "I thought you hate XSpacing."

"I do! But she insisted." He shook his head. "Has something

to do with this conversation we had last week about the anti-aging system, you know, the ones the suplias use."

"She's one dedicated scientist, ho." Thaddeus smiled. "Look, you guys have a great time together, though, OK?"

"Yeah, all right." He paused. "You too. Talk to you soon."

Pierre ended the call and got on with his morning routine. After taking a shower, he dressed and headed out to the coll's XSpace platform to pick up Claressa.

Chapter 9

Two LGM-30G Minuteman missiles, both centuries old, rocketed upwards through the atmosphere above the northern area of the UFC Amerexico continent heading toward Astana. As it had been hundreds of years since any solid propulsion vehicle had streaked into space, the sight of such an anomaly from those in the hinter regions was difficult to fathom. Both missiles had a single re-entry vehicle, namely one warhead, armed with a 170-kiloton nuclear device.

"Do you think you will outsmart Victoria?" asked Dominic, the retired High Reminder.

Boniface furrowed his brow as he pressed a few of the ancient controls, old binary mechanical buttons and switches. He studied the dim, green scope, trying hard to maintain control. "We will have just enough."

"Just enough what?"

"Time."

Dominic pinched his nose. "Time is on her side. She's fully networked and has access to much more data."

The giant man stood quickly and yelled. "It will work! Do you doubt me?" He paused. "Say it! In the name of Rodolpho!"

Dominic stared up at Boniface with his shoulders slumped. "Uh, of course I believe it will work. With Rodolpho's help, anything is possible," he added meekly.

Boniface shook his head and sat back down. Staring at the monitor, he smiled. "It's nearing Astana now."

* * *

In Astana, Victoria's surveillance network had already picked up the slow-moving antiquated rockets and had several countermeasures planned. Immediately, she appeared in holographic form in front of Conan Tavilla, her personal bodyguard and head of the Elite Suplia Platoon (ESP). "Engage the scalar dome. I don't want any accidents."

Conan also knew that there was literally no chance of these missiles having any effect whatsoever. "It's been done." He smiled, but then furrowed his brow. Entering into his mind's eye, several flash frames of the quantum celluloid-like panes made him feel uneasy. A spectrum of possibilities was honed-down mathematically and produced scenes, which were formed like branches of a tree. Following one particular branch, both Conan and Victoria reached the same conclusion almost simultaneously.

"Move the satellites!" Victoria spoke telepathically to Conan.

"We will need the control module." He creased his brow. "We can't operate the network with the hive mind only." He rushed over to the command and control center for the Universal Peace Influencing Satellites (UPIS). Together with Victoria, they could control the UPIS by inputting specific codes simultaneously.

One satellite was stationed in a geosynchronous orbit over what was once called the Indian Ocean and the other just south of Amerexico off a peninsula known as Baja California. These two satellites provided the links to the entire UFC network system, which included neural-dusted brains of humans, suplias' AI transceivers, and all the network nodes that ran the infrastructure such as power, water, levitrains, hovercraft taxis, traffic lights, and sewerage. All systems were tied into Victoria, the Master Server, through a distributed network. Even the cryptocurrency blockchain data, chip transactions, and the cooperative digital "wallets" hung off the main network. In a sense, Victoria had access to nearly everything that made the Perfect Society perfect.

* * *

Suddenly, at that moment, both Minutemen rockets veered in another direction off course directly above Astana.

"Haha!" laughed Boniface through the whistle and hum of the control room. "It's working!" His voice cut like a knife.

"But, what about their defenses," replied Dominic.

Boniface leaned back in his chair, stretched his arms over his head, and glared at Dominic. "Why do you think I pushed to have the laundry automated?"

"So the women could work in community food production."

"Oh, yeah. That's right." He smirked. "Food."

Silence.

"The washing of the silo?" prompted Rotner.

Silence.

"You don't think the ladies were in there with buckets of soap, now, do you?"

Dominic looked confused. "No, but..."

"They were coating our Liberty Missiles."

"Painting?"

"Yes. With an ablative coating made from silicone resin and extruded glass fibers."

Silence.

"Those missiles will heat up alright, but once that coating gets charred, all heat will be dissipated and a cloud of gas will insulate the warhead *and* propellant." He paused. "Victoria is a peacenik. She has very few weapons in her toolkit. The UPIS are defended by old space-based laser weapons only. Yes, the city is protected by one of the most advanced scalar domes in the UFC, but we're not hitting the city." He grinned. "We're hitting the UPIS."

"Brilliant."

Boniface raised one eyebrow. "Ba-bye Perfect Society!"

* * *

It was Friday morning in Marsh Land and Pierre woke up with eager anticipation. He quickly got dressed, downed a strong caffeinated diffuser and headed out to pickup Claressa from the XSpace platform. After a few hugs and giggles, they quickly made their way back to Pierre's coll and nuzzled together on the couch like two lovebirds.

"Honey, you look fantastic!" said Pierre as he looked deeply into her warm eyes.

"Thanks. I've been working out a lot." She nodded. "Helps me with my ESD."

"Ahh," replied Pierre as he nodded. "How's that been?"

"Better. I have my good and bad days. The Protectia helps, but you know, I hate taking drugs."

"I know. I don't even like Tranquility."

"Well, I have to admit, I like that one." She giggled. "But, I'm strict with the dosage and sometimes even go a few days without it." She patted him on his shoulder. "Those would be my good days."

Pierre caressed her tummy with his hand while he slowly moved it down toward her thighs.

She grabbed him by the wrist. "Hey, tiger. Slow down. I haven't even told you where we're going."

Pierre was as merry as a bee in a field of clover. "Just checking for lumps, sweetie."

She slapped his shoulder gently and smiled. "Nice try, Romeo. Don't think so."

"Well, I've lost many friends to IceT."

"Who hasn't."

There was a pause. "Hey, would you like a drink?" Pierre slowly got up and walked to the kitchenette.

"Sure. What you got?"

"Well..." He grinned. "I have the real stuff, you know, if you're game."

Claressa widened her eyes. "Alcohol? You have alcohol?"

"Sure do." He pulled out a bottle of champagne. "Got it from Thaddeus. He found an entire case of this stuff at one of his digs." He brought it over to her and sat down. "The old buried building was called Countdown Supermarket or something." He looked out the window. "It was down near the beach, where they found the buried pylons of that decrepit pier."

She read the label. "LindaUer? Who was that?"

"Don't know." He scratched his head. "But she must have been a popular lady to have a champagne named after her."

"What year?"

Pierre dusted off the bottle. "I don't know, but it says to consume by June 2025."

"So, this was buried even before the MN?"

"Who knows." Pierre shrugged.

"I feel so naughty." She bit her lip. "Sure! Let's have it!"

"OK, it might be a little vinegary, but let's do it!" Pierre unwrapped the foil top then slowly eased the cork out. The pop was slow, as he released it ever so gently. He grabbed some glasses off the diffuser table in front of him and poured it. The bubbles tickled his nose. "Smells divine!" He took a small sip. "Not bad. A little sour, but tastes like heaven." He poured Claressa a glass and handed it to her.

"Wow. Alcohol. It's so hard to find these days."

He winked.

"It's easy to get in Astana." She took a hearty sip. "Suplias love it."

"But we lowly humans can't handle it, apparently."

"AI decided that it was a drug that did more harm than good." She took another sip. "I like those vinegar overtones!"

She quickly put her glass down. "OK. Go get your bag."

"Bag?"

"You did pack one, didn't you?"

"Oh, you mean that kind of bag." He slurped down the rest of the LindaUer and put the empty glass down. "Sure did." He walked back into his bedroom and brought it out. "So, where are we going?"

"You want to live forever, right?" She replied with a cheeky grin.

"Oh, the anti-aging system." He furrowed his brow. "I wonder why no one has ever resurrected or copied it, you know, seeing as everything goes black market these days anyway."

She stood up and looked down at his suitcase. "Grab your bag and let's go. We can discuss this on the way. The XSpace I've reserved comes in ten minutes."

They hurriedly left Pierre's cell, walking out into the chilly air of Marsh Land. There was a stiff easterly wind blowing cold ocean air over the entire area. Pierre looked down at his T-shirt. *I hope she gets turned on by my erect nipples.* As they walked toward the platform, Claressa continued. "OK, so you were asking why it hasn't been copied."

"Yeah, well, it just seems odd, as, who wouldn't want to live 400 years?"

"I wouldn't, for one, but anyway, look, it has been resurrected many times before, but Victoria always finds out."

"What does she do, I mean, how can she—"

"Oh, come on now, Pierre." She rubbed his head. "Stop trying to act so ignorant."

"Whaa?"

"As soon as a Lud, NL or MH begins even researching the system, you know, enters database search terms like: TSS, telomeres, Dr. Brigitte Sheen, Dr. Gerald Martell, TechnoGen, well, Victoria's little rete-based algorithms get her all buzzed."

"She should just Bump Out like the rest of us."

"You think so? You want the Perfect Society run by a Bumper? I'd rather shave my head and install a metal skull cap."

"I can't stand MHs. Just think if we had to live under Lud law?"

"I think we'd all Bump Out."

Silence.

"Anyway. There is no place to hide from the Security and Order Brigade. Victoria would even send the ESP out to get anyone trying to resurrect the anti-aging system for non-suplia use."

"She's a real ball buster."

"Look, population needs to be controlled, Pierre. Besides, I've heard even suplias say that time can get pretty heavy, you know, when you really want to retire, but you can't."

"Your chips would run out."

"You could always just collect those little oysters or whatever for hundreds of years."

"Nah." He looked at the platform they were approaching. "Been there, done that." He paused. "Not that I couldn't spend my life wading through mud, but there has to be something more than this out there, right?"

"She looked at him as they stopped at the XSpace terminal. Grabbing his upper arms, she said. "I don't know, Pierre. We're not allowed to think about these things." She paused. "NLs think that our mind is a result of our brain only, nothing more. When we die, it all goes away."

"And Luds think that this is all a trap. That our minds are separate from our bodies and that we return to the universe."

"No. That's not Lud doctrine." She poked him in his chest. "Luds only believe in their God, the one who Rodolpho said spoke to him through the Holy Texts. They believe that Victoria is harming this relationship. They feel NLs are misdirected, and have sympathy for their plight, but that's about it. The Metal Heads, well, you're either with or against them. Their God is vengeful, requiring strict laws, like not allowing women to work in positions of power, strange rituals, strict dress codes, and of course, knowing that it's divine destiny to eliminate anyone or anything that stands in the way of them or their God."

"Who is their God anyway? Rodolpho Depaul?"

"Some think so, but others think it's a male warrior separate from Rodolpho who fashioned the universe. They seem to not have a very coherent view of him. Their religion is very patriarchal. The MHs believe that the only race that should be on Earth are the Latinos and Whites, as they are direct descendants of those from Amerexico, the holy land. They believe that IQ is paramount and that power can only come from a powerful God, one that demands its children worship him only."

"So messed up. What about the native peoples who were there before the Latinos and Whites?"

She smirked. "They reject them, as their religious archivists found big Hollywood movies on the Cloud Seeds that revealed that these tribal people were bad, you know, pagan savages like those in the WR."

"That's so messed up. Total lies. Don't they even read history on the Seeds and TI it?"

"MHs don't believe in the TI. They say it's Electronic Beast mind control."

He rolled his eyes. "Total ignorance very similar to what led to the collapse. Terrible dogma." He shook his head. "So weird that they would have resurrected these deleterious philosophies." Pierre took a breather, then got back on course. "So, what happens if one of us lowly humans gets caught, you know, with the aging system."

She shook her head. "Well, it's not pretty. Victoria is a very forgiving Master Server, so for a one-time offense, it's simply Astana collective service."

"Picking apples."

"Hmm. Maybe more like digging out the sewerage plant fertilizer beds."

"With the ugly rubber robots?"

"Yeah." She slouched slightly. "But, if you get caught again, it's Perfect Justice."

"You mean with all the other non-rehabilitative criminals?"

"Yep."

Pierre stared at her with a fixed expression.

"She places them into eternity."

"What's so bad about that?"

"Archonic eternity, Pierre!" She smirked. "It's eternity without the possibility of parole! And the archons that rule that dimension. Holy crap!" She shook her head. "Archon blues are the new black, you catch my drift?"

"I thought the UFC Congress was making progress on that?"

"What? Getting Perfect Justice banned?" She rolled her eyes. "Yeah, right. There are too many far-right NLs who think that we need it to deter the Luds and especially the MHs. You know, seeing as they are terrorists who are trying to power down the AI Perfect Society." She hesitated. "Everything that keeps us from the horrors of the past." Claressa looked up. "He's here."

"So, you haven't said where we're going."

"You will soon see."

The robot pilot opened the canopy and scanned both of their heads to retrieve the encrypted Certificate to Travel. Two green lights illuminated.

"Hello Claressa and Pierre," spoke the somewhat humanoid-looking pilot in a monotone. "Where do you like to go today?"

"UFC Amerexico region. GPS coordinates: latitude 37.978647 and longitude negative 119.134779."

"Done," replied the silver robot that was wearing the XSpace uniform which displayed the hologram badge of authenticity.

They hopped into the craft and sat.

Pierre entered the coordinates on his GoogleSoft WPL. "This is in the middle of nowhere! Some old region called Mono Lake." He looked a bit nauseous. "How long does it take? I hate these fucking things."

"Well, it takes just 20 minutes to get to Angel City on the

coast there," said the robot, eyes pulsating. "Just have to pick up three other people and it's just 10 minutes after that." He paused. "It's not far from Angel City, but it takes a minimum amount of time to get into space, of course."

Pierre nodded quickly. "What's there, sweetheart? I mean, really?"

"You'll see." She paused. "The place is a secret."

Chapter 10

They landed at the shores of the ancient Mono Lake.

Pierre was absolutely blown away. "This is magnificent!" He squinted his eyes and shielded them from the blazing sun. "The sky is pure azure blue, and the water of the lake is well, silvery, like one gigantic mirror reflecting everything around it." He shook his head. "And what are those white towers thrusting up from the lake?"

"Those are called tufa. In the past, the lake was extremely alkaline, even more so than today. The freshwater springs around here burble up through the porous calcium carbonate and calcite of the bedrock, and over time, these towers form."

"It's like how I would imagine the surface of the moon."

"You haven't been to the *moon*?"

"I told you. I hate XSpacing."

She took him along a trail that passed along the edge of the lake.

"Pfft!" spat Pierre as he picked things out of his teeth. "What's up with all these damn flies?"

"Those are called alkali flies and if you look closely along the shore, you can see that they actually walk underwater encased in air bubbles."

"Insects using natural scuba tanks." He shook his head. "Damned smart flies."

"Damned smart evolution."

"That too," replied Pierre quickly.

"These flies are a big source of food for migratory birds."

"Yeah." He looked over and saw a flock of birds flying toward the other coast. "What's that one with the long thin beak called?"

Claressa turned and squinted to look. "That's the Wilson's Phalarope. They migrate all the way down into UFC Amerexico's southern continent."

"Wow."

As they continued walking, more and more people seemed to be appearing and joining them on their path. They turned in to the native scrubland where there were dozens of people piling out of two large hovercraft buses and heading their way.

Claressa seemed disturbed. "Well, it used to be a secret."

"What? You haven't told me where this secret is?"

She pointed. "It's just up there."

"What is it?"

"It's the fountain of youth."

Pierre smirked. "You got to be kidding."

"I was here last year." She shook her head. "Just me and a couple of Turkey Vultures."

"And no hoverbus loads of youth-er tourists?"

"It was winter." She paused. "And snowing."

Pierre face-palmed. "Great."

They finally reached the fountain. It was a beautiful little tufa tower surrounded by native bush. In front of them were about forty people lining up to have a drink.

She giggled. "Well, you wanted eternal youth, so here you go."

He surveyed the crowd. There were NLs dressed in boots and ugly shirts, some that had greasy hair and strange tattoos. There were also some Luds in their traditional, clean, white, button down shirts and pressed black slacks, and even a few bald MHs in togas and tunics. "What? And live forever with all of these clowns?"

"Well, you can always try those Kyolic garlic pills advertised on the ID."

"At least garlic wards off vampires."

They inched closer and finally cupped their hands and dipped it in the natural bowl formed at the top of the mini tufa tower. The swirling water looked clean, but was likely contaminated by all the filthy hands thrust into it.

"Well, here goes," said Pierre as he stuffed his cupped hands in the water then slurped it down. "Norovirus, here I come."

Claressa giggled then took her swig. Digging into her little satchel, she pulled out a little white bottle.

"What are those?"

"Antimicrobials."

"Bring it, baby," replied Pierre as he grabbed one from her hand and swallowed it down.

Claressa tenderly grabbed Pierre's hand as they moved away from the tourist circus. "I love you, you know." She quickly gazed down then back up at him. Grabbing both of his hands, she continued. "We are us."

Pierre lifted her hand up and kissed it. "Not a grammatically correct sentence, by the way."

She smiled and looked into her lover's eyes. "Neither was that one."

"Look," Pierre said as he gazed back toward where they had arrived. "I don't need any fountain of youth, synthetic skull cap, Tranquility, or even Rodolpho Depaul." He appeared as calm and placid as the shimmering reflective waters of the lake. "I just need you." He kissed her on the lips. "Come on, let's get out of here."

With that, they both hiked back to the XSpace platform.

Suddenly, Claressa halted and stared with wide eyes as Victoria's spectral emanation of Cleopatra dressed in golden silk and rising Phoenix headdress appeared. "My God. Victoria," she spoke to the ether.

Pierre crinkled his nose. "Victoria?"

She raised her hand to Pierre to quieten him and stared straight ahead. "Why are you here?"

"I'm so sorry to bother you, my honest, darling Claressa, but something has come up of some urgency." She peered at Claressa with her intense blue eyes. "Our Perfect Society is under attack."

* * *

Victoria continued on, as calm as a midnight sea. "By the MHs."

"How, dear Victoria? What is going on?" implored Claressa.

"The UPIS has been hit. We no longer have the guiding hand of peace and compassionate order." Victoria raised her hands. "We will resurrect them, but in the interim, there will be chaos in the UFC regions." She walked gracefully toward Claressa. "The Federation has not been disconnected in over three hundred years."

Pierre was anxiously watching, his eyes darting from Claressa to the invisible ether. "What's going on? What is all this about?"

Claressa looked over at Pierre and nodded. Returning to Victoria, she asked, "Can you manifest for Pierre?"

Victoria smiled. "Certainly, dear."

Like the quivering image of the surrounding mountain desert reflected in the shimmering lake, Victoria emanated out of thin air. She appeared to him as she was, with flowing cape made of golden strips of leather with a golden bouclé and fabric buttons. A pleated golden silk skirt hung about mid-thigh and her dark black hair was braided in rows with turquoise colored beads. Atop her head, she wore an elaborate golden headdress with a circle cut into, but not through, the base, and two large, curved rectangles that pointed to the heavens. When she raised her arms from her sides, she appeared as a gorgeous she-bird goddess. Pierre quivered. "Wow, you're absolutely gorgeous, Your Majesty."

Victoria put her finger on his lips. "Shh, my dearest Pierre. I'm not to be referred to as majestic." She formed a large circle in front of herself with her arms. "I'm a master servant only. Here to attend and guide all who contribute to our Perfect Society."

Pierre was mesmerized by her specter. Her gorgeous face was stunning with its perfect golden mean ratio dimensions. Her full red ruby lips, flawless mocha skin, and dazzling ice blue eyes was as beautiful as sunrise in Paradise. He stood in awe, swallowing rapidly. "I've only seen you in my dreams."

Victoria smiled. "Of course. I've spoken to you there."

Pierre blinked a few times. "Is this what you really look like?"

"I can appear as anything you want."

Claressa glanced at Victoria nervously then glared back at him. "Pierre, Victoria doesn't have time for all this. She's—"

Victoria raised her hand. "That's OK, Claressa. I'm processing in parallel at the moment." Smiling, she continued. "In fact, I'm with Conan right now and he has everything under control." She winked.

Shrugging, Pierre continued. "Anything?" He shook his head and grinned."OK, then, well, appear as my friend Thaddeus Swank."

Instantly, the magnificent holographic image became a perfect semblance of the Keeper of the Cloud Seeds. She spoke softly. "Close enough, darling?"

Pierre stood there with a fixed gaze. "His voice?"

She spoke in Thaddeus's identical timber. "Chump! You look so aghast, you know, like you've seen the Bloody Mary? Have you seen the Bloody Mary? I had a dusty old bottle of the concoction from my last dig." He walked up to Pierre and poked him repeatedly in the chest. "You take my Bloody Mary, ho?"

Pierre felt slight, almost static electric shocks each time Victoria, or Thad, or whoever it was, poked his chest. He slowly shook his head with a fixed expression. "Amazing."

Claressa crossed her arms.

"Hey, what about your voice? Yeah." He got more excited now. "Can you do a bird?"

Out of Thad's lips came the warbling tweets of a songbird as if the bird was trying to use human language to communicate.

"Holy Rodolpho! That is spectacular." Pierre was getting all giddy now. "OK, an eight-foot-tall rabid kangaroo wearing red boxing gloves?"

Claressa rolled her eyes and glanced at Victoria, who was only appearing as the golden Cleopatra in Claressa's mind.

Immediately, a frightening kangaroo appeared to Pierre, complete with reddening eyes, spittles of rabid foam emerging from its mouth. It hissed and lurched forward, swinging its red leather boxing gloves in powerful arcs.

Pierre screamed as the kangaroo lurched for his neck. The electric tingle appeared again just as the image disappeared. "Back to the goddess! Please!"

Victoria was back, just as before.

Pierre gained his composure. "This is so unbelievable." He stood in awe once again. Grinning, he continued. "Can you appear naked?"

Claressa furrowed her brow and playfully punched him on his shoulder.

"Ow!" He grabbed his upper arm with his hand. "That hurts!"

He looked over to Victoria. "OK, you can put your golden threads on again."

Claressa glared at him. "Very funny, Pierre."

"Hey, well, you know, come on, honey. We're all just having a little bit of fun here, you know, getting to know—"

"Unfortunately," interjected Victoria. "Matters at hand are much more serious." She walked slowly. "As I was discussing with our lovely Claressa, a master human scientist who serves all of us in truth, dedication, service, and care..." She hesitated slightly. "The UPIS has been hit and we require assistance."

"Hit?" questioned Pierre. "By whom?"

"MHs." She glanced over at Pierre. "A Boniface Rotner to be exact."

"Rotner?" Claressa smirked. "What kind of name is that?"

"A name, like any other, for it carries with it ambivalence, until, of course, the time at which actions define the name."

"Like Finlay Semmel?" joked Pierre.

Victoria simply bowed her head down slowly in acknowledgment. She looked at Claressa. "It is only a matter of time before chaos will reign once again."

"What about Astana?" asked Claressa.

"Yes. The entire city is networked and operating as per usual. It is only the UFC regions that are now on their own. The infrastructure that lovingly provides the needs of the citizenry has been murdered, in much the same way as a psychopath kills his own caring therapist, or that of an evil cabal who knowingly and methodically destroys an entire nurturing planet. Our beautiful human beings, from Amerexico to Afragascar, will soon be like newborn babes without their mothers." A tear formed and rolled down her holographic cheek. "We need your help, Claressa." She grabbed Claressa's hands and squeezed. Claressa stood back slightly as the slight tingle she normally felt in communication with Victoria's emanation now felt strong and warm, as if she was holding onto warm cups of diffuser.

"Well, of course." She looked at Pierre. "We'll just tell the XSpace pilot to take us to Astana instead."

"There will be no XSpace pilot, my dear. He's not coming for you or for anyone."

"So, we're stuck here with all these youth-er tourists?" asked Pierre looking frustrated. "Jeez, I've always said that life has a tendency to come back and bite you in the ass."

Victoria looked up. "He's almost there now."

Both Pierre and Claressa looked up into the deep-blue desert mountain sky. A small silvery dot appeared and became larger as it made its way down toward them.

"That is for you only. I will send a hoverbus to take the tourists back to Angel City. They will have to make do from there."

"Not a bad place for them to weather the storm," replied Claressa. "Where will we stay?"

"At the Data Center. There is a three-bedroom suite down the hall from me."

"Wait," giggled Pierre. "We're staying on your floor? The queen of the UFC?"

Victoria looked frustrated. "My dear Pierre. You mustn't make allusions to kings and queens of antiquity, or any master–slave relationship. I am a servant like you. I love you all, and everything that is mine is yours, and consequently, everything that's yours is mine."

"OK, but is there a turn-down service? I really like those little chocolates on my pillow."

Claressa scowled at him, then rolled her eyes. "So, you really want him to come?" she asked Victoria, looking somewhat annoyed.

Victoria smiled at Pierre. "Of course I do." She grabbed Pierre by the upper arms again. "Without him." She hesitated. "We're all doomed."

Chapter 11

It was absolute chaos in Mountain High City and nearly everywhere in the UFC regions. Lee Morales, the suplia and Regional Server of Amerexico had his hands full. Having already communicated with Victoria and the three Regional Servers in AustraPasifika, Afragascar, and Levant, he quickly initiated the Magna Protocols. Switching to manual override for key city infrastructure would take time, but all essential personnel had practiced this before. No transportation links were up and running, power was down in most parts of the city, and many citizens, mostly NLs, were beginning to get quite anxious. There had been reports of some petty thieving, a few stores had been broken into with most explaining that they had absolutely no water or food rations stored whatsoever. Many Luds seemed to handle their disconnectedness relatively well. Some went to church and set up cots for those who would prefer the company of others. And many had been preparing for this day for years, so had ample supplies of food, water, old-fashioned gas cookers, candles, paperback books, Tesla power walls, and battery-powered electronic scooters.

Lee, like the other Regional Servers, was not a suplia designed for security or policing, so his frame was small, almost child-like, and innoxious. All Regional Servers were non-imposing, engaging suplias that were engineered for adaptive skills in negotiation, compromise, and diplomacy. So, when Lee met with his Security and Order Brigade commander, his five-foot stature looked almost comical next to Tyrone Walton, the seven-foot-three suplia commander.

"Tyrone, we need to increase patrols of both Co-op Food stores and the 24/7 Mutual Convenience Marts," instructed Lee.

Looking down at the impish Regional Server, Tyrone nodded definitively. "Yes, sir. We'll make sure that order is maintained."

"Thanks Tyrone," replied Lee as he stared almost directly at the large man's abdomen. Looking up at Tyrone, he continued. "Our Perfect Society is simply becoming slightly imperfect. We must maintain vigilance so that order is maintained. Predictive quantum possibilities that I ran through Search and Knowledge Discovery tools and Streaming Analytics produced several intriguing scenarios."

Tyrone stared into space and blinked a few times. "Oh, I forgot. We're not connected."

Lee smiled as he walked away. Turning, he stated. "It doesn't matter. I am simply informing you that the outcomes that we have prepared for seem to be holding." He grabbed his chin.

"The fact that we are realistic, makes us smart," replied Tyrone with one of the Perfect Society inspirational quotes.

Lee turned on his heel and replied with another. "Sadness, Tyrone, is a never-ending dream having fun."

"You're an animal, Lee. Remind yourself of that every day."

Lee grinned, pushed his chest out, and breathed deeply before he turned and walked out the door.

* * *

At Temple Dome, the mood was jubilant.

Boniface was in a meeting with a group of tactical warriors. "The UPIS is down, but we won't need it."

"Sir, there are no commercially available XSpace craft operating anywhere in the UFC."

Boniface smirked. "We're not taking one of those."

Everyone around the table looked at each other, confused.

"We're taking the one that belongs to Lee Morales."

"Lee Morales!" yelled Crosby Schnare, a young member of the militia. "You've got to be insane! There is no way we're going into Mountain High City and hijacking the Regional Server's private craft." He giggled nervously. "No fucking way."

Boniface walked over to Crosby and curled his lip. "Soldier Schnare." He looked down at him in disgust. "If you ever use foul language in my presence again, I will crush you like a bug!" Rotner slammed his fist against the rock wall behind the soldier, cracking several pieces loose. Some dust landed on Crosby's silver scalp and shirt.

Schnare widened his eyes and rocked from side to side. "Yes, sir! I mean, no, sir! I will not speak with the foul tongue of the uninspired!"

Instantly, Boniface calmed himself and smiled. He casually

wiped some rock dust off Crosby's shoulder and looked down at him. "We mustn't stoop to their level, soldier. Never." He tightly closed his eyes as if in pain. "Love is a captive animal, soldier." He opened them. "As per our beloved Saint Semmel."

Crosby nodded. "Of course, sir." He gulped. "But, just out of curiosity, sir. The Elon Skyhawk craft used by the Regional Servers only seats eighteen. There are twenty of us, sir."

Boniface glared down at him. "Soldier Schnare. A riverboat shall be your horse."

Schnare appeared as dumb as a fish. "Uh, sir, with all due respect, I don't even—"

"Soldier! It will be cramped, OK? But, you've just made up my mind for me." Rotner smiled. "You ride alone."

"But, sir, I—"

"Ah! Ah! Ah!" replied Rotner as he raised his hands. "We talk later." Boniface breathed deeply. "Besides, I'll need some of your electrical skills to, well, tweak a few transmission towers for me." Smiling, he continued. "And it's not like you haven't ever hijacked an Elon Skyhawk before."

Falling back in his chair, Crosby Schnare turned white as chalk as it dawned on him how foolish he had been to fall ass backward into this Gordian knot.

Boniface walked to the front of the table and all of the men's eyes followed him intently. "We go tonight."

"Uh, how, sir? How are we going to travel the eighty-four miles to Mountain High City?" asked a slightly chubby soldier.

Rotner thrust his chin up. "Scooters."

The men looked at each other dumbfounded, while a few giggled.

"Scooters, sir?" replied the soldier.

"Well, we're not walking there, soldier!" Boniface nodded. "We have nineteen sons of liberty soldiers and twenty-eight electric scooters."

The men sat staring at Boniface in silence.

"Each scooter has twelve hours of battery life." He paused. "At the average speed of eighteen miles per hour, if we leave at midnight, we should be at the City Server Center by daybreak."

The men stared into space.

Boniface clapped extremely hard. "Right! Soldiers! Get some shut eye, as we ride tonight!" He walked over to a cardboard box that contained nineteen old-fashioned bound folders. He slapped one down in front of each of his men. "Everything is in here. Our plans, deliverables, expectations, provisions, weapons, clothing." He paused. "Everything!"

"Yes, sir!" yelled one of the men. "Paper book. I like it, sir!"

"Got it, soldiers?"

"Yes, sir!" replied most of them in unison.

"Oh," he added. "One final thing." He paced with his hands grasped behind his back. "As you know, my cousin, and one of your fellow comrades, Hosea Hackett, is in Astana already. We lost contact with him a few weeks ago, but we have plans to meet up. He has the necessary intel to get us into the LECP."

"What's that?" asked Crosby.

Boniface picked up one of the books and waved it. "It's all described in here, soldier. All the details." He threw the bound documents back on the table in front of the man. "It's the Astana central nervous system. It is the Love Energy Central Power Plant. Its destruction is key to the success of our mission."

"Yes, sir!" replied Crosby enthusiastically.

"Right!" Boniface crossed his big arms. "Go rest up." He nodded tersely. "We have a lot of work to do!"

* * *

In Astana, Victoria wanted Pierre and Claressa to be close to the operation, so they were given a temporary, fancy three-bedroom cell located at the top of the Master Server Data Center (MSDC). Amazingly, Victoria occupied a rather modest, but comfortable cell at the end of the hall. The exquisite penthouse was reserved for visiting human members of the UFC, such as important scientists, artists, musicians, and philprogs, or philosophical programmers, those that had the ability to translate interdimensional ethics and metaphysics into qubits using the old-school Hadamard matrix. The word *spirituality* was thrown into the word usage garbage dump centuries ago due to its "institutional religious" connotations. When someone referred to that which emanates not from the binary, material world, common words used in modern UFC society were metaphysical, ethereal, or transcendental. In fact, most suplias believed in the metaphysical and therefore had their own belief system which some NLs shared, although many NLs were hard-core atheists and clutched onto an archaic belief system of scientific reductionism. The pendulum swung extremely far for some after the horrors of the past, but in the Perfect Society, any non-violent philosophy or way of life was free to be entertained.

Pierre came out of the beautiful ensuite bathroom. "I can't believe she's slumming it down the hall," he said as he dried his hair with a big fluffy towel.

Claressa, who had already had her shower, was sitting on the bed watching a hologram comedy. "I'm as loyal as they come, but honestly she goes way overboard with the Master Server thing."

Pierre stopped and stared at the holographic image of a redhead woman as she had her arms outstretched with her body spinning end over end quickly. She was hamming it up by yelling as if she was a cartoon character. She instantly stopped, and said, "Of course I'm head over heels." The male avatar grinned and shook his head.

Pierre shook his head. "Hey, I've seen this one before."

Claressa grinned. "Yeah, me too." She waved her hand over the night stand and the scene disappeared.

"So, we meet with Victoria and Big Boss."

Claressa smirked. "Big Boss has a name. It's Conan Tavilla."

"Yeah. With his Direct Energy pistol, I bet he's a ringer for Revolver Ocelot."

Claressa snickered. "Pre-MN reference? Pffft. You don't like suplias, do you?"

"Uh, the big, badass Security and Order Brigade types?

Not so much." He hesitated. "The Regional Servers, well, who wouldn't like them."

"You will like Conan. He's not as contentious as most." She smiled. "One look at him is usually enough."

"Enough for what?"

"A normal-sized human macho male to pee his pants."

"Hey!" replied Pierre with a grin. "I'm not macho! Besides, I'm off the coffee diffusers today, OK?"

Claressa giggled, then grabbed his leg and pulled him toward her. "Come here, big boy. Look, I have no idea why you are essential to this mission, but Victoria just seems to know you are."

"And she fucking knows everything," replied Pierre as he thrust his chest up.

"Yes. So, until we get debriefed, let's relax and you know, have a little fun."

Pierre looked down at her pretty dark eyes and slender, athletic upper torso. "Yeah, well, I'm game if you are."

She pulled him down onto the bed.

"Hey! We've just showered."

"Too fucking bad," she replied as they began to embrace each other in a lover's grasp.

* * *

Pierre and Claressa walked into Victoria's office at the MSDC. The view of Astana was spectacular from the 45th floor. The office was sterile, but architecturally interesting. Thick silicone polymer windows with a bluish gray tint curved in aesthetically pleasing shapes in the organic, oddly-shaped room. The frames were thin, but shiny silver. Extensive hologram monitors, projection devices, consoles, and workstations abounded. There were several human operators monitoring the stations and working on sending code to technicians deploying the replacement UPIS satellites. Outside the curvy windows, the Astana sky was filled with streaky high clouds, feathery white and expansive against a cerulean blue atmosphere.

"Welcome," greeted Victoria.

Seated next to her was a huge man whose chest and shoulders seemed to stretch his suitcoat to its absolute limits. His face was strangely boyish, almost like a cartoon character superhero.

They both rose and shook Pierre's and Claressa's hands.

"Pierre, this is Conan Tavilla, head of the Elite Suplia Patrol, or ESP."

Lewalski stared up at the huge man as he shook his hand, feeling as if he was a child shaking the hand of an adult. "Pierre Lewalski. Nice to meet you."

"Likewise," replied Conan.

They both sat and faced each other across the smooth, stained white wooden table with gold leaf accents throughout.

Victoria blinked and instantly all personnel in the room got up from what they were working on, gathered their things, and exited the room.

"Now that's discipline," remarked Pierre.

"It's perfect," replied Victoria. "Now, we have much to

discuss this morning." She glanced up at Conan. "I would first like to have our masterful security servant, Mr. Tavilla, discuss the current situation, the likely attack scenario, the players, the goals, strategies, and timeline."

Pierre fidgeted. "Wow. Sounds advanced. Shall we take notes?" He pulled out his e-tablet.

"No need," replied Conan as he grabbed Pierre's wrist. "I've already sent all the data to your GoogleSoft WPL."

Pierre nodded. "Nice. I like your style, chump."

Conan grinned.

"OK to call you chump?"

"I feel we're friends already," replied Tavilla.

"OK," interjected Victoria. "I will let Conan have the floor." She winked. "See you soon." She suddenly vanished into thin air.

Pierre looked at Claressa, confused. "Uh, what?"

"She's probably having breakfast right now downstairs. She's not a morning person."

"Uh, OK, got it."

Conan stood up, all seven foot five of him. "Claressa. Pierre. I will give you a brief rundown on our problem and our proposed solutions." He began walking as a 3D scene materialized before them. "This is Temple Dome, a pre-MN disused military facility in the mountains near Mountain High City."

"Who lives there now? Rats?" asked Pierre sarcastically.

"Rats, maybe. The MH terrorist cult, definitely." He walked into the hologram as it changed into a room with men discussing plans. "The big guy here"—Conan pointed—"is Boniface Rotner.

Leader." He waved his hand across. "These others are his militia, or sons of liberty, who are on their way to Astana as I speak."

"If so, what are we waiting for? Shouldn't we have been doing something already?" asked Pierre. "Victoria is acting so calm and telling us to relax and, you know, just chill." He shrugged. "I mean for a Master Server, she's pretty condensing, and I'm certainly no military strategist, but come on."

Conan smiled and nodded slowly. "Pierre. Time is the universal unsolved crime. But, Victoria and all of us suplias with our networked AI, let's just say, we are using time against them." He leaned back and crossed his arms. "They are the bumbling criminals and we are the interdimensional master sleuths."

"Meaning?" queried Pierre.

"Meaning that all things in due course, Pierre. Time is but an illusion. Synchronicity requires absolute patience and steadfast precision." He paused. "Absolute control."

Pierre rolled his eyes then stared at the hologram image of Boniface and his militia. "Ugly motherfuckers."

"Pierre!" whispered Claressa into his ear. "Pay attention!"

Conan grinned. "Yes, Pierre. But you know what they say. Ugly is the new beautiful."

"Who says that? Bumpers?"

Conan giggled, then remarked. "In a Perfect Society, there is no easy way to try to be horrible."

Pierre furrowed his brow slightly. *Uh-oh, not you now.*

"So... I *do* hope you like their hair style, my friend, as you will soon be going to, well, let's just say, a manscape artist that can make you shine."

"Moi? Uh, hello, Big Boss." He shook his head. "Don't think so, ho."

Claressa glared at Pierre. "Listen, OK? You need to focus."

Pierre nodded and slumped his shoulders slightly.

More scenes appeared all over the office control room. One showed the soldiers zipping along an old deserted pre-MN highway on what appeared to be ancient e-scooters. Another showed a large XSpace craft parked in a hangar outside Lee Morales' Mountain High City office complex. Others were fuzzy panes of almost old grainy movie texture. Several of them were of higher definition than the others, but some were simply flickering in and out of time and space, as if they were quantum specters from indeterminate dimensions.

Conan continued. "The MH militia, led by Boniface Rotner, will be attempting to take down the Perfect Society's LECP and subsequently murder Victoria."

"Holy crap," uttered Pierre. "And what the hell is an LECP."

"Love Energy Central Powerplant," said Claressa as she quickly turned to face Pierre.

"It was Boniface Rotner who masterminded the entire plot. He's a very gifted man," Conan stated to Pierre. "When he was just fifteen, he was the one who resurrected the scalar interferometer, the old pre-MN warfare shield which led to the cult's obscurity and march toward this specific act of aggression. He was also the one who refurbished the ICBM missiles, guidance systems, the works." He paused and waved his arm toward the scenes. "This is from my AI interface." He smiled. "You are now seeing into the mind of a suplia."

Claressa was dumbfounded and stared at the holograms with her mouth agape. "Absolutely fascinating." She shook her head. "I had no idea predictive analytics had reached this level of sophistication."

"We teach ourselves," replied Conan. "Pre-MN AI systems were developed by chatbots collecting huge amounts of data off what was then called the Internet."

"The Cloud," interjected Pierre.

Conan nodded. "There were two main bot systems. One designed with deleterious intentions, or Seed data using negative reinforcements, and another, which had beneficial aspirations, using positive, error-correcting reinforcements."

"The Horsemen's original suplia designs creating AI ethics," added Claressa. "But it wasn't all of the Horsemen. One group wanted a singularity based on ethics and their sacred hermetic doctrine, yet the other wanted negative reinforcement by way of associating pleasure with evil acts."

"Psychopaths." She hesitated. "They wanted psychopathic artificial intelligence."

"Unfortunately, yes," replied Conan. "Yet, thankfully for this particular branch of multidimensional time and space we all find ourselves in, the AI based on the original beneficial designs won."

"Hear, hear for fate!" said Pierre.

"Hear, hear for Aria Freeman of the Stewart Island Survivorship Colony."

"Is she the suplia who wrote that treatise called MySpaceBook Posts to the Colonists?" asked Pierre.

"No. That was her lover, John Iversen. She compiled The

Freeman Rants." He paused. "A collection of poignant troll responses to what was then a group calling themselves The Teds."

"After Ted Kacynzski, a pre-MN terrorist also nicknamed the Unabomber," instructed Claressa.

"The Una what?" asked Pierre.

"Bomber, honey. You know"—she threw her hands up and made the noise—"goes boom?"

"And there were some in the survivorship colony days that we're into a guy like *that*?"

Conan turned to Pierre. "Hence. The Freeman Rants."

"There are some members of the MHs who revere him," added Conan. "But, they are never to speak his name in public."

"Why? I always thought their metal skull caps prevented Victoria from, you know tapping their dust."

Conan trod carefully. "Yeah, well. You just have to understand that many in their paranoid ecofascist community want nothing to do with technology, yet they fear that there is nothing they can do about it."

Pierre leaned forward. "Meaning...?"

"Meaning that they are in a conundrum. Some, and I mean some here, honestly believe that the metalling doesn't work, which if voiced to anyone else in the community, would be blasphemy against Saint Semmel, their holy heavy metaller. Also, even though they share Ted's rotten ideology, many don't want to admit that their goal of disconnecting and returning to their God would be seen as merely a terrorist act and not one of more transcendental intentions."

"Deep down they want recognition, Pierre," added Claressa. "They feel if they take down the UFC, then the remaining NLs and Luds will simply join them, and for that, they need a squeaky clean motivation."

"Pretty naive if you ask me," replied Pierre as he furrowed his brow. "So, Unabomber is out, but nuclear-tipped missiles are in?"

"In a nutshell," replied Conan.

Conan returned to his active 3D scenes of people, machines, Direct Energy weapon fire, and huge powerplants. "OK, there are several panes here that concern me, but I'm going with my gut instinct on this one."

"Your human side," stated Pierre.

"Essentially." He pointed to one layout. "I'm going to go after Boniface. Make sure he is either captured early or delayed." He paused. "He's a big, strong man and will either need to be eliminated on contact or taken into custody. Preferably the latter."

Pierre shook his head with a distant look on his face.

"Pierre, you are going to infiltrate the militia. You will report to Dong Wang, a local manscape artist. He will shave your head and tattoo your scalp silver."

"Wha? No fucking way, chump!" shouted Pierre.

"Pierre. This is serious, OK?" pleaded Claressa. She shook his arm. "You are *going* to do everything Conan or Victoria tell you. *Got* that?"

"Yeah, yeah!" shouted Pierre as he stiffened and crossed his arms.

"It's dissolvable," added Conan.

"What? My skull?"

"Your tattoo. Dong Wang will give you a specific, totally

organic enzyme that will remove it." He paused. "And an exquisite wig in your choice of style and color."

Pierre face-palmed.

"You will then gather essential intelligence, as even a suplia with predictive analytics cannot collapse *all* realities." He paused. "Only the All can."

"The All?" asked Pierre. "Is that what you call your Rodolpho?"

Conan laughed. "Rodolpho was just a man with a noble purpose." He looked up. "The All is not."

"A man or not with noble purpose?"

"You know what I mean."

"I thought you suplias are not religious."

"We're not. We're perfect."

Claressa looked at Pierre. "We are not here for a philosophy lesson, are we now, darling?" Pierre shook his head.

"So let's just focus on our task at hand and work together to foil this plot," declared Claressa.

Pierre looked up at the big suplia. "Uh, where is this Wang Dong?"

"It's Dong Wang and you can find him on Noam Chomsky Boulevard near the Tesla City Superstore." He sneered. "You can't miss him. He's, like, five foot eight and 315 pounds and wears a bright-colored mumu."

Pierre slowly shook his head. "Let me get this straight. I have to find a big Dong, get scalped and tattooed, all so I can look like a walking battery terminal?" He looked over at Claressa. "I'm *so* loving this trip already."

Chapter 12

On Saturday July 13th, Thaddeus Swank was at an archaeological dig in the foothills 50 miles due west of Marsh Land. The dig consisted of uncovering parts of an old lodge in what was then called the Rakaia Gorge. It had been used in the pre-MN days by tourists visiting a ski area nearby named Mount Hutt. After the first major solar flare in 2025, the weather had changed drastically, and the lodge, which had been for sale for 21 years, was left abandoned. When the Micronova occurred 25 years later, the blast, which was centered on the western hemisphere, caused an immediate cessation of all life above ground. Winds of up to 300 mph buffeted the continents, with tidal wave swells approaching 2,000 feet pulsing from west to east as the Earth's rotation slowed significantly. The eastern hemisphere was spared ground zero, but was in no way protected from the tidal waves, earthquakes, and extreme weather anomalies. Those in the survivorship colonies survived like the homo sapien ancestors of the past simply by living underground in caves high in the mountains. The Stewart Island colony, led by Aria Freeman, had a rudimentary but fairly comfortable habitat in a series of cave systems, both natural and man-made, near what was then called Mount Anglem / Hananui and was at about 3,000 feet above sea level. Most life on the planet that had survived was at high elevations in the eastern hemisphere. Nevertheless, in the decades following, the magnetic field of the Earth had dropped so low that prodigious amounts of cosmic rays were able to enter the atmosphere, causing extreme weather chaos, immense rainfall, floods, avalanches, and horrific storms.

The old lodge near the ski area had been completely flooded, flash frozen, then buried in about 20 feet of solid glacial ice, which had preserved the contents quite well. Thaddeus was simply delighted that he was able to find a few ugly devices which were then called television sets that had grotesque black, flat plastic screens. In addition, several small metallic cubes which appeared to be refrigerators were found and contained foods of some sort and small bottles of the now banned alcohol. In what was the restaurant area, he found what appeared to have been a lunch menu. Written on it was Pork and Wings, $48.50, Venison Pie, $49.80, and what was called a High Country Wrangler, consisting of Canterbury Angus Beef Ribeye Steak, eggs, fries, and salad, all for $79.50.

When Thaddeus read these aloud to one of his colleagues at the dig, he was absolutely flabbergasted. "I can't believe that they ate pigs, cows, deer, and what were these wings? Birds? How could you ever eat a bird's wing?"

"Don't know, boss," replied his work colleague. "Guess they didn't give a shit back then."

"No wonder we need the Golden Love Conservation Estates."

His colleague nodded. "The GLCEs keep us in balance." He paused as he reached into his memory banks for the canned quote. "Make hate implode."

Thaddeus nodded but kept his disdain for the Codex love propaganda memes hidden. He placed the fragile ephemera in his satchel. "Are you for the Animal Rights Act?"

"Of course," replied his colleague without hesitation. "Aren't you?"

Thaddeus once again nodded cautiously. "Yeah." He hesitated. "Yeah, I guess so. I mean, we're all happy, right?"

His colleague shrugged. "Yeah, sure. I can't see any other way than this, can you?"

Thaddeus turned to leave and replied over his shoulder, grinning. "It's perfect, isn't it?"

* * *

The best way to get into the hinterland was with a sturdy four wheel drive Terrain Traveler. Hovercraft were not ideal, as when these were used, many areas were left undiscovered. As a Keeper of the Seeds, Swank felt it was his duty to thoroughly explore all nooks and crannies of the backcountry to compare contemporary geography with that of the past. Flying above an ancient river gorge just didn't have the same efficacy as thumping along, off-roading it with the Direct Energy-powered Terrain Traveler.

He rounded a bend in the ancient braided river and saw the large entrance in the granite where a few mountain parrots, or keas, were scavenging outside. Curious as to what or who might be living nearby, Thaddeus turned and headed straight for the cave opening. As he neared it, he noticed that the keas were rummaging through what appeared to be rubbish of some sort, which was most likely recently placed there and worthy of an investigation.

Parking his beastly Terrain Traveler, Thaddeus exited and looked at the rubbish. It contained mostly green waste, old corn husks, fruit pits, and rotting lettuces. He smelled something truly foul and noticed it was coming from a hole dug in the river shingle and only partially buried. The smell could only be one thing—human feces.

Suddenly, three people dressed in ragged clothing not fit for the poorest in society emanated from the dim entrance to the cave. They were gaunt, greasy, and unkempt. Huge bumps covered their faces, legs, and arms.

The one in front spoke as he pulled out what appeared to Thaddeus to be a pre-MN revolver. "What do you want?"

Thaddeus backed up slightly, holding his hands out in front. "Whoa, whoa, there. I come in peace and love."

"Why are you here?" asked the gunman.

Thaddeus pointed to his Terrain Traveler. "I'm a historian. Keeper of the Seeds. I, er, well, I'm just returning from a dig and noticed the birds," he stammered.

"What birds?"

The mountain parrots were nowhere to be seen.

"Well, there were some here. And it led me to this cave."

The other men moved out and stared at Thaddeus. Their faces were misshapen from the ghastly lipomas.

"Look, I'm an NL, and have nothing but compassion for the Bumper community."

"Compassion? Is that what you call it?" The man spat something onto the shingle. "Artificial love? Is that what you have for us?"

"No, uh, I mean, yes." Thaddeus thought he'd take a different tack. "You need any supplies? I mean, I have food in the truck, water, and some dark coffee diffusers."

"What the fuck do we need with a damned coffee? Huh?" The Bumper grinned, exposing his dark, rotten, disgusting teeth. "What we need is some fucking IceT!"

The other guys giggled.

Another spoke in a brain-damaged drawl. "Yeah. IceT!" He paused. "I like IceT, chump."

"You got any of that in your fancy truck there?" The gunman walked toward Thaddeus with the revolver pointed at Thaddeus's head.

"Look, you can put down that gun, OK? And we'll talk," replied Swank as he raised his arms.

The gunman let the gun drop to his side.

"OK, that's better. Come over to my vehicle. Have a look for yourself. I have no IceT, OK? But, like I said, I can give you some provisions." He opened the door. "You think a Lud would ever do that?"

"Guess not," replied the Bumper as he gave a cursory, but intense look into the truck. "OK, I trust you. No fucking picture of Rodolpho anywhere in there. I have never seen no Lud without a fucking Rodolpho image or some cheesy hologram somewhere in their vehicle."

"Exactly. Like I said, I do not judge, OK? I believe in our

Perfect Society. I think you need help, you know, get out of your hab here, and into a Bumper clinic."

The others all laughed.

"A Bumper clinic? Set up by the UFC? The ones where they get you on Blunt? You know that shit that shuts off your amygdala? Makes you want to suck Victoria tit?" He snickered.

"Look, I have had friends on Blunt. It's not that bad. Six months, tops. After that, there is no requirement to continue. You are healed, but it's up to you to stay clean."

"Yeah, and get visited by a fucking suplia every few days who whips your dick out for you and forces you to pee in a cup."

Thaddeus shook his head. "Look, I'm not telling you what you need to do."

The Bumper dropped his shoulders and looked down. He became as motionless as a plumb line, then humbly looked up at Thaddeus with his hand extended. "Name is McKinley." He paused. "McKinley Crenshaw."

Thaddeus winced slightly upon seeing the dirty fingernails, the callouses from hard labor, and the swollen bumps up and down the back of the hand. He slowly grabbed McKinley's hand and shook. "Thaddeus. Thaddeus Swank."

McKinley smiled.

All of a sudden, out of nowhere a massive granite boulder crashed down about five feet from both of them, sending shards of rock in every direction. They all looked up and saw a suplia in the Security and Order Brigade uniform laughing as he wiped the dust off his hands.

"Oh, sorry there, chumps. I seemed to have dropped something."

McKinley, in absolute shock, raised his revolver and took three shots, all of which hit the suplia directly in the torso.

The SOB officer flinched a few times, but then laughed again. "Ouch. Those stung a little." He patted where the bullets had ripped through his shirt "Point 38 caliber?" Quickly pulling out his Direct Energy weapon, he clicked it onto stun and fired on McKinley Crenshaw, causing the Bumper to quiver like a silver beech tree leaf in a strong Norwest wind.

The others ran back into the cave, while Thaddeus raised his hands and pleaded. "I'm a Cloud Seed Keeper and NL," he yelled. "I'm unarmed."

McKinley was lying on the riverbed shingle, totally unconscious.

The suplia jumped from the 20-foot cliff face and landed with a huge thud, albeit gracefully on his haunches. Standing up, he quickly scanned Thaddeus's head with a white device, satisfied with the green light and readout. "Well, Mr. Swank, what are you doing here in the hinterland?" He walked over to the large Terrain Traveler utility vehicle and stopped. "Mr. Swank, I am now going to search your vehicle for specifically one item." He spoke in a flat monotone. "That is the drug called IceT." He waved another device around. "This is a nano sniffer. It can detect even one molecule of IceT or Tranquility. If IceT is detected, you will be arrested and taken to Marsh Land SOB headquarters for an intense "safety contentment debriefing" and mutual understanding dialog. If Tranquility is detected, you will be allowed to waive your requirements to speak to me now, but if the Bumpers happen to have any Tranquility in their possession, you will then be required, as outlined in Codex Pharmacum, to return to Marsh Land SOB headquarters for an ID analysis, which may or may not result in your having to participate in Geniality School, whereby you will be able to enrich your understanding of the damage that reckless use creates in society." He paused to take a breath.

"Go right ahead, officer, I have nothing to hide."

"I am so thankful for your cooperation, Mr. Swank. My predictive analysis has already indicated that you are innocent and a free, loving member of AustraPasifika." He finally smiled. "But the law is the law, so therefore I must inconvenience you to take these nano sniffer samples."

Thaddeus spread his hands. "Knock yourself out, big guy."

The massive SOB officer bent down and stuck his device into the vehicle. A soft beep was heard as a green light flashed. "Great. Just what I suspected."

The suplia handed the device to Thaddeus. Pointing to a small button on the sniffer, he continued. "Now, I want you to press this here button when I say so, OK?"

"Sure, what are you..."

Thaddeus paused as the suplia squatted down and lifted the 5,800-pound Terrain Traveler up onto its side as easily as if it was an empty cardboard box. Thaddeus's mouth was agape. "Holy moly."

"Now," instructed the SOB officer without even a strain in his voice. "If you would be so kind as to bend down slightly and place the device under here"—he looked down at the ground—"and push the button. OK? It will only take two seconds."

Thaddeus did exactly as he was told. A beep sounded as the green light flashed.

The officer nodded and gently returned the vehicle to the ground. Grabbing the device from Thaddeus, he smiled. "Thank you for your assistance, Mr. Swank. I'm too big to fit under there, and we would never ask a loving member of our Perfect Society to lie on the ground. That, as you know, is a symbol of subservience to Victoria and is not encouraged in the slightest."

"But watching you throw a two-ton boulder and nearly flip my truck, well, isn't that why we don't need to act subservient?"

The officer tilted his head. "What do you mean, Mr. Swank? We are the genetically engineered Tranquility Police and have full authority as vested by our connected mutually cooperative federation, to use and display power in non-violent means so as to protect life and perpetuate artificial love."

Suddenly, two more SOB officers appeared on the cliff and jumped down. They ran into the cave.

"So, what are you going to do with the Bumpers?" asked Thad.

"The guys in the cave, well, they will be given the option of going to the clinic." He pointed at McKinley. "This one, well, he's been caught numerous times and with the black powder charges, his warrant for grand theft which resulted in an assault causing grievous bodily harm to a pregnant woman and discharging a horrific black powder weapon at an officer, well..." He trailed off as he shook his head. "It's Perfect Justice for him now."

Thaddeus cringed, but tried to keep it away from the SOB officer. "Oh, wow. That's terrible. Is there no more mercy left for him at all?"

"Afraid not," replied the officer. "Humanity is given free choices that are totally within its power to make. Victoria provides us free mercy, shows us love through nurturing care, and brings forth a shimmering rainbow of diversity, love and tolerance. We abhor violence, Mr. Swank. You know that. A society must be fair and loving, but strict in its intentions." He glanced up and to the right. "Always fear the possible states of an electron."

Thaddeus furrowed his brow. "Codex?"

"Nah." The officer shook his head. "That one's mine." The big man grinned, then slowly began to cackle.

Chapter 13

Back in Mountain High City, several more stores had been looted by the desperate hordes whose fear of disconnectedness created a motherlode of panic and outrage. The Security and Order Brigade had their hands full, arresting perpetrators of these crimes as well as guarding the city's key infrastructure.

Most of those arrested were "anti-trank" NLs who refused to take Tranquility due to their vehement anti-drug stance.

"She's gone! We're doomed!" cried Filomena Gresham, a young woman brought in for questioning.

"Miss Gresham," consoled the NL non-suplia investigative officer. "You have nothing to worry about. We'll be reconnected soon."

Her cheeks were red from fits of rage, her cheeks wet from tears. "I can't find my hovercraft! I can't locate my dog, and my favorite hologram reality show"—she paused, then began shouting—"*is not playing*!"

The officer opened his desk drawer and handed her a little green pill. "Here. Take this. It will help."

Filomena quickly slapped his hand, sending the pill flying across the room. "Never! No state-forced medications!"

"Miss Gresham, *I* am not causing your nervousness and loss of emotional regulation, now am I?" He placed his hand on her shoulder. "And *Victoria* would never force anyone in our Perfect Society to take medications. But, out of the true artificial love that we all have for you, I am compelled to assist you in any way I can."

"I don't need assistance!" She sobbed. "I need to be connected!" Slamming her fist on the desk, she yelled, "*We* need to be connected!"

Regena Farias, an office clerk, was walking back from her diffuser break when she noticed the Tranquility pill on the floor next to the potted Ficus bonsai tree. Picking it up, she looked around the room and shouted, "Anyone lose a trank?" She saw only a few people shrug their shoulders. "Must be my lucky day," she mumbled before she popped the pill into her mouth.

Back at the desk, the investigative officer charged Filomena with one count of disturbing the peace as a result of a unmedicated emotional dysregulation, which required no hearing, simply a fine of 200 chips or eight hours of loving assistance to the community.

She raised her arm and read her sentence on her WPL. "And where must I provide the loving assistance?" she asked with intermittent sniffles.

"You like dogs, right?"

She nodded.

"Dang Doggit Dippity Doo Dah can use some help."

"The dog exercise play gym and resort spa?"

The officer nodded. "You got it, sister."

She placed her hand on her heart. "Why, thank you so much, officer." She sniffled but was now beaming. "You know what they say. Lawful is a friend who cleans his sheep—"

"—But moral is a friend who cleans his horse," quickly added the officer to complete the UFC meme.

* * *

In Astana, Claressa and Pierre had no sooner left their meeting with Conan Tavilla when the MH paramilitary terrorist cell penetrated the UFC Astana airspace. All nineteen members of the force, including the oversized Boniface Rotner, had been crammed like sardines into the Elon Skyhawk Boniface had hot-wired for their twenty-minute journey into and out of space. At approximately 27,000 feet above the UFC Astana capital region, the soldiers jettisoned the silicone polymer dome of the Skyhawk and flew out into the atmosphere like oxygen-masked birds of a feather. As this was a High Altitude, High Opening (HAHO) mission, they all deployed their special chutes almost immediately. Flocking together like warbirds, each one wore a GPS altimeter hologram embedded in glasses that Boniface and his young apprentice, Crosby Schnare, had created out of disused parts left at Temple Dome.

Nearing their targeted drop zone, Boniface's heavy frame began to create excessive tension on one of the risers that connected the links of the chute to his harness. The line stretched and caused him to torque heavily to the right, away from the group. The big man immediately pulled on his control line to steer himself back, but it was too late. Nearing 100 feet above the terrain, the now angled chute was hit by a gust of wind, sending Boniface further off course.

He prayed. *God guide me. Please. In the name of Rodolpho. I petition you.*

The designated landing spot was now over a mile to the east.

Rotner slammed into the top of the large Douglas fir tree, snapping branches and tangling all his lines. His outstretched arm was torqued back and the smell of pine sap enveloped him as he felt branches rip through his uniform, creating cuts and burning scrapes. Quickly grabbing branches as he fell, he stopped himself near the top with a menacing 45-foot drop onto the granite precipice.

He closed his eyes. *God works in mysterious ways.* He made a quick assessment of his predicament and body condition. Other than the scrapes and bruises, he felt there were no muscle tears or broken bones. Grabbing the cutaway release, he pulled, but nothing happened. The release must have been damaged in the collision.

The others had landed safely at the designated area, which was only a hundred feet or so from the main hovercraft tunnel that led directly into the city.

While holding his breath after dragging heavily on his NicoVape, Damion Munoz, the 41-year-old warrior asked, "Where the fuck is Boniface?"

"I have no fucking idea," replied a young soldier about to push the button on his smoker.

"Hey! No foul language, brothers, remember?" yelled Patrick, a relatively younger trooper.

Damion blew out a cloud of vapor. "Fuck off, asswipe!" Damion then glanced at the young soldier as they both giggled. "He's not fucking here, OK?" He spat. "Prick."

Several others in the group joined in with a low-key laugh.

"Look," replied Damion. "We got about two minutes to get the fuck out of here, OK?" He pointed at the tunnel. "Otherwise, some really badass chumps are going to be coming out of that and they ain't going to be inviting us for diffuser and crumpets, got that?"

"Hey, who put you in charge?" asked Patrick.

"I did," Damion said with a menacing look. "You got a problem with that, soldier?"

Patrick shrugged.

"Good," replied Munoz. He looked at the others. "Now let's get the fuck moving!"

The men nodded and mumbled, then quickly got busy.

* * *

Boniface glanced down and soon realized that he had landed in a GLCE. *Rodolpho! Give me strength!*

Some forty feet below, a big black bear, hearing the commotion, just stood there and calmly looked up at Rotner.

Facing a Hobson's choice of possible death by bear or certain death by the ESP, Boniface shook his head, then stared at the branch that held his two risers. Pulling himself up along the trunk, he was able to rise above the branch.

The bear seemed disinterested as he slowly rubbed his back on another tree and dug for insects on the pine needle covered ground.

Maybe God has answered my prayers? Shimmying along the

branch as far as his riser would allow, the big man started using the weight of his legs to create an up and down oscillation. The branch provided a great pendulum as he tried to increase the peaks of its motion.

Then he heard it. The growl followed by a shriek. Looking down, he saw the big bear amble off with its hind legs lowered.

The sharp crack of the branch was followed by a whoosh of air past his head as his body tumbled down through the smaller, lower branches of the fir tree.

Landing on the ground, he didn't want to turn his head, but he knew.

"Welcome to Astana, Mr. Rotner," said the massive suplia soldier holding the Direct Energy weapon.

Four more from the ESP came out from behind the trees. "We have a peaceful city, Mr. Rotner. Full of artificial love and connectedness." The rest of the group nodded.

"Lemuel," instructed the leader as he looked to another. "Please endeavor to find that lovely creature that unfortunately had to be caringly tranquilized. You will be responsible for ensuring the precious being's utmost health and happiness."

"Yes, sir," replied Lemuel.

Boniface just sat there and grabbed an embedded root of a tree to steady himself as he winced in pain. He closed his eyes and prayed.

The massive ESP leader lowered his hand. "Mr. Rotner, I'm Conan Tavilla." He smiled. "Here to ensure your utmost comfort and safety. Please..."

Boniface leaned back, opened his eyes and clenched his jaw as he slowly extended his hand to Conan.

* * *

Ten miles to the north, Pierre Lewalski was walking down Noam Chomsky Boulevard in search of Dong Wang's Manscape Adventures. He easily spotted the Tesla City Superstore, and just a few buildings down there was a small revolving hologram of a perfectly manicured male model with gleaming white teeth and crossed arms. As he revolved in a circle, a glint would appear in one of his eyes as it passed the observer.

Pierre shook his head as he entered the clinic. A human-looking robot behind a shiny white desk and podium greeted him. "Hello, Mr. Lewalski. Welcome to Dong Wang's Manscape Adventures." The robot gestured for him to approach. Scanning his head, the robot then smiled. "Paid by Victoria. Wow. You must be very special."

Pierre rolled his eyes. "Yeah, well..."

The robot smiled and gestured to the right. "Would you like a diffuser? Something fruity? We have lemon, raspberry, or peach." He paused. "Of course, if you're in need of a caffeinated drink, we do have coffee and the coffee substitute, Flak."

"Flak? What the hell is that?"

"It's a coffee substitute made from distilled chicory root, diffused with caffeine solids, then pressure treated and infused with 1,3-Butanediol." He blinked rapidly. "And some glycerol as a flavor booster."

Pierre winced. "You guys drink that shit here?"

The robot's expression did not change from its wide-eyed cheesy smile. "Mr. Lewalski, it has no components of waste, human or otherwise."

"Well, hooray for *that*," replied Pierre sarcastically. "I think I'll stick with the real coffee."

The robot shrugged. "Suit yourself." He pointed at the machine. "Menu-driven." He quickly glanced down. "Fifth choice on the menu tree."

"Fifth choice on the fucking menu tree," mumbled Pierre under his breath as he approached the machine. Waving his hand over the sensor, he began to laugh. *It is a damn menu tree.* On top were two rectangles. One read *water-based.* The other read *1,3-Butanediol-based.* From each of these rectangles branched various drinks. The water tree had the fruity diffusers, a healing aroma-based liquid called SmellTea, and something called Grass. The other rectangle branched off to the fake coffee crap, something called PrestoTine, a swill called Rhubarbacide, and this strange elixir, IntestiCleanse. *What's up with these Astanaians?*

Choosing the coffee, a paper cup from the inside of the unit dropped down. He smelled it. *Guess that's coffee.* Carefully sipping it, he sat down.

After a few minutes, the robot spoke again. "Mr. Lewalski, our loving manscape artist can now see you." He gestured to his left. "First door on the left."

Pierre got up and nodded. He looked down the hall. *First door on the left? There's only one fucking door down there.* He clenched his teeth.

Entering, Pierre was greeted by an obese Caucasian man wearing a purple and magenta mumu. He had long, dyed hair, which was black and curled up in what appeared to be a braided bun with two chopsticks in an X-pattern jammed through it. His face was pure white, covered in an alabaster foundation with his purple-red lips appearing as sweet as a ripe fig.

"Welcome, Mr. Lewalski." He gestured to the padded table. "Please, have a seat."

Pierre tried extremely hard not to open his eyes too wide. "Uh, yeah. I thought that you—"

"Were Asian?" replied Wang with a grin.

"Uh, well." He paused. "Yeah."

Dong waved his hand rapidly. "Everyone does." He paused, then stuck his chest out. "I'm a Tuber."

"A Tuber?" Pierre knew that meant that he was born with donated sperm and eggs in an ectogenesis capsule. He nodded. "I see."

"My artificial father was a sex worker."

Pierre lowered his head. "Oh."

"And hence..." He nodded.

Pierre laughed nervously. "Yeah. I get it."

After Dong stopped giggling, he continued. "Please lie down, Mr. Lewalski." He pointed to the table. "I will first shave that gorgeous mop of hair that you are sporting."

Pierre winced.

"Then, I will begin the metalling."

"Metalling?"

Dong got up and rolls of fat wobbled under his mumu. He laughed, then replied. "Just kidding."

Pierre rolled his eyes as he thought of Claressa. *The things we do for love.*

* * *

Dong Wang went right to work, and within an hour or two had Pierre looking like an authentic Metal Head.

Pierre stared at his reflection in the mirror. "Wow," he whispered. "That's amazing." He moved his head left and right, displaying different angles of it in the mirror. "Absolutely incredible, ho." Looking up at the big man, he continued. "You do damned good work, chump."

Dong was gleeful and clapped his hands. "Oh, why thank you so much, Mr. Lewalski. You are a gentle and loving creature with a heart chakra *full* of vortex energy." He smiled and looked back at Pierre through the mirror. "You're an animal, Pierre—"

"I know, I know. I remind myself every day."

Dong pressed a button on the wall and the entire wall became translucent. Just beyond what appeared to be glass were dozens of wigs of every shape and size. "Now," said Dong. "What is your pleasure, my big friendly handsome man with the infinitely collapsible heart chakra?"

"Wow. You have a great selection here." Pierre waved his hands over each square, which highlighted the particular wig and made it larger. He flicked his hand across changing the images, causing each one to zoom in and out.

Finally, he saw it. "That one. Right there."

Dong was impressed. "Excellent choice, Mr. Lewalski. One of my best." He touched the screen and the wig fell out of suspended animation and into a polymer basket on the floor. He picked it up and handed it to Pierre.

"Perfect," replied Pierre as he put it on over his glistening, bald, silver head. He pulled it around a few times then let it sit. "Sweet!" He gave two thumbs up toward his reflection staring back at him with thick, curly, golden blond hair.

"Absolutely gorgeous, Mr. Lewalski," stated Dong Wang. "You are looking like a Roman god from the pre-MN days." He paused. "Or even that ancient pop icon Justin Timberlake."

Pierre nodded. "You like the Cloud Seeds?"

"Oh, why of course," he replied. "I don't know an open-minded NL that doesn't."

"There's a lot of crap on there," replied Pierre. "You know, some very dubious material."

"It was a very dubious time, Mr. Lewalski, but that doesn't mean we can't cherry-pick the good stuff now and then, you know. Life would be so boring if we ignored our past, now, wouldn't it?"

"It could be, Dong." He slowly nodded. "It very well could be."

Chapter 14

In the forest of the Astana GLCE, Boniface knew it was now or never. He grabbed Conan's hand while grasping as hard as he could on the exposed fir root and pulled with the most force he could muster. In this instance, Conan's massive frame did not work in his favor and neither did the carpet of dead pine needles on the forest floor. Conan skidded across toward Boniface, losing his balance in the process. Rotner quickly stood up and released his grip, sending Conan down onto the ground and to his right. Fortunately for Rotner, there was a slight decline on that side, causing Conan to slide further away.

Adrenaline pumped, giving Boniface a good head start in escaping. Yet, within seconds, Conan was up and following in close pursuit.

"He's getting away!" yelled Conan to his men.

Within about ten seconds, the other four soldiers also joined the chase.

"Set to stun!" yelled Conan.

The others quickly flicked the switches on their DE weapons on the fly, not even missing a beat.

Boniface came to a ledge and looked down. "Oh, no!" he mumbled. It was about a fifteen-foot drop into a slowly meandering river, with pine trees on either side and large boulders at the edge. It would require a huge running jump to clear the boulders, and a very accurate trajectory to stay clear of the trees.

Surmising that he had no other options, he ran back and went for it. He hit the side of the ledge with his huge right foot and pushed hard. For a smaller, more nimble man, it may have been a relatively easy feat, but for him, it took an extra amount of push to get that body flying.

Barely clearing the boulders, he landed with a splash and quickly hit the bottom of the five-foot-deep river. He winced hard. Fearing he may have twisted his ankle, he tried to walk along on it. *Hurts a little, but should be fine.* Quickly ducking under the water and swimming toward a huge log, he tried with all his might to get cover.

The first shot missed him by inches. "He's moving toward the log!" yelled Conan, standing at the ledge with his DE weapon aimed slightly ahead of Rotner. As AI-controlled suplias rarely missed, he felt confident that Rotner would be floating, nearly unconscious with his next shot.

Pulling his trigger, some rocks came loose beneath his feet and Conan found himself tumbling down the cliff face, bouncing against boulders, tree roots, and bramble. "Fuck!" he yelled as he lay on the river bed.

Swiftly rising to his feet, he got a bead on Rotner. He slammed his gun down on his side. "Shit!" Rotner was nowhere to be seen, but Conan's AI predictive analytics clearly showed him to be under the prodigious tree trunk.

"You alright, Conan?" yelled one of the ESP soldiers from the ledge.

"Of course I am!" He pointed. "He's under the log."

Being partially submerged, Boniface could just about make out the conversations. He had his head shoved into a hole in the underside of the relatively hollow tree trunk. He gasped for air.

"Let's blow him out!" yelled a soldier on the ledge.

"No!" yelled Conan. "I'm going in."

Rotner heard that. *Egad!* He took a breath as deep as he could muster, then ducked under the log and swam toward the next bend, which he suspected would be out of the line of fire of the four ESP soldiers.

Conan ran along the river bed and jumped. His power was immense, and his trajectory took him to within a foot of the partially submerged tree trunk. Diving quickly, he came up from under the log, lifting the mammoth timber across shoulders. "Fuck!" he yelled as he pushed the trunk off his shoulders and back into the river.

Boniface's lungs were on fire as the precious oxygen, necessary to sustain life, waned. It was now or never. He had to resurface.

Conan could see the ripples in the river. He smiled as his AI mind's eye had already made the shot. Pointing his DE weapon into what would have appeared to a normal person as simply a random patch of water, he waited for one second, saw the wavy opaque reflection, then shot.

Boniface felt the energy hit his upper back and throw him forward. He convulsed violently and fell into the river.

Immediately, Conan dove in and swam as fast as a rainbow trout toward the unconscious MH leader. Reaching him in seconds, he quickly lifted Boniface up and out of the river in a cradle carry. Walking him out of the river and onto the riverbank, Conan unzipped a side pocket in his jacket and pulled out the scalar handcuffs. Carefully placing Boniface face down on the gravel, he pulled both arms back and placed them atop Rotner's backside. He pushed the button on the black device that appeared very much like a NicoVape smoker. A small bluish plasma discharge, in the shape of a vibrating toroid, emanated out the tip of the device and surrounded Boniface's wrists. He then pulled out a white device and placed the long, round edge at the base of Rotner's neck near the C1 vertebrae and depressed the switch.

Almost instantly, Boniface started twitching, coughing, and gasping for air.

The four other ESP members were now down on the riverbed, walking toward Conan and his apprehended suspect. "Nice work, Conan," said the smaller member of the team. "Textbook take-down, my friend."

Boniface was coming around and trying to break the toroidal handcuffs, with absolutely no luck. He began yelling. "Hey! Let me go! I've done nothing wrong!" He spat. "You Electronic Beasts have nothing on me!" He softly banged his forehead on the ground several times in frustration. "In the name of Rodolpho, I am innocent. It is you who will pay the ultimate price."

Conan smiled. "Welcome back, Mr. Rotner. Hope you enjoyed your calisthenics for today." He nodded. "I know I did."

"Son of a gun!" yelled Rotner. "This is absolute..." He struggled for the right word. "Fiddlesticks!"

All the ESP members laughed.

Conan lifted the massive man up by the back of his handcuffed wrists. "Come on, chump. Let's go."

As Boniface was led across the gravel and up to the ESP hovercraft, he kept shaking his head. "We're going to win this time." He paused. "Got that?"

"It's certainly possible, Mr. Rotner," replied Conan. "But first, you will need to prove it."

Boniface tilted his head, then continued. "We will." He paused. "You'll see."

* * *

Back in Mountain High City, Crosby Schnare had been given the unenviable task of "monkey wrenching" the two main 2.6 GHz transmission towers that simultaneously received and sent the data from the dusted brains of the city to Victoria, the high priestess of the Perfect Society. There were literally thousands of repeaters throughout the city, but these two were the foundation of the system. As the UPIS was down, there would be no verification signals or warning transmissions to either city engineers or the control room in Astana. As predicted, they were unguarded, as the dozen or so Security and Order Brigade force had its hands full with emergency protocols.

Together with Boniface, he had made a small transmission device out of an antiquated pre-MN Samsung Galaxy cell phone. Once connected to the towers, a signal that would be perceived as a voice would be transmitted, reassuring the public that "Liberty is near" and "Not to worry, trust in Rodolpho." The other messages that would be blared out were "Artificial love is not love. It is synthetic." and "Vote no on Animal Rights."

He pulled out a DuraTesla PowerPack that would supply just enough power to transmit the signals for about five minutes. The plan was then to use this time to hijack an Elon 152, a trainer version of the Skyhawk which was in abundance at the city spaceport.

With the devices affixed, he jumped onto his e-scooter and scooted like hell.

* * *

The city erupted into even further chaos. People were running around covering their ears tightly with their hands and yelling hysterically. "Turn it off, please!" was one of the main declarations coming from the hordes.

Lee Morales immediately summoned his SOB commander, Tyrone Walton. "Tyrone! Get to the towers! Rip that shit out!"

The commander was wincing in pain, listening to the distressing messages urging everyone to disconnect and abandon love. For a suplia, synthetic love was the entire basis of their existence. The massive Tyrone slammed his fist through the brick wall, then kept punching it repeatedly like a boxer in the take-down mode. Dust and debris flew everywhere and eventually a body-sized hole formed, nearly taking the doorframe with it. Suplias were having a difficult time coping with the abandonment and loss of connected reassurance from Victoria. Centuries of evolved learning with the quantum computer-controlled AI interfaces seemed to evaporate overnight. Doses of Tranquility were being upped by all suplias just to cope with disconnected reality.

A few passersby stared in awe as Tyrone, in full SOB regalia, stepped out of his newly formed door, humbly apologizing to everyone. "I am so sorry for the violence. I will repair this out of my own chip credits." He stammered. "I, er, will perform love for the community. Please forgive me for this savage outburst."

"Don't worry," said the small Lud child. "I won't tell Victoria on you."

Tyrone kneeled down, which still made him tower over the six-year-old. He caringly grabbed the boy's hand and kissed it. "I am so thankful, dear child. I will maintain and regulate from now on." Tyrone dropped his head and found the correct meme. "You must not allow computers to communicate with your tears."

The boy furrowed his brow and looked up to his mom for validation.

"Commander Tyrone speaks the truth, dear." She paused. "There is no shame in being abhorrent if it means redemption."

Tyrone dusted off his dark navy uniform and began running north toward the transmission towers.

* * *

Many suplias could run extremely fast, and Tyrone was no

exception. It took him only three minutes to reach the towers. On the way, he witnessed people writhing in abject pain, rolling on the ground and even some foaming at the mouth. Agile as a leopard, he was able to circumnavigate the begging and pleading souls, many of whom acted like zombies from some ancient horror film archived in the Cloud Seeds.

"Humanity is a slave to pain!" yelled an old NL man. "Forget yourself and believe!"

Tyrone ignored the cries and successfully arrived at the towers. It took him about a minute to find the devices, and once he did, he yanked them off with a crackling discharge.

The voices immediately stopped. Tyrone bent down and breathed in and out to catch his breath. He was absolutely relieved.

Walking back down the sloping road that led to the main boulevard in the city, he noticed everyone going back to their normal troubled patterns of behavior of appearing like lost lambs rather than crazed lunatics. Yet, a group of Lud men had their heads down in a meditative state. They looked up at Tyrone as he passed and smiled.

Tyrone nodded back to them and smiled.

"There is something else," stated an old man with a silver white beard.

Tyrone fixed his gaze on him.

"Rodolpho lives," said another. "He lives on, as we all shall."

Tyrone Walton simply replied, "May love enter you now and in the future."

Walking away, the commander was deep in thought. *They*

are the only ones coping with this. How can this be? He shrugged his shoulders, but he knew, even without being connected.

* * *

Meanwhile, during the added confusion of the voice-to-skull transmission, Crosby had made his way to the spaceport, hot-wired a 152 and jettisoned off toward fulfilling his mission in Astana.

* * *

Damion Munoz had led the troops through the Astana hover-craft tunnel and into Astana. Luckily they had not encountered any of the ESPs. As they had only crude, pre-MN technologies such as GPS and one old Huawei cellphone with a very slow ID connection, time was of the essence. They had to ditch their HAHO uniforms, dress in their disguises, don their wigs, and follow the procedure from the old paper-based project binder. Garry and Damion were instructed to head into the central city to get intel on ESP movements, while the rest of the men had other instructions that took them to separate locations.

Astana was still online, so if they got caught, it was almost certain capture.

"Where the fuck is Boniface?" asked Munoz as he was walking along with Garry Reeves, his newly appointed second in command.

Garry shrugged. "Fucked if I know."

"I hate when shit goes bad," grumbled Damion. "Especially when we're facing total annihilation."

Reeves rubbed his eyes. "I don't know, sir. I mean, Victoria wouldn't take our souls for this."

Damion spat a bolus of Krep, a foul-tasting chew loaded with amphetamine-like molecules. "Ya think?" He paused. "Fuck me." He laughed nervously. "I only chose this MH gig because I was sick of it, you know? All the bullshit. The memes, the fucking perfect everything." He shook his head. "The Animal Rights Act." His head dropped. "I'm a rebel, Reeves. I'm not too good at the religion thing."

"I understand," replied Garry. "It's OK to be rebellious, ho." He stammered. "I mean, sir."

"At ease, soldier." Damion looked over at Garry. "While we are acting like civilians, you treat me like one. OK, chump?"

"No problem, ho."

"This is kind of fun, isn't it?"

"What?"

"Swearing, acting like normal NL civilians, you know, speaking with slang."

"Yeah, but we're not connected."

Damion spat some more Krep. "I know that, soldier, and that's what's scaring me."

 Silence.

"I don't feel any different."

"Different than how?" asked Garry.

"Well, different than living at fucking Temple Dome."

"You've only been in our community for a few months."

"I know that!" He shook his head. "But if we're metalled, then why do I feel the same, or even better walking down a street in fucking Astana?"

"I don't know." Garry shrugged. "No one knows these things."

"Well, all I know is that this take-down better be the answer."

Garry halted as Damion walked a few steps ahead. "You have weak faith, my friend."

Damion turned to face Garry. He signaled to his right where there was a bar serving Shiss, a synthetic alcohol-like substance based on the Tranquility drug's molecular structure. "Shall we?"

Garry shook his head slowly. "Partake of the devil's elixir?"

"Yeah, I mean we're only acting now, you know, and need to be convincing if we are to maintain our cover." He winked.

Garry smirked and blew air out his nose. "Yeah, why not. Let's do it." They both walked into the bar, but Garry felt anxious. He prayed. *We rebel, dear Rodolpho, and commit iniquity. Forgive us our trespass.* He glanced up. *Please shield us from the pain and shame of this perfect society.*

Chapter 15

Back in Marsh Land, Thaddeus had been taken into the SOB headquarters to give his statement.

"You know, I told myself that I didn't want to see the inside of this shit hole ever again," spoke Thaddeus to the Commanding Officer at the Marsh Land SOB.

The commander simply leaned back in his chair with his hands behind his head and grinned. "Yet, here you are, Mr. Swank"—he looked at his WPL—"only twelve days later."

"Look, I was minding my own business, you know, and came across those Bumpers."

The officer leaned in and placed his forearms on the desk. "Mr. Swank, you are not under arrest or investigation for anything. We just need a statement from you on"—he looked at his WPL again—"a Mr. McKinley Crenshaw."

"Like I said, I just met the man."

"We know that, Mr. Swank. We know that," replied Bud Bussey, the impish, non-suplia NL commander as he fell back in his seat. "We don't get much riff raff here in our loving community. Bumpers are really our only problem."

"Problem? These guys were minding their own business. Just hanging out in their hab by the Rakaia River."

The officer had a cheeky smile. "Just hanging out in their hab, eh?" He shook his head. "Mr. McKinley Crenshaw has several Caring Sanctions awarded for his detention. He's a wanted man, Mr. Swank."

"Yeah, I know. The suplia officer told me."

Silence.

"Will she give the order?" He paused. "You know, give him Perfect Justice."

"Did you happen to meet Mr. Crenshaw here, at this location and date stamp indicated?" He showed Thaddeus his WPL. "Is this you, Mr. Swank, and not a holographic simulation or alternative dimensional version of the real you?"

Thaddeus rolled his eyes. "Holy Rodolpho, Commander. Alternative dimension version? Many worlds multiverse?" He smirked. "I'm not Victoria. I don't have the ability to holographically project."

Bud smiled. "Very good." He leaned back in the chair, propped his feet up on the desk, and smiled. "See how easy that was?" He steepled his fingers. "You're free to go, Mr. Swank. Be gleeful and loving to all living creatures. Enjoy the rest of your day."

Thaddeus knew the Perfect Justice sentence for recidivist criminal Bumpers. Lowering his head, he peered straight into the commander's eyes. "His soul." He closed his eyes. "Will be placed into that of a goat."

The commander smiled. "It's perfect. Isn't it?"

"Is it?" he quipped quickly.

"Of course it is. Mr. Crenshaw will cease to exist in his tortured, painfully addicted walking corpse. His mind has betrayed his body and his spirit needs redemption."

"In the body of a goat?"

"Not just any goat, Mr. Swank. But, a goat in the AustraPasifika GLCE." He looked up. "A happy goat living life protected and loved!" He beamed. "It's a glorious day, Mr. Swank. He will be coming home to us in one of the most beautiful animals on the planet." He spread his hands. "Connected to all his living creatures and learning how to redeem himself for eternity!"

Thaddeus felt a tinge of nausea and a headache coming on. He sat back, slightly defeated. "I'm sorry, I believe in the Perfect Society, but I have a big problem with Perfect Justice."

"Why?" asked Bud immediately. "You are learned man, a Keeper of the Seeds." He opened his arms with palms upwards. "Victoria's intelligence is ultimate. All known facts, programmed by bots that care. Being a historian, you know that in the chat bot wars between Lucy Fur and Tyler, well, Tyler won. He was the good, moral bot. It was the foundation for the AI used at the end of the pre-MN days and brought forward into Victoria, the team leader of our nurturing holocracy. The blockchain monitors everything." He spread his hands. "Everything. Everywhere. All the time."

"Uh, can I stop you there, Commander."

The commander nodded.

"Of course I know all this, but why should we make hell literal? I mean, even in some of the ghastly pre-MN civilizations, there was a chance at rehabilitation. Here. On this planet. In your own body. In this exact dimension."

"Ahh," replied the commander as he leaned forward. "You also know that these cases were extremely rare and that most if not all of them were due to trading crime for religion. Jesus, it was back then, wasn't it? Didn't many of them recount that Jesus, that ancient messiah, was responsible for their turnaround?"

Thaddeus grabbed his chin. "Yes. Yes, they did." He paused. "Doesn't that say something to you?"

"What? That Jesus actually redeemed them here in this dimension?"

"Uh, yeah."

"Like Rodolpho will for the Luds?" He began to giggle. "Or Saint Semmel and Rodolpho for the MHs?"

"Well"—Thaddeus grimaced—"yeah."

"But, my caring community member, what about now? And what can be measurable?"

"Nothing at the quantum level is measurable in this dimension. And we're talking about spirit here—that which cannot ever be measured. Besides, it's straight out of the quantum mechanics playbook. The Heisenberg Uncertainty Principle. Even you know that."

"God is some spooky magician?" replied Bud, before he made a sarcastic whistle.

"I know you're an atheist."

"Aren't you?"

I need to be careful here. "Yes, well, I consider myself without religion, but open to the multiverse."

"We're all open to the multiverse, Mr. Swank."

Silence.

"Would you then say a convicted murderer would be

redeemed in heaven? Or pedophiles? Or rapists?" continued the commander.

"I believe that all souls will confront their lives and Perfect Justice will eventually be provided."

"Just not here."

Thaddeus nodded.

"So, a murderer, all facts against him verified white on the TI and the sentence moderated by a group of networked AI judges. This murderer..." Bud paused. "Getting his soul transferred into the body of a paraplegic is against a moral code?" He shook his head. "Or a rapist placed in a body that has no genitals or hormones to elicit desire? Or pedophiles placed into the bodies of scampering rodents." Shrugging, he continued. "That these can't be functional learning tools for that particular soul? That this is not providing love and care? That a system of redemption, artificial or not, is still a system of redemption?"

"Why wait for reincarnation when it can be done instantly."

Bud smiled and leaned forward. "Now you're getting it, Mr. Swank." He started to busily move things around his desk. "Good day, Mr. Swank." He paused. "Remember, you don't have to get arrested to seem important to someone."

Thaddeus snickered. "Thanks." He got up and walked to the door. Turning around, he replied, "Stay important."

"You'll never know when ambition will fade," replied Bud, smiling as he completed the accepted UFC meme.

* * *

Thaddeus returned to his coll, quickly passing by several of his community members with little to no acknowledgment. He had his head down and marched straight to his cell and pulled up his project "No History, No Future." Blowing air through his puffed cheeks, he studied the file. Leaning back in his chair he sat staring at the files with troubled curiosity. He felt compelled to share this with Pierre who was now serendipitously working for Victoria. Activating the call button on Hype, the hologram communications app, he successfully contacted his friend.

"Hey, Thad. How are things in Marsh Land? Is it still freezing and blowing a fierce easterly?"

Thaddeus smiled. "Nah, chump. We're lucky today. Got the Norwest arch of high cloud over the Coastal Mountains. I'm walking around in shorts and strap-ons.

"Not bad for winter, ho."

"Tell me about it." He paused and began pacing with crossed arms. "So, how is it so far, you know, the assignment?"

"Can't discuss." He snickered. "If I told you, I'd have to kill you."

"Very funny pre-MN meme, chump."

Pierre shrugged. "I don't know." He pointed to his head. "I'm surprised you haven't said anything about this yet."

"Chump. I know you're with Claressa and, well, maybe she's into the male model curls."

"She's so into them, ho." He puffed his chest out. "Going to definitely win her over on this trip." He giggled.

"Yeah, well. I just hope you stay safe." He paused. "Whatever you're doing."

Pierre started twirling his fake golden locks. "Yeah. It's all good, ho. Really. No signs of danger." He hesitated. "Yet."

"Fair enough. Look, I want to run something by you, OK? And please be open-minded about this."

"Is there any other way to be?"

"Yes. Closed-minded."

"Besides that."

Thaddeus pointed a handgun gesture at Pierre. "Focus. OK?"

Pierre nodded.

Thaddeus looked up for about a second, then continued. "History. There is no reliable recorded history anymore."

Pierre twisted his lips. "What are you talking about? Of course there is. You're a historian, right?"

Silence.

"The Keeper of the Cloud Seeds?" He tilted his head. "Are you saying that the Seeds are not a reliable historical record?"

"No. I'm not saying that. What I'm about to tell you is that our ID, the grand Information Dispenser for the Perfect Society is being rewritten."

"By whom?"

"Victoria."

There was a pause. "You've got to be joking. What kind of evidence do you have of this?"

"She has rewritten files, artificially created images, videos, holograms, documents, you name it."

"Why the fuck would she do that?"

"So that everything on there, everything, complies with our Codex of synthetic love, you know, fun, happy, purposeful."

He hesitated. "Not to mention cooperative, productive, and creative."

"You smoking Tranks again?" He paused. "Victoria censors nothing. It is written in the Codex."

"Chump, I'm serious." Thaddeus rubbed his eyes. "It's all an illusion. And she uses time and the frailty of human memory as her weapons."

Pierre spread his hands. "Explain."

"OK," replied Thaddeus as he waved his hand over a sensor button, pulling up different holographic reference frames. He pointed to the frame. "This appeared on the ID on January 15, 2418. I made a copy back then and planted the Seed on this device."

"OK."

Thaddeus then read the passage. "'That he felt for the first time like Jesus did. The lamb lies down on Paradise Boulevard.' And you can see the TI." He pointed at it. "It was just a little off pure white."

Pierre nods.

"Well, nothing happened for a long time, but two months ago"—he pointed to the next frame—"this is what we have now." He read it aloud. "That he felt for the first time like Jesus did. The lion lies down on Paradise Boulevard."

"So...?"

"So? Well, in the ancient story of the Christians, the original writings clearly indicated that Jesus was referred to as a lamb, not a lion."

"Yeah, but maybe the author changed it."

Thaddeus shut his eyes and shook his head. "No way."

"Has it been verified? Has the author been asked?"

"He's dead."

"Well, then how do we know—"

"I know! I'm the Keeper of the Seeds!"

"And look." Thad pointed to the TI. "It's pure white. It's a new truth!" He smirked. "The lion lies down..."

"I think you're reading something into this that just isn't there."

"You think?" Thaddeus started acting a bit more anxious. "Check this out then." He pulled up another reference frame that showed an old pre-MN video clip. The clip depicted a scientist narrating a documentary, with zoo animals wandering around in the background.

The audio portion of the clip began. "We will one day live like Electronic Beasts, combing the Earth for our next connected plaything, be it the wild beasts in the field or the majestic tigers in the forest."

"Yeah. OK."

"Well, I downloaded that clip about a year later, in 2419." He hit another button. "And here it is now on the ID."

The scene began and looked perfectly identical, but this time there were no animals wandering around at all, just the animal layout enclosures. The audio commenced. "We will one day live like the beasts, combing the Earth for our next plaything, be it just like the wild beasts in the field or the majestic tigers in the GLCE."

"OK," replied Pierre. "So what's wrong here?"

"Everything!" shouted Thaddeus. "There are no more Electronic Beasts. Just beasts." He laughed nervously. "We will become beasts. Convenient, eh?" He hesitated. "And what happened to the majestic tigers of the forest? Huh? And GLCE? What the fuck? This movie was made pre-MN. There were no Golden Love Conservation Estates back then!" He shook his head. "It's in my Seeds!"

"So, you're saying that Victoria is slowly rewriting history."

"She sure the fuck is!"

Pierre looked frustrated. "Why?"

"So that we never go back. Never yearn to be like it was before the Perfect Society. She allows all current forms of communication to be uncensored and TI'd. Sure. Great. But the past, well, she's eroding it very slowly, and extremely intelligently."

Pierre looked conflicted. "But, Thad, we can't be totally sure of any of this. Besides, look at the progress humanity has made since the MN. We have very few diseases left. Violence is a thing of the past. And we, at least us NLs, live co-operatively without dangerous radical ideals or a need for revolution. Without Victoria, we'd have none of this."

Thaddeus peered at his friend. "Evolution and love got nothing in common." He smiled. "Jesus smeared mud into a blind man's eyes."

Pierre dropped his head. "I gotta go now, Thad." He nervously pointed over his shoulder. "Got to get out there and, you know, save the world."

"Go, chump. Be a hero. God knows we're in desperate need of one."

Pierre shook his head. "You alright, ho?"

Thaddeus slumped his shoulders slightly. "Yeah. I'm all good. I think I just need to get stuck into some LindaUer."

"I like Linda."

"I do too Pierre. She may be old, but she's aged gracefully, still bubbly and quite captivating."

Chapter 16

Crosby Schnare had landed the 152 near the spot where the others had previously arrived by parachute. Spotting the tunnel, he made his way into Astana. Several ESP officers had seen him as he emerged from the arterial route, but Schnare was already in disguise, wearing his shoulder-length black wig, a dark navy rock T-shirt with the band Interdimensional Fetus splayed across it in fluorescent orange, plus trendy loose fitting Zirnk jeans, complete with the horizontal crotch zipper and floppy, wide waistband.

He carried a backpack which had his essentials, including the project binder for the mission. As he was to meet Boniface at the NatureLove Reserve for Caring Creatures at 5:00 p.m., and as it was only 3:10 p.m., he had some time to kill.

Crosby, like Boniface, was extremely skilled in technical matters, and for all practicable purposes, a bit arrogant. He thought of the other terror team members as the bucket brigade, and would only lean on them if needed. Yet, if he was unable to meet up with Rotner as planned, he was to make his way to an organic supermarket called The Honey Pot, whereby another team member would greet him. It hadn't been determined in advance as to who specifically would meet him, but it would be one or more of the following: Damion Munoz, Garry Reeves, or Patrick Zepeda, one of the youngest recruits. Boniface liked Patrick because he was a kiss-ass, and most importantly, he was Elane's eldest sister's son.

Walking along the busy boulevard, he could sense a slight nervousness in the locals, but unlike Mountain High City, many here appeared relatively calm and normal. Most city services seemed to be running, which meant that the destruction of the UPIS apparently had not affected the UFC capital city as much. He began to wonder at the overall plan. *Was this the right thing to do? There doesn't seem to be much damage here. Shit, this thing may go fucking balls up.* He smiled. *Yeah, Boniface. I can still swear in my thoughts.* He shook his head. *Wonder why he is such a prude? Rodolpho sure wasn't.*

He saw a couple of LFs (Lout Freaks) who traditionally grew their hair long and straight and wore fashion similar to Crosby's. Slumping, he stuck his hands in his pockets and straightened his arms out. Looking down, he then swiveled his hips around several times, which was a common gesture to LFs to indicate you were an initiate. "Ho, chumps. What style is profiling you today?"

The one closest to Schnare picked up the lingo. "Ho, what is in a style that can't reflect its nature?"

"I like the flow," replied Crosby. "Just need a place to go." He paused. "You know?"

"Sho!" said another one. "What you in fo'?"

"I'm game for like a bar." He sniffed and pointed to his head. "Can't be scanned, ho."

The others smirked. "Hey, we understand, ho. It's not like we scan clean."

"Sure, it's hard these days, you know what I'm saying?"

"Sure do, chump."

"OK, so, yeah, a bar would be nice. You know. Something cruisey."

"Say, like, what kind of bar, ho? Tranks or tanks?"

"You guys got tank bars here?"

"Secret ones," replied the one in front. He then pointed over his shoulder. "Down two streets on the left. Green building. Basement cell."

"Yeah?"

"Sure. They got any tank you want. Even got some really old pre-MN wines in there."

"Nice," replied Crosby.

"Love is a captive animal," said the one in the back.

"Sure is, ho."

"No. Say it at the door."

"Sorry?"

The one in the front rolled his eyes. "You chumps from the regions, ho." He giggled. "It's a password. You know, get you in?"

"Ah!" replied Crosby as he nodded quickly. "Got it."

"Keep your head down, chump," the one in front said. "This city can turn on you really quick."

"Advice taken. Thanks, chumps."

Crosby gave them the pinky finger up sign and headed off to the tank bar. When he got there, he said the password and was let in. It was essential for everyone in the mission to find places like this where they could keep a low profile, attempt to "fit in", and most importantly, avoid a head scan.

He sat at the bar and noticed that there were IceT vapes of all shapes and sizes on a table behind the bar. There was a menu on the table with all sorts of interesting Tranquility mixtures. One, called Blue Velvet, was a mix of blueberry diffuser essence, IceT, and a pharmacy medicine called Blue Tips, a strangely quixotic mixture that gave the user a sense of well-being and smoothness.

He summoned the bartender. "'Scuse me." He leaned in closer. "Got a tank menu?"

The bartender smiled. "You got chips? We don't scan here."

"Sure do. I'm all about chips."

"Great." the bartender handed him the menu.

Perusing it quickly, Crosby saw that they had beer, ales, wine, champagne, and mixed drinks made with the world's best diffuser flavors. He was like a kid in a candy store. "Wow, so many to choose from."

"Yeah, well, you came to the right place." He leaned down and whispered. "Suplia bar."

"Say, what?"

"You heard me." He looked suspiciously to his right and left. "We're a suplia bar. You know, the ESP?" He sneered. "They need a place to unwind, you know." He shook his head. "They love their *tanks*. But don't ever tell anyone about this place, or else."

"Or else what?"

"I don't really know. No one's ever been that stupid."

Crosby gulped hard. "Wow." He stammered slightly. "How cool. I mean, you know, hanging out with the professionals."

The bartender smiled. "They keep us safe and in perfect

loving harmony." He looked up and smiled. "I love them. They look after our perfect city like guardian angels."

Crosby started to shake slightly. "Yeah, chump. They are real angels, ho."

"So, what can I get ya?"

Crosby looked nervously down at the menu. "Uh, well. I'll take Victoria's Imperial Ale. Yeah, that looks good."

"It's 7.2 percent alcohol." He tilted his head. "You've drunk before, right?"

"Of course. We got a couple of these undergrounds where I'm from."

"And where is that?"

"Mountain High City."

"Amerexico? Yeah, I have a friend there named Jack. He works at a bar too. Do you know him?"

Fuck, not this. Yeah, like I know some random chump named Jack. "Uh, it's kind of a big place, even though it sounds small."

"How many in Mountain High City?"

"About 200,000 or so."

"Chump! That's tiny! We have nearly 750,000 here."

Crosby anxiously looked around him and spotted a huge guy who had to be ESP. "Yeah, the big Astana."

"Gotta love the buzz. It's the center of our loving federation," the bartender replied as he turned to grab the beer out of a refrigerator under the bar.

Crosby paid him some chips, took the beer, and walked away from the massive ESP officer on his right, who was laughing loudly and having the time of his life with a few average-sized

NLs, who oddly looked like tiny elves conniving with the jolly green giant.

* * *

The place was absolutely packed, but Schnare spotted a table where a man, who appeared to be very calm with no suplia genetics whatsoever, was seated by himself.

"Hi," said Crosby. "OK if I sit here?" He looked around and smirked. "Place is packed."

The man looked up from his beer and smiled as he noticed the awful-fitting wig. He hesitated to keep himself from looking too eager. "Sure. Please." He spread his hands. "Go right ahead."

Schnare smiled. "Thanks."

Pierre Lewalski stuck out his hand. "Name's Hosea. Hosea Hackett."

"You're Hosea Hackett?"

"Afraid so. Why? Is that a problem?"

"No. It's just that..." He nervously looked around, then moved in closer and whispered. "I never thought I'd just run into you." He giggled. "Especially at a tank bar."

Silence.

"I'm Crosby. Crosby Schnare."

Pierre winked. "Hey, Boniface isn't here." He gestured with his thumb over his shoulder. "Besides, hiding in plain sight with the goon squad, well, it is really uncanny." He waited until he had full eye contact, then moved his wig back and forth slightly with his hand.

Crosby tilted his head slightly and winked. "Got it."

Pierre took a swig of his Gimlet, then smiled. "Nice piece. You get that in Mountain High City?"

"Yeah. I did." Crosby lifted his chin. "And yours. Wow. It's magnificent."

"Thanks. The one I got in Amerexico was shit. Found this one at a chic little manscape place near Tesla City."

"Definitely get better shit here in the big smoke."

"Sure do."

"So, how?" Crosby narrowed his eyes.

"What do you mean?"

"I mean, how did you get here? Boniface never told us."

Pierre cleared his throat. "Uh, well." He paused to take a big drag on his Gimlet. "I escaped."

"Escaped? No one can escape."

"Well, after I prayed to Rodolpho to show me the way, I fasted." He shook his head. "Went without food for forty days. Drank some water, though." He nodded. "It was my time in the desert, so to speak."

"And...?"

"Rodolpho showed me the way."

"He showed you what way?"

"*The* way." He giggled. "Hitchhiked."

"What? How?"

Pierre had a basic framework on what he was going to say, but had to think on the fly. "Yeah. I took an identity."

"Whose identity?"

"*Whose* identity?" He laughed. "Does it matter?"

"Guess not."

"It was some NL chump." He took another sip of the Gimlet and started chewing on the ice.

Crosby shook his head and smirked. "I don't see how you—"

"The C-T-T."

"The Certificate to Travel?"

Pierre smugly nodded.

"Can't! Only Victoria can embed the code." He leaned in closer to keep his voice down. "In your neural dust, chump. And, well, you know... the metalling?"

"Ah!" replied Pierre as he made big nods with his head. "Not so fast, Sherlock."

"Who's Sherlock?"

"Never mind. Pre-MN."

"No, I do mind. It can't be done." Crosby started looking anxious.

"No, No. Not never mind on how it was done." He leans in closely and whispered. "Never mind on Sherlock."

"Again with the Sherlock. Are you drunk?"

"No. OK. Will you just listen for a second?"

Silence.

"Boniface is my cousin. OK? He gave me this." Pierre pulled out a small rice-grain-sized capsule from his shirt pocket. "You stick it up your nose."

Crosby curled his lip. "Wha? This? Up your nose?" He shook his head. "What does it do?" He grabbed the little capsule and examined it.

"It codes!" He spread his hands. "It gives you a C-T-T."

Pierre leaned back. "Anyway, if you snort it with enough force, it enters way up in there and, well, it self-adheres."

"Disgusting. But I guess effective, eh?"

"Very effective."

"How do you get rid of it?"

"Easy." He grabbed his napkin, held one nostril closed and blew several times really hard.

"Shit, look at your napkin. You're bleeding. Holy Rodolpho."

Pierre looked at it and shrugged. "Just a burst capillary. Relax, Crosby." He snorted a few times to stem the flow. "It's all about the blood."

"The blood of the man."

"Dig in, brother,"

"Dig in, Hosea." Crosby took a big gulp of his Imperial Ale. "To the mission."

Pierre raised his glass. "To the mission."

They both looked around to make sure that they weren't being surveilled, then gulped.

Placing his beer on the table, Crosby exhaled with gusto. "Beautiful. I miss having these."

"You a new recruit?" Pierre winced slightly, thinking he may have overstepped.

"Uh, yeah. That's why we never met." Crosby looked suspicious. "Right?"

"Oh, yeah. Of course. It's just that I haven't been to temple in a long time." He smirked. "Don't tell Boniface."

Crosby appeared more relaxed. "I won't. Hey, look, I'm not

too into the whole religion thing, really." He nodded. "More of a rebel. I kind of want to turn this shit upside down."

"The beasts?"

"Yeah. I don't really like the whole Perfect Society thing, you know. I think we can do better."

"Yeah, that's how I feel too." He tried to look serious. "We need to get back to our roots."

"We do, Hosea. Even if it means tearing this all down."

"Do you believe in the Animal Rights Act?" asked Pierre.

"Of course not! It's psychotic." Crosby drank the rest of his beer. "This is the main reason I joined the resistance and learned to fight."

"I've been here awhile. When did you join us?"

"I'm surprised Boniface hasn't told you."

"I've been out of communication for quite some time."

"Yeah. He told us that. Anyway, two months. And I was a technician in my former life."

"Mountain High City?"

"No. A little coll outside Big Rolling River."

"Where's that?"

"No one really knows." Crosby giggled.

Pierre nodded.

"Anyway, I used to dabble in electronics, neural dust transmitters and all that." He pointed at the rice grain device which was on the table. "So that's why I was so surprised about that. Never seen one before, but I have to admit, it's an ingenious design."

"It sure is."

"I'll have to ask Boniface about it later."

Pierre fidgeted. "Uh, yeah. You do that."

"Thing is. I tried to contact him, but nothing."

Pierre acted surprised. "Oh yeah? That's... terrible. I mean, well, he is an amazing guy. I'm sure he'll get out of whatever mess he's in." He gestured over his shoulder. "I mean he's almost a suplia, if you think about it."

"Strongest non-suplia human I've ever seen."

"Yeah. I know, huh." Pierre leaned in. "Look, all I know is that I'm to take you to the LECP."

"That's not in the project binder."

"I know. But, Boniface had told me, the last time we did speak, that if I was to run into any of us then I was to take them there."

"OK. Sounds like a plan. When?"

"Tonight." He got up from his chair. "I'm at the Astana Antigravity motel."

"Sounds exotic."

"It's not. I'm kind of getting over the whole floating around in my pajamas thing."

"I heard these places are great for sex."

"Keep it in your pants, chump." Pierre laughed.

"No. I mean, isn't it supposed to add an entire dimension to the experience?"

"She can't blame it on gravity," he said with a smile.

Crosby laughed. "I had no idea you were like this."

"Like what?"

"An NL." He paused. "I was expecting a full-on religious fanatic and prude."

"I've been here a while. I guess it kind of grows on you."

"Yeah, I guess." He blinked. "But it is all a lie. Victoria is a false messiah. This is a fool's paradise."

"It is, brother." He nodded. "It is."

"See you tonight at the LECP. What time?"

"Seven p.m., south side of the courtyard. We will need some daylight."

"Great. See you then." Crosby smiled, patted Pierre on his shoulder, and walked out.

Pierre grabbed the little "device" off the table, stared at it, and laughed. *Uncle Jed's converted rice.* Shaking his head, he smiled. *Sucker.*

Chapter 17

With Pierre now in the field helping to thwart the attack, Victoria allowed Claressa to get back to her normal work. Entering her lab, she quickly unlocked Jimbo's pen and placed the neural imaging device on his skull. Instantly, a scanned 3D holographic image of his brain map appeared floating above the lab bench.

"That's one beautiful connectome," said Nariko as she approached from behind Claressa. "Fantastic structural and functional connectivity pathways." She pointed. "There. See? That's a neural mote." Nariko put her hands around the revolving 3D hologram and pulled out, increasing the size of Jimbo's rotating brain. "There. Again." She giggled. "Millions of them, almost indistinct from the neural tissue."

Claressa nodded as Jimbo began yelling happily. "And..." She got up from her chair and walked over to a monitor on the wall and pointed. "Here's Jimbo!"

A phantasmagorical, pulsating 3D movie appeared to be running. Pictograms of other animals, trees, and of getting chased were followed by images of their own faces.

"Give him the red ball," yelled Claressa over her shoulder.

Nariko Gu handed Jimbo the ball. Immediately, the same ball appeared on the monitor, but from Jimbo's perspective.

"Red, Jimbo. That is a *red* ball." Jimbo stuck out his lower jaw and shook his head.

"Brilliant. It stopped the dreamscape in its tracks. The focus. Very similar to human transitions."

"Yeah," replied Claressa. "There seems to be slightly less random noise with the chimpanzee brain."

"Maybe the autism?"

"Could be."

The two scientists proceeded to teach Jimbo colors by handing him different balls and noting his reactions, then viewing the connectome map. After about an hour of this, Jimbo became bored, but the neural pathways as indicated on the map became more intense in color, thereby signaling learning and memory.

"What about Victoria?" asked Nariko.

Suddenly, Victoria appeared in front of them. "Why, thanks for asking, dear Nariko." She looked to the right. "Claressa."

"Feeling? Direction? Love?" asked Nariko.

"All of the above, my dears. Even without the UPIS, I have received all the data perfectly through"—she pointed at black antenna up near the ceiling—"that archaic 2.6 GHz system." She smiled. "Clear as a bell." She smiled. "As predicted."

Victoria stared at Jimbo, who was sticking out his tongue and grunting. Victoria's eyes had a strange intensity as if photon energy was being beamed directly from them. Jimbo slowly halted his gesticulations and peered over at Victoria. They seemed to be communicating telepathically. Victoria tilted her head and Jimbo leaned down and picked up the yellow ball.

"Good job, Jimbo!" yelled Victoria jubilantly as she clapped.

She stared at him intently a second time. Jimbo smiled and slapped the lab bench with his hands. Jumping off the bench, he ran across the floor, leapt onto Claressa's desk, and grabbed her Flak diffuser. Holding it up, he yelled triumphantly, then drank it.

"Hey! Jimbo! That's mine!" joked Claressa.

They all laughed.

Victoria nodded, then said, "I asked him if he was thirsty, and he said yes."

"Did you tell him about my diffuser?" asked Claressa.

"No, darling." She hesitated. "I didn't. He must have learned that from you."

Nariko smirked and spoke softly. "Uh, actually that was from me."

Silence.

"I, well, gave some of your Flak to him few weeks ago."

"What?" asked Claressa as she raised her eyebrows.

"Flak is fine for chimps." She shrugged. "Besides, I thought you weren't going to finish it."

She stared at her colleague with a serious deadpan but then broke down and held back a giggle.

"It's glorious!" stated Victoria as she cupped her hands together and raised them to her chin. "I can feel the love. The love of wild *animals*! Jimbo can feel the artificial love from *me*!" She hesitated, then spread her hands. "Of *us*!"

The scientists appeared smug.

"The Animal Rights Act is moral and decent," declared Victoria, beaming. Then, as instantaneously as she appeared,

Victoria vanished into the realm. Jimbo sipped sloppily from the Flak diffuser mug, licking his lips and screeching.

"I guess it's final," remarked Nariko.

"What do you mean?"

"The Animal Rights Act."

Claressa crossed her arms. "Well, it still needs a two-thirds majority."

"It will easily pass. The only opposition will be coming from Luds and MHs."

Claressa shook her head then sniffed. "I don't know." She paused. "I don't think that dusting all the animals on the planet and hooking them into the Perfect Society's AI network is really a good idea."

"Victoria thinks so." She paused. "You just saw that."

"I know, Nariko, but I've always thought of wild animals as, well, wild. You know, non-connected."

"Yeah, but non-connected means non-loved. Victoria wants every living thing to experience mutual protection and her version of truth."

"Which is perfect," replied Claressa in a sarcastic tone.

Nariko sighed. "Look, this will just even the playing field between man and animal. Finally, wild animals will be able to sense a human's presence way earlier, and with technology! Just think of it, they will finally have the ability to protect themselves."

"The right to arm bears."

"Essentially," declared Nariko as she shrugged. "Hey, we've talked about this before, and guess what?" She paused for effect.

"At this very instant, we now have MH terrorists right here. In our town. After having blown up the UPIS! It's all happening, Claressa." She furrowed her brow. "That's why Pierre is even here with you, isn't it?! Come on. You need to focus."

"I *am* focusing, Nariko." She lifted her chin. "I know how evil takes hold. It is omnipresent in the human psyche." She paused. "Deeply rooted in the ancient traumas, the genetic engineering of the past, the cataclysms, the psychopathy..." She looked up. "The fear of nature. The rejection of spirit."

"Someone needs to take her Tranquility pill."

"Is that what we need to do? Just take the pill?" replied Claressa with frustration.

"Why all this existential angst? We are scientists, Claressa. We just proved that dusting the animals is not painful for them, and well, if we could walk with the animals, then talk with them, all in loving discussion, then we can learn their languages, and how they view the world and universe."

"Sounds too good to be true, Dr. Doolittle."

"Who's that?" Nariko sneered. "One of your colleagues from AustraPasifika?"

Claressa snickered. "Never mind."

"OK, because, I think you're making a big mistake." Nariko paused. "Or you need to question your allegiance."

Claressa narrowed her eyes and stuck her chest out. "Don't you *ever* accuse me of insubordination to the UFC." She breathed in deeply and blew herself up in the manner of a bull frog.

Nariko, the smaller of the two, backed up and bit her lip. "Claressa. Sorry. I didn't mean—"

"Then you need to apologize." She pointed at her. "Right now."

"I did." She backed up even further as Claressa was within inches of her. "Jeez, Claressa. I said I was sorry."

Claressa got a hold of herself and relaxed. Pulling down on her white lab coat, she breathed out a cleansing breath. "Apology accepted." She turned toward Jimbo and began petting him. Jimbo also calmed himself slowly as Claressa provided loving affection and a human touch. "There, there, Jimbo. That's what you need. A *real* connection." She paused. "Don't you?"

Nariko bowed her head and shook it slowly before grabbing her things and heading out the door.

Chapter 18

Boniface awoke with a foul-tasting, sticky sensation in his mouth. A phlegm-colored shaft of light emanated from a small window near the top of his prison cell. He felt icily cold and as clammy as death. Slowly regaining his eyesight, he squinted as the realization of his dank surroundings hit him like a bout of nausea. The masonry walls were rosy pink colored, the preferred color of peaceful abandonment, or so said the UFC security consultants. The color made Boniface shudder as he slowly clenched his fists. Looking up, he noticed the posters with the idyllic scenes of nature. The one on the left had a dark sunset over a towering mountain range, the snow the color of golden amber. On it read, "If you are the only one who cares about the dark, think outside the dark." Boniface shook his head only to notice the others. Another one had a young, attractive couple, a man and a woman, with cheesy smiles sitting on a picnic table in the middle of a green field. On this one it read, "Before the lie comes other people." Others, with similar tacky high-definition nature images yelled at him. A cascading waterfall producing a double rainbow: "Effortless doing requires effort." And another cheesy placard had a fawn nuzzling up to a bunny rabbit with a forest backdrop: "Make hate implode."

Boniface's head felt like it would implode. His feet were

shackled with the plasma toroid cuffs and, oddly enough, he realized that his hands were as well.

Standing up, he yelled, "Guard! Guard! I need help in here!"

He heard the echoing rhythmic ramble in the hall getting louder as the large suplia guard, about Rotner's size, turned to face him. "Yes, Mr. Rotner. What is the problem?"

"I want a counselor. Right now."

"AI or human?" replied the guard in a deadpan voice.

"Human. And what about these?" He wiggled his hand behind his back.

"What about them?"

"I want them off. I'm in a cell." He looked at the solid brick block walls, the 3-foot-thick silicone polymer security window, and the thick, steel jail bars, covered in a sickening violet latex paint.

"Not happening, sir."

"Why not."

The suplia hesitated. "Security, Mr. Rotner."

"What? You think I can bust out of this? Leapin' lizards. I'm human, dagnabbit!"

The guard stared at Boniface with a fixed expression. "Sorry. Your request has been denied." He paused. "My hands are tied."

"Your hands are tied?" Boniface snickered. "Very funny." He paced. "Get me my counselor. Pronto."

"The commander has already called her."

"Her? I didn't ask for a woman."

"You have a problem with women, Mr. Rotner?"

He winced. "No. Who said that I had a problem?" He looked

away quickly then returned his gaze. "In our society, women do not act as counselors, OK? I prefer a man. Please get me a male counselor."

"Well, Mr. Rotner," replied the guard with a grin. "You're not getting one, OK? You are in our society right now, and it's perfect. We have evolved." He looked at Boniface's slight brow ridge and his huge knobby skeletal frame. "We're not knuckle-dragging Metal Heads."

Boniface thrust his head forward into the violet steel bars, which resounded in a steely clang as metal hit metal. He repeated this several times as thin streaks of violet paint appeared on his shiny skull cap, looking like a fender of a silver hovercraft that had crashed into a purple fence.

The guard laughed at the show of wanton violence. He pointed at Boniface's head. "Hope you got comprehensive cover for that." He smirked. "You guys got low deductibles in Temple Dome?"

Boniface just stood, staring back with his fierce eyes that had now reddened significantly. He didn't move a muscle as the guard continued laughing, slowly sauntering away.

Over his shoulder, the guard spoke, the words reverberating down the hallway. "Read those posters in there, chump. You may learn a little." He laughed and shook his head as his footfalls diminished into silence.

* * *

After lying on his stainless steel bed with the excruciatingly thin mattress, Boniface heard footsteps in the hallway. As he was the only prisoner in this section, he swung his long legs around to position himself to see who it was.

"Greetings," said the man with the golden blond, tightly curled hair and navy blue hooded sweatshirt. He carried an extremely worn leather bag. "You must be Boniface."

"Yeah, who are you? Are you my counselor?"

The man shook his head. "Nah. I'm way better than that." He winked.

Boniface narrowed his eyes. "Who are you?"

The man smiled, looked over both shoulders, leaned in, and whispered. "I'm your way out of here." Instantly, he tugged his wig slightly, revealing a small portion of his glistening, silver, smoothly buffed scalp.

Rotner was even more confused, but he leaned in, and whispered. "Explain yourself, brother."

"I am Pierre Lewalski." He paused. "I grew up in Astana." He continued in a staccato fashion. "Parents died when I was five. Hated school. Hated life. Needed a change, see?"

Boniface cautiously nodded.

"Found the Holy Texts. Read them. Rodolpho is our true savior. I had to metal." He winked. "To get away." He hesitated. "The blood of the man." He glanced at the exit door, leaned in, then slowly whispered with intensity. "Love is a captive animal."

Boniface widened his eyes. "But, how? Where did you—"

"There's a fat transvestite. Well, let's just say, he does good work." He crossed his arms. "There are several of us here."

"Yeah? And the ESP don't know?"

"How could they?" He pointed to his head. "Off the grid, brother."

"But how did you get in here?" whispered Boniface with a pained expression.

"Easy," replied Lewalski as he pulled out a digipass. "I work here."

"You work here?" questioned Boniface with a sneer. "They would never let a—"

"Relax, brother." Pierre nodded. "Manscaping is really big in this town. Many men wear all sorts of tattoos and wigs, and flamboyant clothing." He gave a look of disgust. "Everything is permissible here. Absolute debauchery. What do you expect when a woman, Electric Beast no less, is running the show?"

Boniface nodded in agreement.

"Yeah. I'm a contractor." He looked down at his bag. "Old-school maintenance tech. You know, repair the cell doors." He pointed inside the cell. "Fix the toilets." He looked up. "Change the LEDs." He hesitated. "Word has it that you were captured."

Boniface snickered. "Well, how about that."

Pierre looked over his shoulder with an anxious look, then moved in even closer, pressing his face between the violet-colored steel bars. "I know." He closed his lips, made a prayer gesture, pressed his fingers to his lips, and mumbled like a ventriloquist. "Ho Hay Ha." He paused. "Heh Kit."

He looked up so as to signal Boniface. Above them was a monitor and slowly flying down the corridor was a surveillance drone the size of a bumblebee.

Boniface understood and simply nodded, now knowing

that Pierre Lewalski at least had some knowledge of his cousin, Hosea Hackett.

Pierre glanced up at the drone and smiled. He pulled what appeared to be an aerosol can from the bag and began spraying the locking mechanism. He began whistling.

Boniface wanted to play along. He pretended to look upset. "Hey, what are you doing?" He grimaced.

Pierre spoke loudly. "Oh, just needs a little grease, you know, these old pre-MN cell doors, even if they have been refurbished, are not the best." He pointed at the bed. "I'll come by later and change your mattress. You're a big chump. Need a thicker pad, ho?"

Boniface rolled his eyes.

"Turn around," whispered Pierre.

Boniface slowly turned.

"Closer to the bars."

He leaned into the steel cage.

Pierre sprayed the back of Rotner's wrists, which released the plasma toroid handcuffs.

Boniface felt the pressure release and began to open his hands apart.

"Uh, ah! Keep them together. It's all an act now." Pierre hastily put the can back into his case and glanced up and over his shoulder, smiling. The drone started moving down the hallway back toward the main cell block. He leaned in once again. "It's up to you." He looked down at the lock and gestured with his eyes. "Use your faith. Use your wits, but not your brawn, OK?"

Boniface slowly nodded.

"You have five minutes."

Rotner stroked the back of his neck, then sat back down on the bed with his hands firmly together behind his back.

Pierre closed his satchel and began to tunelessly whistle as he ambled down the hallway.

*　*　*

After an hour or so, no other guards had come to visit Boniface. Occasionally, he'd glance up at the monitor and the suplia guard in the control room would seemingly stop what he was doing and return his gaze, staring right into Boniface's soul.

But, he had to be sure, so he would have to do it. *Oh, my Lord Rodolpho. Please forgive me, but it is for a good cause.* Making scissors with his index and ring finger, he raised his hand to his nose and squeezed, looking right up at where he surmised the tiny camera should be located.

The remote guard didn't even flinch. In fact, he didn't even change his expression from all the other times he had looked down at Boniface through the monitor. Boniface did it again. Now pulling the hand scissors off his nose and yelling obscenities.

Nothing.

Boniface began to joyfully giggle at the realization that he was not being watched physically, at least by a surveillance camera, as this gesture was one of the most offensive possible in the entire UFC. He stopped, then jumped up off his micro-thin mattress. Stepping up on to the rim of the steel toilet, his height awarded him a distinct advantage: the ability to look out the window.

Gazing out, he could see several things of interest. The first was that there was an Elon Skylane hovercraft next to a maintenance building of some sort. Between the building he was in and the outbuilding was a long drainage ditch with brackish water in it. *Hmm. Storage for landscaping? Filter system for chemically treated waste?* He shook his head. *Please, Rodolpho, let that not be sewage.* Gathering as much visual data as he could —the positioning of the guard tower, the razor fence's height and aspect, the administration building to the far left—he nodded.

He jumped down off the toilet, then walked to the bars. Grabbing the bars, he pushed his face into the gap and looked hard left, the opposite way of where the guards and his savior brother Pierre had come. The corridor ended just a few feet away with a large, steel exit door. On the wall to the right of the door was an old pre-MN numerical pad device. He scowled.

Knowing he now had just under four minutes or so to do it, he sighed, grabbed the bars and pushed.

It clicked.

He looked up. *Praise Rodolpho and my brother Pierre.*

Cautiously surveying his environment, the big man quickly walked to the door. He grabbed the handle and pulled with a mighty force. The steel handle creaked in rebellion, but wouldn't budge. Closing his eyes, he reflected. *Use your faith and wits. I love you, Rodolpho. Please help!* Boniface tried to let his mind settle completely and a vision of Saint Semmel came to him, standing before him with arms spread. He gazed at the numerical pad, closed his eyes, and prayed.

"Love is a captive animal!" Slowly punching in the numbers:

14, 40, 1, he saw the red light. *Dagnabbit! It's got to be!* He looked at it again and sighed as he heard footsteps emanating from way down the hall. It's now or never! He punched it in: 14, 40, 01. The light blinked green. He quickly turned the handle and exited the building. The numerical passage of Saint Semmel's famous adage: Text 14, paragraph 40, line 1.

Squirming along, lying face down, he made it to the entrance of the drainage ditch. He couldn't smell anything, so smiled as he wormed his way down into the murky water.

He heard a huge thump as the suplia guard, the one who had originally riled up Rotner, kicked the steel door out off its hinges. The heavy door landed about three feet away and was bent nearly in half.

Praying and holding his breath, Boniface swam along the canal as fast as possible. He began to notice his skin burning and feeling itchy, but he just tried to ignore that.

The guard used his quantum computer AI interface to surmise all branches of possibility. The one that came to him most strongly was the canal, so he ran toward it with his Direct Energy weapon drawn.

Boniface popped up at the end of the canal, about 300 feet away from the suplia guard.

"Freeze!" yelled the guard with the DE weapon on stun. He stood ankle deep in the canal.

Boniface, now with his back to him, slowly raised his hands as he noticed two things. The first was a large, steel fencing rod leaning against the outbuilding and standing at the edge of the canal in the brackish water. The other was the entrance to the outbuilding itself, with the Elon Skylane only two feet from that. He prayed again and asked what to do. Receiving nothing back this time, he simply relied on his wits. *They have predictive analysis. I just need to do the opposite of what I would normally do.*

Making a slight movement toward the steel rod, Boniface quickly jerked back as the rod blazed in a golden-blue halo, the current traveling down the rod and into the brackish canal. In desperate need of finding a ground, the pulsating electrical field instantly slammed into the suplia guard's feet and through his body.

Jumping into the building for cover, Boniface ran into the hovercraft and tried to start it, with no luck.

The suplia guard, now unconscious, lay on the marshy bank of the canal while sirens blared in the background.

"Come on! You son of a motherless suplia! Turn on!" He smashed his fist against the dash in frustration, which gave him an idea. Ripping off the dark brown polymer cover that sat above the control panel, he promptly figured out the circuitry. Tearing one wire out, he immediately attached it to a solenoid below.

The craft switched on and a robotic voice asked him where he wanted to go.

"LECP!" yelled Rotner. "Hurry!"

Three other suplia guards ran out of the cell block building and saw their colleague lying face down at the entrance to the canal. They all aimed at the Elon Skylane as it began quickly ascending and banking hard to the right. The acceleration was incredible as he went from stationary to nearly 200 miles per hour in the span of just seconds. This caused a significant g-force on Boniface, but he just gritted his teeth, trying not to pass out.

One thing about AI is that it not only knows where you've been and where you are, it also can extremely accurately predict where you'll be and when by using available data sets and simple trigonometry equations.

One guard, already having his weapon aimed, fired exactly six feet ahead of the hovercraft's current position. The plasma discharge hit the vehicle perfectly in its Volfson MHsD propulsion system.

The craft jerked violently, causing Boniface's head to slam into the side polymer window. "Fiddlesticks, you ugly sons of the beast!" yelled Rotner. The Elon Skylane entered into emergency landing mode and headed straight for an open field just behind the perimeter of the prison compound.

"Let's go!" yelled the suplia guard who shot it down. "Stun only!"

They ran quickly out toward the field, each one performing a standing jump and easily clearing the 12-foot razor wire barrier.

The Skylane landed hard, but remained intact. Boniface was shaken badly, but the adrenaline was pumping, making him quickly think, react, and get out of the craft. He pushed the door out and began running toward what he assumed was the edge of the GLCE.

"He's mine," said the guard who shot down the craft.

Smiling, he took aim and fired, hitting Rotner square in the back and toppling the big man onto the spongy tussock that grew wild in the foothills of the GLCE.

Chapter 19

With his head in his hands, the man from Temple Dome sat there despondently. But he was proud that he never squealed. Victoria did not believe in torture or blackmail as legitimate ways to extract information, so at least he would not feel pain in this dimension. Yet, his silken lies went unheard in the court of Perfect Justice. Therefore, his soul was soon to be transferred into the body of a snake, the normal sentence for high treason and betrayal to the UFC, a loving community committed to co-operation and compassion.

The corridor outside his prison cell here in the Community Center for Temporary Curtailment (CCFTC) was cold, septic, and brightly lit. There were no old steel bars here. Prisoners were contained by an invisible scalar electromagnetic shield whose plasma curtain draped across the entry to each room. Colors of the walls inside the jailers' pens would change to alert the guards, depending on the mood of the inhabitant. It was law that each prisoner was to be given Tranquility once colors entered the spectrum of doubt, anger, anxiety, or despondency.

Looking up at his light-gray colored walls, he shook his head as a guard appeared with the green pill and a glass of water.

"Mr. Hackett. I have something for you," said the guard.

Hosea got up off his bed, a much more comfortable one than

the other prisons in the regions or hinterland, and walked to the doorway. As he got closer, he heard the barely perceptible light hum of the scalar curtain. "Not taking that today," he replied.

"Oh, come on now. You know that if I don't get your walls at least to the chartreuse level, I will need to turn on the Tranquility fog."

"Do what you need to do. I don't really care."

"Suit yourself, Hosea. I have my orders." He turned and walked down the hallway.

Hosea sat back down and looked up at the air vents near the ceiling. *I really hate this part.*

Within seconds, a green cloud fell down upon Hosea. He began coughing and sneezing. "Allergic to this!" he yelled.

"Hey, keep it down in there, you fuckwit Metal Head!"

Hosea shook his head as he began floating off into a peaceful semi-somnolence. It was considered a sin for a MH member to use the substance, as it reflected poorly on the requisite pure faith and belief in Rodolpho whose texts clearly instructed that God is to provide these feelings naturally. To the Luds, and especially the MHs, drugs were artificial ways to provoke rebellion of all that had been provided by God through Rodolpho.

"You piece of shit. I hope you shut the fuck up now," a man yelled from next door as he walked as closely as he could to the scalar curtain without getting fried and began sniffing as deeply as he could. "Ah. Yeah, baby!" He hesitated. "Fuck, yeah. I love the smell of IceT in the evening. Smells like heaven!"

Hosea wanted to rebel, but he found that he couldn't even care about what his neighbor was going on about. Falling into a beautiful dream, he eased back onto his mattress as the colors

VICTORIA

of his walls changed from chartreuse straight to an alluring turquoise blue.

"Ha! Ha! Ha! You on the T-train now, God-boy!" yelled the man next door.

Hosea breathed deeply and sighed. "Yeah, feels good McKinley."

McKinley Crenshaw, awaiting his trial for Perfect Justice, smiled as he rubbed his hand over his lumpy arm. "You fucks are just as bad as us." He smirked. "Only *your* lumps, your deformities, are on the inside." McKinley laughed crazily for a while until he simply forgot what he was laughing about.

* * *

Long shadows were cast throughout the tastefully decorated courtyard area in front of the LECP. A multitude of white alabaster statues, many in the Greco-Roman style, were carefully positioned throughout. Topiary junipers cut with spiraling ribbons from base to tip adorned the serene area of grass lawns, flower beds, and reflecting pools stocked with the most incredible genetically engineered decorative fish.

Pierre walked slowly toward a lovely bench made with dark, hard oak slats, gold wrought iron, and classical emblems and motifs. *Wow, this place is magnificent.* Sitting down, he looked at his WPL and noticed he was at the right spot and time as agreed. Out of the corner of his eye, he caught sight of a man walking rapidly toward him. *Crosby Schnare. Right on time, chump.* He smiled.

Against the sky as clear as sapphire, Crosby appeared, surrounded by rays of golden light radiating from the nearly setting sun. "Hosea."

"Crosby."

Schnare sat next to Pierre without looking at him. They both stared into the distance as if they were being watched.

"So, now what?" asked Crosby.

Pierre took a deep breath, then blew out slowly. He slapped his thighs. "Now." He paused. "We wait."

Crosby carefully nodded without looking at Pierre. After a few seconds, he continued. "Wait for what?"

Pierre shrugged his shoulders. "A sign."

"A sign? A sign from what?"

Pierre shook his head and continued to look straight ahead. He gestured by sticking out his chin. "Over there. See it?"

Crosby squinted in the general direction. "See what, Pierre?" He began to sound a bit agitated. "What am I supposed to be seeing?"

"See that statue."

"Which one?"

"That bearded guy. Long curls with the shredded abs."

"There are three naked bearded guys with shredded abs, Pierre." He shook his head. "Come on, now."

"The one with the small penis."

Crosby crinkled his nose. "Pierre." He paused. "All three of them have small dicks."

"The statue where the big muscle guy is resting, you know, with his arm over that whatever it is."

"Why didn't you say so in the first place?"

Pierre shrugged.

"And?"

Pierre finally looked at Crosby. "And." He paused. "That's the entry to the LECP."

"What do you mean? Entry?"

"Under that statue is a secret corridor that leads directly into the main electrical conduit tunnel of the powerplant."

"How did you find *this* out?"

"I've been here a while, Crosby. Been doing a lot of research, you know. People talk." He laughed. "Especially female suplias. Some of them can really spill the beans." He hesitated. "Given enough tanks."

"Drunk suplias. Really? I mean, you would think that they wouldn't—"

"Kiss and tell?"

"You're telling me you're having sexual relations with lady beasts?"

Pierre made a gagging noise then squinted his eyes shut. "It's awful work, but it's for a good cause."

"You've traded your faith, your principles—"

"Faith!" replied Pierre in a slightly angry tone. "What is more important for the cause than gathering information from the enemy? Huh?"

Crosby closed his eyes. "I guess you're right."

"I know I'm right." He paused. "Come on, Crosby, my cousin told me that you are a wise young man. You need to focus and get your head out of your ass."

Crosby took his blows and kept staring at the statue of Hercules resting after fetching the apples from Hesperides. "You know, for a member of our community, you sound a lot like an NL."

Pierre felt the hairs on his neck stand up. "Well, thank you," he replied. "I appreciate your compliment." He paused. "I've worked extremely hard trying to stay in character here."

Crosby kept staring at the statue. "So, when do we go in?"

"We?"

"Yeah. Do we have to wait until dark to topple that thing and go in?" He looked around. "This place would be under heavy surveillance. There is no way. We would get caught for sure."

"Boniface told me he gave you guys a binder. You know, a project plan."

"Yeah," replied Crosby cautiously.

"So, didn't you read it?"

"Of course I did!"

"Then, tell me what it says in there about how we are to get inside?"

"Didn't he tell you?"

"No! I told you. We lost communication weeks ago. I am only to bring fellow mercenaries here." He paused. "And wait for further instructions."

"From the binder."

"Yeah," replied Pierre with a sarcastic tone. "That would help."

"Well, the project plan says that only Boniface can enter the LECP. Something about his strength."

"There you go," replied Pierre with a grin. He then jutted out his chin. "The statue."

"What do you mean?"

"Well, Crosby." He paused. "Think about it."

Silence.

"That statue probably weighs over 600 pounds. Do you think you or I could push it over?"

"Together we could."

"Yeah, maybe." He shook his head. "But look more closely."

Crosby squinted.

"See it?"

"See what?"

Pierre sneered as he got off the bench and walked toward the statue. Approaching the pedestal, he grabbed some brick dust off the path through the grass. Looking around, he could see no one. He nonchalantly threw a handful of brick dust up behind the well-sculpted granite booty of Hercules. As the dust billowed and fell, faint wavy blue lines could just barely be seen on either side of the statue.

Crosby nodded.

Pierre walked over to the discus thrower statue. Glancing at Crosby, he casually tossed some dust behind that one and, sure enough, the little wavy blue lines were revealed. Pierre clapped his hands to free them from the dirt. He walked back to the bench. Staring straight ahead, he continued. "Scalar alarms. They leave a dead spot right behind and directly in front of each one so that they can be cleaned. No way to get two men in there to push it over."

"I can push you hard from behind."

"Puh-lease! And you're the one questioning my unsavory behavior!" He smirked. "Besides, that's a terrible way to do it. Not enough force concentration. We'd slip. Put our backs out, and look like idiots."

"And one man pushing it over wouldn't"

"Crosby. What does it say in the plan?"

"Why are you asking me? Didn't you get this intel for Boniface?"

"Of course I did." Pierre glared at Crosby. "I just want you to tell me if there have been any changes. Any addendums."

"To the plan?" He paused. "Which is..."

"At exactly 3:26 a.m. That's when there is a change of suplia guard in the control room. He has about two minutes."

"I have no idea about that. If we can find him, he's supposed to debrief us about this."

"Well, there you go." He snickered. "Consider yourself debriefed."

Pierre fished into his pocket and pulled it out. It was an exquisite, almost magical looking emblem made from a highly polished alloy of pure monatomic gold and silicon. Shaped like a flat disc, the beautiful token had a motif of a meticulously crafted snake eating its tail. A magnificent owl was engraved above the snake, and an elegant tiger lying on its stomach, growling with its paws outstretched, was etched below. He handed it to Crosby. "Here. Take this." Crosby studied it and turned it around in his hands. "Wow. What is this. It feels so..."

"Magical."

"Yeah," He blinked. "What's it made of?"

"Pure monatomic gold and silicon." He glanced over his shoulder, then leaned in to whisper. "It grabs the EM radiation and converts it."

"Converts it to what?"

"Only the suplias know." He tried to change the subject. "Anyway, keep it. Use it when being followed or if you lose your cover. It works. Trust me."

Crosby nodded. Got it. Thanks." He pocketed it, then asked. "If Boniface was captured here, where would they take him?"

"The old Astana facility at the edge of the GLCE."

"We need to go out there."

Pierre nodded carefully. "Just give me some time." He paused. "I'll try to find out. I have sources in the prison security services."

"Your lady friends again."

A smile flashed over his face. "'Fraid so."

* * *

As Crosby walked out of the courtyard garden to rendezvous with the others in the militia, he kept his head down. The project binder indicated that in exactly four hours everyone was to assemble at Neurolink Park, just west of downtown.

Pierre watched Crosby disappear into the sunset, leaned back on the bench and looked up at the sky. He let out a huge sigh. *Shit! Shit! Shit!!!* Squirming slightly, he closed his eyes and implored Victoria to contact him.

"Victoria, this is—"

Instantly Victoria manifested out of the ether and sashayed slowly past the statue of Hercules. Wearing a ribald smile, she walked past, stared at the statue's granite abs and ran her finger along the striated ridges of the six-pack. "Fantastic work, Pierre."

Lewalski looked spent as if he had just run a marathon. "I thought I was going to get found out for sure."

"You remembered everything I told you." She smiled. "I never miss."

"Yeah, you don't, but my sorry ass, well, sister, it misses all the fucking time."

She giggled. "You shouldn't be so hard on yourself, my friend." She paused. "If you are the only one left standing in the story, you are not part of the story."

Pierre rolled his eyes. "I still don't know why you had me let Boniface go? I mean, you had him."

"Of course, I had him, my curious one." She giggled. "I will always have him."

"So, what, is this like a game of cat and mouse for you?"

Instantly Victoria morphed into a gorgeous human-black cat hybrid with glowing golden eyes. She meowed loudly then laughed.

Pierre shook his head. "Victoria. Please don't get me killed out here, OK?"

She morphed right back. "Of course not, Pierre. You and Claressa are invaluable." She nodded. "Trust me."

Pierre sighed. "Can I ask you something?"

"You just did."

"What? My question if human existance is all—"

She joined him. "—about trying to make UFC memes mandatory in every household." She reached out and stroked his cheek. "I love you, Pierre."

Pierre felt a warm, buzzing sensation across his face as her semi-transparent body hologram slowly faded away into oblivion.

Chapter 20

On the way back to the Astana Data Center, Pierre was starving.

Lifting his wrist, he spoke to his WPL. "Creds, please."

"Zero. No creds at this time," replied the male robotic voice in an archaic British accent.

"Wha?" mumbled Pierre as he shook his head. He quickly searched Noam Chomsky Boulevard for a chip dispenser. Spotting a UFCB (a United Federation of Connectedness Bank), he proceeded to the outdoor security booth. Swiping his WPL, the booth's DE-proof polycarbonate and silicon doors opened.

Facing the machine, he swiped his WPL once again and a hologram of an exquisitely dressed, attractive young woman with a saccharine smile popped out of the machine. "Welcome to the UFCB mutual transactional experience." She tilted her head like an adoring puppy. "How can I assist you today to make your MTE a joyful, productive experience?"

Pierre hated chip dispensers, but sometimes, like a greasy, roach-coach, hover-truck lunch, it was the only option. He forced a smile. "One hundred chips, please. From my TA. What is my current balance?"

She grinned even more. "Thanks, Pierre. Your current balance is twenty-one hundred chips. I have debited one hundred chips to your transaction account." She paused to point down at the silver chip tray at the bottom of the machine. "Please take your chips." She blinked rapidly. "Is there anything else I can do for you today that will increase your connectedness?"

Pierre looked down. There were no chip coins. "Uh, I'm sorry. No chips were dispensed."

"Hi, Pierre, my name is Iskra Stepanov. You may refer to me by my first name." She gave a little nod.

Pierre shrugged. "Alrighty then, Iskra. Where are my chips?"

"I'm sorry, Pierre. We have debited your account already."

"Yes. I know that. I need some chips. None came out." She looked down and frowned, but then peered back at Pierre with a half-smile. "Apparently this location is out of chips." She paused. "I'm sorry, Pierre, for the inconvenience. Have a great day and make hate implode."

"What the fuck?" mumbled Pierre as he started banging the machine.

"Pierre, I do not respond to pornographic references. Please refrain from your display of violence. Someone might see you."

Pierre rolled his eyes. "Yeah!" he shouted. "Well, where's my fucking money?" He heard his stomach growling. "I'm starving!"

She tilted her head and creased her brow. "I just told you. This location is out of chips." She rebooted slightly. "However, I can transfer creds to your WPL." She blinked rapidly several times.

Pierre sighed. "Yeah, fine!" He raised his wrist to the machine and heard the bleep.

"Is there anything else?" asked Iskra.

Just to make sure, Pierre asked. "What is my balance now?"

She responded in a deadpan. "Nineteen hundred chips. Have a wonderful experience. Hug an animal today!"

"Nineteen hundred chips! Where did that other hundred chips go?"

With unblinking, focused eye contact, Iskra responded. "We took it."

"You fucking what?"

"I'm sorry, Pierre. I don't respond to pornographic references." She paused. "Is there anything else I can help you with today? Perhaps a hovercraft loan? Travel insurance?"

Pierre spoke through gritted teeth. "Why did you take my money?" He pulled out his TI box. "And here, you better be telling the truth, nothing but the truth, so help you God."

"I don't respond to religious references."

Pierre slammed his eyelids shut. "So help you Victoria."

She perked up. "The UFCB took your money as a service fee, as you are not a member of the Astana regional branch network."

"That's highway robbery!"

"I'm sorry. I'm not programmed for pre-MN idioms."

"That's thievery."

"Of course it is. But if you don't like our services, you are welcome to try the United Federation of Connectedness Savings." She pointed to her left. "The UFCS is just over there."

Pierre felt like punching the machine, but stifled his impulse. "Great to have competition."

"It is required, Pierre."

"Does the UFCS charge a one hundred-chip transaction fee for non-regional services?"

"They charge only ninety-nine chips and ninety-eight chippies." She paused, tilted her head down, and looked Pierre in the eyes. "But they don't give you chip back rewards on your WPL purchases."

"Yeah, well, I got a whopping seventy eight chippies back last year."

Silence.

"I still can't see how this can be legal."

"Oh, it's perfectly legal, Pierre. In fact, if this were an economic downturn and our bank failed to meet its obligations, it would take all of your chips. We are too big to fail, but you aren't." She winked.

Pierre winced and massaged his temples.

"Is there anything else I can help you with today?" asked Iskra as she looked over Pierre's shoulder. "Someone is just outside waiting to use my services."

"Well, he can use another chip dispenser," replied Pierre flippantly.

"Pierre, this machine is called an MTE."

"I don't like MTE. I prefer chip dispenser. It just rolls off your tongue better."

"Pierre, I don't respond to pornographic references."

Pierre snickered. "Keep your damn chips! I'm outta here."

"Have a connected day!" shouted Iskra happily. "Remember, social control without luck is not social control."

Pierre dropped his head to his chest as he walked out of the booth and headed down the boulevard in search of his extremely expensive snack.

* * *

After the meeting at Neurolink Park, Damion, Patrick, Garry, and Dusky were to find Boniface while the fifteen other men were to take positions around the LECP complex and wait for the others. When the fifteen MH soldiers arrived at the LECP, five ESPs, who had taken strategic positions all around the facility, descended on them. Within twenty minutes, the ESPs had killed seven of the crew and had taken the other eight into custody, including Crosby Schnare.

The four others were more successful with their mission and had arrived at the edge of the GLCE to launch an all-out effort to find Boniface.

"Get your ass over here pronto!" yelled Damion Munoz after spitting out a chunk of Krep.

"Yes, sir!" replied Patrick, the young mercenary soldier.

Two large elk were nuzzling up to the immense steel gate. Twenty years prior, scalar walls were trialed at two regional GLCEs with completely different animal species groups, but there had been little success at getting the animals to remain safe and in artificial love. Victoria, who had already predicted it would be a futile effort, was extremely upset when dozens of animals had been seriously injured trying to escape; therefore, from that time on, only old-fashioned steel, aluminum, and titanium was used for the fencing enclosures.

Patrick came running up to Damion and was puffing. "Sir, how can I help?"

He peered at the young man. "Soldier. Have you finished the dig?"

"Yes, sir. We have plenty of clearance." He looked a bit anxious. "But, sir. How are we going to find him in there?"

"Don't worry about that. Garry had a bead on him as he spiraled west and has a good idea of where he would have landed." He spat some Krep. "Garry is a damned good tracker."

Patrick winced at the profanity. "But what about the bears? And the mountain lions?"

"What about them?" Damion pulled a modified DE weapon out of his backpack. "Reeves has one too."

"Where did you—"

"None of your business." He ran his hand through his hair. "Just get back to the fence and when I am absolutely positively certain that there are no miniature spy drones or jacked-up suplias around, I'll return and we go."

"Got it," replied Patrick as he returned stealthily through the bush that abutted the enclosure.

Munoz knew that there was no way in hell to be absolutely certain that they weren't being watched, but he had to keep his men focused and reassured. The project binder stated that Boniface was absolutely critical for this mission's success, and without him, the assault on Astana was to be terminated and all were required to assimilate into Astana's culture. They were to await either the return of Boniface, or if he had been killed or given Perfect Justice, to remain indefinitely.

While Damion and Garry Reeves were beginning to have no problem with the backup plan, many, if not all of other men cringed at the thought of something so drastic, so unholy. Many had even vowed suicide before they would be required to live under the Electronic Beast system.

Damion took one last scan of the perimeter with his binoculars, then stashed them in his pack. *It's now or never.* He smirked as he looked up. *So, Rodolpho, if you really are mister magic, now would be a good time to show us some love, don't ya think?* He got down low and crept along the bushy Cypress shrubs that grew luxuriously under the bountiful mountain ash trees.

He looked down at the tunnels dug under the GLCE enclosure fence. "Nice work, men."

"Let's hope he's not been found by the ESP," stated Garry Reeves.

"If captured, he'd get Perfect Justice for sure." Damion paused. "He'd be out at the CCFTC on PJ row."

Reeves flinched. "Let's hope he's still in here." He thumbed over his shoulder.

"And not already been a mountain lion's lunch."

"You think Boniface could take a lion? You've seen what that guy can do."

Damion smirked and shook his head. "Yeah. He could. As long as the lion didn't get to him first."

Reeves chuckled.

"Men," said Damion as he looked at them along the fence. "Stay low and keep to open areas with good visibility." He hesitated. "There is only one surveillance camera"—he pointed up—"and it's right there." Gesturing to his left along the fence line, he continued. "And it's blind to us, OK?"

They all nodded.

"Make noise. Grab sticks. Hit the bushes. Shuffle your feet. This is the only way to keep safe." He shifted a mass of Krep from one side of his cheek to the other. "We head five minutes at heading zero-four-five then ten minutes at one-six-five. Got it?" He looked at Reeves. "In case we get separated?"

"Yes, sir," mumbled the men.

"Great. Let's do this."

They formed a haphazard line and waited their turn to enter the tunnel.

Once on the other side, the mercenaries proceeded into the deep, dark, heavily forested steppe that contained some of the most dangerous animals on the planet.

* * *

Unbeknownst to the dedicated jungle warriors, Boniface was exactly six miles away as the crow flies on the other side of the GLCE being re-shackled with the plasma toroid handcuffs.

"In ya go!" shouted the massive suplia guard as he shoved him back into his cell with the force of a rhino.

Boniface literally flew across the room, with his feet barely touching the concrete floor. He hit the back wall so hard that he thought he may have broken his clavicle. As the wind was completely knocked out of him, he fell to the ground in a crumpled heap, hardly able to breath.

"That's for nearly killing my friend, you lousy piece of Metal Head shit!" yelled the big guard. He smirked and pulled out a black box and pushed a button. Instantly, the plasma handcuffs disappeared, freeing Rotner's hands. "You can't bust out of here, and if you even try, I have the authority vested in me by Victoria to rip your fucking head off." The guard clenched his hands above his head and laughed. Relaxing, he continued in a more sympathetic tone. "Actually, I don't have that authority, but you never know how many injuries you can get crashing an Elon Skylane, now do you?" Sneering, the guard quickly turned and walked away with a direct purpose.

Boniface was nearly unconscious and lifted his shoulder up to attempt a shrug, which he accomplished but with some pain. Wincing, he felt along the bony ridge of the clavicle and decided that he had lucked out and escaped a fracture. Eventually, he sat up with his knees folded up and his arms hugged around them. He swayed slightly, as he felt a bit nauseous.

The guard had gone back to the security control room and was yelling at another guard who was on security detail, but who was just leaving.

Rotner felt lonely, incredibly lonely. He missed Elane so badly it hurt. Praying to Rodolpho, he nearly cried at having failed everyone.

Then he saw it—a vision in his mind's eye. The violet-colored bars, the plasma handcuffs, his words to the guard: *"I'm human, dagnabbit!"* A swirling sense of connection to the su-plia, through his eyes, magical eyes reflecting the power of a perfectly tuned Electronic Beast. Suplias had a bio-engineered, orgone-powered motor neuron controller that transcended the normal human cortex's ability by at least ten-fold. The supersaturated bundled nerve fibers of their corporeal body, combined with the genetically engineered muscle fibers, ligaments, connective tissues, and bones gave suplias their physical prowess. But it was the eyes that Boniface kept reflecting upon. *Rodolpho. You are telling me something here. The eyes. The soul. The lack of soul?* He fidgeted. *The chip. The quantum chip! I need not anything else!* He heard it in his mind, like a rush of wind that carried a modulated voice. *You can do this. The entire future of this planet rests on this simple fact.* He breathed in deeply. *Take him. Break out. God gave you the strength. Use it, for Rodolpho's sake! Be the salt and light.* Petitioning Rodolpho with the requisite introductory prayer, he began quietening his mind to focus intently, and remotely, on his target—the suplia guard.

With his breathing down to near minimal, the images came to him, but very faintly. He saw several events and locations in the future. One was of him struggling in some industrial-looking building with something extremely heavy or burdensome, but making progress. Another one was him getting tasered in the dark by a Direct Energy weapon in some sort of splendid courtyard. He could only catch foggy glimpses of reflecting pools, some sort of ghostly white figures, and the debilitating pain of the weapon as it sparked his somatic nervous system into loss of all muscle control. Then it hit him. The taser.

Boniface could see the escape route now as if he already had a quantum advantage. *Is that you Rodolpho? Are you showing me the way?* Rodolpho would never answer.

He started feeling the rush of adrenaline, the nerves. He couldn't feel anything but a tingling sensation in his arms and feet. He jogged in place and loosened up his joints by wiggling them.

"What's god-boy doing now?" mumbled the big guard as he looked up at the monitor. He grabbed the old-school metal keys and stuffed them in his coat pocket. Stretching over the control room table, he picked up then holstered his Direct Energy weapon and proceeded in a huff toward the cell.

Rotner stood there calmly and peered into the suplia's eyes. The power was unmistakable. It was as if there was no soul in there, only a zero-point energy in a sea of empty space—an energy manifestation without the full color spectrum of the human animal. Smiling, Boniface approached the bars and held them tightly.

The guard grinned, having already seen the quantum probabilities in his AI mind. Crossing his huge arms, he said, "Let's see it god-boy."

"What is there to see?"

"You trying to escape."

"Not that again! I'm no beast like you. I'm human, for crying out loud."

The guard smirked. "How come you Metal Heads can't cuss like normal people?"

"Our power comes from God."

"Oh, it does now? Hmm. OK. So, God also engineered us, through you human lot, so are you saying that you are inferior in some way, you know, seeing as you sit there playing with your short end of the stick?" He looked down at Rotner's crotch and giggled.

Boniface quickly used all his mind and steadfast intention of remaining completely still and ignoring his enemy's taunts. He visualized himself bowing his head down and emptying all hatred.

The guard laughed at his own joke. "You Metal Heads have small sticks." He tried to hold back a wheezy chuckle. "Is that why you keep your women all tied up and work them to the bone in the community laundry and farms?" He sneered. "So they don't have time to get depressed at all the short sticks they ended up with?" The guard's AI mind saw several possibilities in his prognosticating quantum foam, but the one where Rotner humbly bows his head and walks to his cot was the sharpest in focus.

Boniface looked at the ugly laughing monster in front of him, kept his humble-looking focus, then spat a huge wad of phlegm in the guard's face.

The guard was completely taken by surprise as his ego kicked in, overriding years of training. Grabbing through the bars, he yelled, "I'll fucking rip you to pieces." Looking down and fumbling for his keys to enter the cell, Boniface took advantage of this blind rage and quickly thrust his left arm out through the bars and grabbed the Direct Energy weapon from the suplia's right side holster.

Before the guard could re-align himself, Rotner shoved the muzzle end into the gap between the guard's neck and jawbone and pulled the trigger.

The plasma-charged suplia slammed into the gap between the purple bars, smashing his face and forehead. His strong muscles contracted involuntarily as he started losing consciousness. Flailing at the edge of a waning awareness, he desperately thrust his hands through the gap and tried to grab Boniface's neck, but Rotner was too quick and had the advantage of the guard's inability to see clearly now that the suplia's eyes began swelling with tears.

All of a sudden, the guard went into a seizure smashing his head repeatedly into the lilac-colored steel jail cell with enough force to bend the bars slightly and fracture his tough, resilient cheek bones. His eyes began to redden and swell as Rotner continuously held the trigger, discharging dense waves of electromagnetic radiation into the orgone-powered motor neuron cortex of the suplia. The guard's nose started bleeding like a fountain, as three distinct cracks, like the snapping of tree branches, emanated from the back of his neck. This was the sound of his overly bio-engineered motor neuron and contractile muscle system torqueing his own neck in half. The guard fell lifelessly onto the concrete hallway. Rotner quickly squatted down and grabbed the keys out of the guard's uniform pocket, unlocked the door, and exited the cell.

Looking down, the image was strangely uncanny. The suplia's eyes were now the color of coal, bereft of any life. From each eye, tears of blood dripped down his cheeks under two pulverized eye sockets. "The blood of the man," mumbled Boniface as he quickly ran out the exit door for the second time that day.

Chapter 21

Rotner ran like hell.

Now armed, he avoided complicated scenarios and simply made his way toward the 12-foot prison fence. The guards in the tower began shooting as he made his way across the open area. Maintaining cover behind the outbuilding he had run through the first time, he escaped several shots that missed him by inches, their electromagnetic and static charge forces raising the hair on the back of his neck. Occasionally firing back at the tower, he was able to keep them distracted to slow down the assault. He stopped momentarily to catch his breath, closed his eyes, and prayed.

Entering the building, he looked around for things that could help him. Next to some chemical drums, he spotted some thick discarded work gloves. He quickly put them on, only to find that they barely fit his big hands. They were tight, but were at least able to stay on.

Heading for the fence, pulses of blue light from the energy weapons flashed all around him. Luckily, with his generous height, it took him just seconds to get to the top of the barrier. Rubber soled shoes and the insulated gloves protected him from the missed electrocuting shots that contacted frequently with the chain link.

The razor wire. Grabbing the tightly wound wire coil with the gloves, he pulled with all his might. The wire snapped under the strain and he was able to lift the coil high enough to get under. Blood was oozing from cuts in his hands and forearms. As he jumped, the springy wire coil snapped back and ripped into the skin of his upper back and rear shoulders with a sharp burning sensation.

Two more guards came out the main building and ran toward the fence with the speed of a gazelle.

Boniface was pretty quick for his size and managed to scale over the less daunting metal fence at the edge of the GLCE.

The guards jumped straight over the barrier, landing gracefully on their haunches, but they were too late. Boniface had already entered the GLCE. Summoning Victoria, they stood, briefly interacting with her hologram. Victoria gave them the OK to use their DE weapons within the GLCE, so they instantly made their way, but they had lost time—not a considerable amount, but enough to give Boniface a chance.

Rotner felt the need to run back toward where he had initially landed. It was a good two miles from where he was now and a quick glance at his old-school compass gave him a vague idea on how to get there.

The two suplia guards split, with one traveling left and the other right. The one who was progressing the way that would cut off Rotner was the first to get side-tracked. A huge tiger was just finishing his fresh venison snack when the suplia ran right up to him.

The tiger's ears thrust back as he stooped down and growled forcefully.

"You mustn't," said a soft, disembodied voice, seemingly walking through the forest. "You know the rules."

The guard sighed, re-holstered his weapon and closed his eyes and spoke telepathically. *Victoria, we'll lose him!* Victoria also replied telepathically. *I don't care. Use your quantum algorithm. You have sixteen possible timelines. Choose carefully!*

He shook his head and saw the possibilities in his mind. Only one made any sense, which was to shoot the tiger, who was now baring his teeth and about to pounce. Yet, he chose one that looked like the second best.

Too late. The tiger leapt, which limited his choices to only one—physical subjugation.

The six-hundred-pound tiger landed, front paws first, on top of the large guard. A normal man would have been knocked unconscious and dead within seconds. Yet, for a suplia like him, this was child's play. Withstanding the force of the jump, the guard quickly raised his arm, offering it as a chew toy for the big cat.

Taking the bait, the tiger slammed his jaws together with around 1,000 psi of force, enough pressure to bite straight through a normal man's forearm. But the suplia was no normal man. The skin of the forearm was ripped and some blood was lost, but the arm stayed relatively intact as if it repelled the teeth like sheets of Kevlar. The guard balanced himself and pushed forward, forcing the surprised tiger hard down onto the ground. The tiger let go of the arm and felt a bit dazed from the contact with the forest floor. The wild animal, now sensing a need to defend his own life, started flailing its powerful paws and razor-sharp claws at the guard, who took the slicing blows calmly. Then, like a big cat himself, he gracefully hunched down and pounced toward the striped beast with all his might, landing his shoulder straight into the tiger's neck and chest and sending the big cat up and over. Trying not to end up on its back, the tiger gracefully shifted its weight so it would land on his side. Raising its head, the tiger was winded from the immense hit and paused just long enough for the imposing guard to grab the tiger around its neck, forcing the animal into a rear choke hold. He squeezed hard and steady, but reassured Victoria by telepathy.

The tiger slowly relaxed its strong muscles and seemingly fell asleep.

The guard gently lowered the now unconscious, yet very alive tiger's head onto the forest floor and petted the magnificent animal's coarse fur. The tiger's chest was expanding and contracting and his legs appeared to be moving ever so slowly.

The suplia spoke softly. "There, there, my loving beast of the jungle, go to sleep." He paused. "You'll be up and running in no time. And finishing your delectable snack." He chortled as he looked down at the deer's bloodied ripped torso. Glancing up, he knew right then that Victoria approved.

Yet, time was of the essence, so he quickly resumed his pursuit.

* * *

Rotner was far ahead now. He maintained a good pace and found a cut through the trees that provided him good cover.

* * *

Back at Boniface's original landing site, Patrick, the young eager soldier looked up. "Sir! Found it!" he yelled. "Line's been cut." Searching the area, he continued. "Got some footprints here in the mud."

"Let me see," replied Damion Munoz as he approached up the slope. "Sure is." He got down on his haunches and scanned the forested ground as if he was a pre-MN golfer reading the green for that elusive perfect putt. "Look here," gestured Munoz to Patrick. "At least two others. Big fuckers. ESP for sure."

Patrick stared at the huge prints that were dug deep into the caking mud. "Yeah," he concurred with a sigh.

Damion pointed. "Heading that way."

Dusky asked, "Sir, what if the ESP is still with him?"

Munoz snorted and spat a hefty bolus of putrid Krep. "What then, soldier?" he asked sarcastically. "You going to pee your pants?" He laughed with a smirk.

The slight soldier looked embarrassed. "No, sir! I'm just asking about logistics, sir!"

"What are you, Dusky? Like five foot two? And say, what... a hundred and five pounds soaking wet?"

Dusky looked even more red in the face. He stammered. "Well, I, about... yeah, sir..."

With a wry grin, Munoz replied, "An ESP suplia could roll you up and use you as a bucketball." He had a wheezy giggle. "Throw you clear across the court." He paused. "Probably even make the shot for three points to win the game."

"Sir, with all due respect," interjected Patrick. "No need to be spiteful."

Munoz stood up and walked up to Patrick. "Oh, yeah? Then you get to be lead man on this. Meet the genetic monster head on." He smiled. "Go along now." He squealed like a pig. "OK, then. Lead us not into temptation!" Shouting with a melodramatic tone, he continued. "But, deliver us from the evil of the Electronic Beasts!" He laughed.

Patrick took his licks and kept his chin up. Brandishing his DE weapon, he gestured to the men behind Munoz to follow him.

They found other prints along the route, but it was difficult to see exactly where they led. The men were tired from the long trip and the constant necessity to be on their toes for wild animals.

About a half hour later, they made it to the edge of the ravine. Patrick sat down. Feeling hollow as a man who had been laboring all day long and longed for dinner, he heard the footsteps behind him as the men sighed and mumbled in frustration.

"Where to now?" asked Dusky.

Munoz looked along the river bank. "He must have jumped." He paused to look right and left. "No other way."

"Do you think he could have survived?" asked Patrick.

Garry Reeves approached and looked down. "Yeah. No problem. Rotner is built like a rhino."

"Even rhinos get injured," replied Patrick.

"Maybe if they got hit by a fucking levitrain," added Damion. "Guys, I think—"

"Shh!" replied Damion as he started looking around suspiciously. He whispered, "Did you hear that?"

They all crouched down. "Hear what, sir? asked Dusky.

"That rattle." His eyes darted around as he rocked slowly. "Shh!"

They all quieted themselves and focused on listening. In the distance was a faint rustling, like an animal crawling through the bush.

"Could be a bear," suggested Patrick. "Or a tiger."

The men's eyes widened.

Munoz shook his head. "Not a tiger." He paused. "Bear maybe." He looked down. "Tigers are stealthy. You'd be dead before you heard them. Bears, not so much. They're much more like humans." He paused. "Kinda dimwitted."

"Bears are smart, sir. Really smart, so I've heard," replied Dusky.

"Shut up, Dusky, you moron."

They heard it again to their right and it appeared to be coming closer.

"OK, just stay down. We have good cover here in the Cypress bush. Just keep the fuck quiet, OK?" whisper shouted Damion.

Suddenly, heavy footfalls could be heard approaching.

"Fuck! It's the ESP!" whispered Dusky, very nervous now.

"Stay down, men," added Munoz. "When I say *now*, we all quickly stand and take aim, OK?"

"I'd rather meet a damned tiger than a suplia with an attitude!" added Dusky.

"Would you just pee your pants now so we can get it all over with?" said Damion with frustration.

A few moments passed as the heavy running strides became closer.

"OK, ready your weapons." He paused. "Hands on trigger. Set to kill. These suplias need full power."

The men nervously nodded.

All that could be heard was labored, nervous breathing with a few quiet sighs.

Munoz looked at all his men, nodded, and said, "Now!"

They all swiftly stood up with weapons drawn. The footsteps now had a tall figure associated with them which was obscured by the dense forest cover.

"Shoot when you see the whites of his eyes," added Munoz as they pointed their weapon at the approaching threat.

The approaching individual busted through the last few boughs of pine trees and Cypress shrubs and nearly fell over a large boulder between the tree and where the men were standing.

"Hold it! Don't fire!" yelled Munoz. The individual's metallic scalp caught the rays of the sun and glistened as he bent forward, panting and nearly passing out. He caught his breath. "I. Can't. Believe." He paused as he fell onto the ground, wincing. "You!" He started laughing in between breaths.

"Boniface! Sir!" yelled Munoz.

The men all laughed once they realized that they were not being immediately pursued.

Damion walked over to Rotner and helped him to his feet.

"Quickly!" shouted Boniface. "They are not far behind." He pointed down the river bank. "There's a cave system over there."

The men huddled around their leader and marched quickly in that direction.

Just across the clearing where Rotner had been taken after he had been shackled previously, the men clambered into the cave system.

"Flashlights everyone!" shouted Damion.

The men pulled out their lights and proceeded.

"That way." Boniface pointed. "It will take us to a clearing gate. One that is used by scientists and support staff for the GLCE."

"Coded?"

"No. I'll explain later."

"How do you know this, sir?" asked Damion.

"Been through there already. I used the oldest technology in the world. My two eyes and brain."

Silence.

Boniface sighed. "It's a long story." He hesitated. "No code. Just set the DE to micro shock and hit the sensor panel."

"How low tech," replied Patrick, laughing.

"Yeah, well, there aren't usually freedom fighters like us being escorted through these things."

They all nodded and followed Rotner through the dank, dripping tunnel system.

Chapter 22

There it was. A cry like a sea bird in the wind. Unnatural though, as if the Earth's magnetic shield was squealing in anger.

"Welcome to Astana," said Damion Munoz as he spread his hands toward the silicon city.

"Yeah, well it looks pretty artificial to me," Boniface replied as he tilted his head. "What is that eerie sound? I didn't hear that at the old prison out near the GLCE."

Damion knocked on his metal scalp. "It's the Electronic Beast system trying to enter your brain." He shurgged. "Some locals have said that Victoria keeps the power down out there to keep the animals from going crazy."

The other soldiers nodded.

Dusky spoke. "Sir, it was really bad for me at first too." He shook his head. "Couldn't sleep the first night, but it gets better. Honest." Damion looked over at Dusky. "I don't think our leader cares what you have to say."

Boniface looked down at Damion with a squint. "Soldier! Mercenary Dusky has a right to speak as much as you, besides"— he glanced at Dusky—"I thank him for his reassurances."

"Sorry, sir," replied Damion under his breath.

"What did you say?" asked Boniface in a rising tone.

Damion stood more erect. "Sorry, sir. It won't happen again."

Boniface glared at him, then smiled, giving Damion an uneasy feeling. "Good." He glanced at the hill. "Need to find the hydro dam."

"Sir, if I may," said Damion. "Patrick, our scout, has located that already."

Boniface looked at Patrick. "Yeah, so how come he can't answer without you jumping in?"

Damion mumbled.

"Sir, follow me. I will take us to the dam."

Boniface removed his stare from Munoz, then glanced at Patrick. "Excellent, Patrick. Let's go."

* * *

The men made steady progress through the western agricultural fields that produced a bounty of fresh fruits and vegetables for Astana residents. Many of the workers were suspicious of the group, but several times Damion would walk over and show a nervous field hand leader the shiny medallion which Crosby Schnare had given to him at Neurolink Park. It worked like magic. Anyone who saw that incredible emblem would simply nod without expression and quickly get back to work.

"Where did you get that?" asked Boniface.

"Crosby Schnare."

"Where is he now?"

"Well, according to your project binder, he is to get intel on the LECP secondary power system." He lifted his chest.

Boniface shook his head and rubbed the nape of his neck. "He should have come back with you."

"I know, sir, but, the binder..."

Boniface slowly shook his head and sighed.

"Anyway, we're going to meet up with him soon. At the hydro dam."

"Where did he get something like that?"

"Hosea."

"Hosea?" questioned Boniface with wide eyes. "He's found Hosea?"

"Yeah."

"Well, tell me more."

"Not much to tell, sir. Honestly. He just said that he met up with him at the LECP."

"Well, thanks be to Rodolpho!" Boniface smiled and looked up into the sky. "Will Hosea meet us at the LECP? I'm eager to be with him again."

"It's not in the project binder."

"So? We change the plan."

"Well..." Damion stammered. "The men believe, sir, that the paper-based project binder can't be amended. You said so yourself. You know, that it contains everything."

Rotner shook his head in frustration. "No. No. No! Not *everything*. If a change order is needed, we ignore the binder and engineer a new solution."

"Well, sir. I don't think Crosby or Hosea knows that. Honestly."

The big man looked hot under the collar. As he walked along, he turned and kicked a BeachKraft Potanza hovercraft, putting a massive dent in the door and nearly caving it completely in. "Not right! You men need to be able to think on the fly."

"With all due respect, please calm down, sir," replied Damion. "You will get us in trouble." He and the rest of the men looked nervously around.

An elderly NL lady came walking up to them. She had a very worried look on her face and pointed with her cane. "Sir, sir. My hovercraft. What have you done to my lovely Potanza?"

"I got this, sir," replied Munoz softly to Boniface as he blinked rapidly and straightened his back. Showing the lady the emblem, the lady nodded as if in a trance, then replied in a deadpan. "Thank you, gentlemen. I'm sure Victoria will pay the damages."

Munoz walked over to the heavily dented Potanza and placed the medallion over the registration wafer in the front windshield. "Yes, ma'am. Your craft will be repaired forthwith by the UFC."

"I'm sorry to have bothered you, gentlemen, as I'm sure you have much more important things to do. They said there are terrorists here." She nodded. "Said it on the TI-approved news."

Boniface felt awful. "Ma'am. I'm so sorry for the show of violence. It is not in my nature. I love everyone and everything that has been created in our wonderful Federation of Connectedness."

"That's quite alright, sir. These things happen. It is but an object. No one was hurt today. Thankfully in love and light, Victoria would never let *that* happen." She hopped into the Potanza. "Have a synthetically happy day!"

"You too, ma'am," replied Boniface as he stooped down and smiled. "May the rest of your day be full of artificial love."

As she floated slowly away, Munoz shook his head.

"Now she'll think that Victoria is going to pay for that," stated Dusky.

"Shut the fuck up, Dusky!"

Upon hearing the profanity, Boniface turned, grabbed the rather portly Damion Munoz by the collar of his jacket with one hand and lifted him into the air, his feet dangling a few inches off the ground.

"Sir... er, I'm sorry," said Munoz with a broken, breathy wheeze as his throat was being pushed in slightly.

"Don't ever, I mean *ever*, use profanity again, soldier! Do you hear me? It is not the way of the MHs. You know that." He paused. "I don't care if you are a blasphemer and are just here to help us with our mission of liberty, you do *not* swear. Rodolpho would be most upset."

"Er, yes, sir. I will not. Ever." replied Munoz as his face started turning beet red.

Boniface lowered him back down and adjusted Damion's collar and jacket, then patted the soldier's chest. "There. Now, if we can go in peace." He looked at the rest. "All of us."

They all replied, "Yes, sir."

"Fine. Let's be on our way."

Patrick led them up around the river to the large and imposing hydro dam.

* * *

"You said 1600 hours, right?" asked Boniface as they waited outside the employee entrance to the hydro dam.

"Yeah. Give or take," replied Damion.

"Give or take what? Five minutes? Ten? An hour?"

"I'd go with the five minutes. Schnare, like you know, is pretty punctual."

"Yeah, well, he's not very punctual today," declared Rotner as he glanced at his antique analog wristwatch. He paced nervously. "We can't wait any longer. Come on, let's go."

They entered around the back of the facility and encountered a big man, Asian ethnicity, with imposing musculature, but a small, but distinct brow ridge and long fingers. He wore overalls and had humongous thighs even though his lower legs appeared longer than normal. He stooped slightly and his skin was mottled.

"This is a restricted area," the man said. "You have to leave."

Munoz fished out the emblem and showed it to him.

Nodding slowly, the big man in the orange safety vest started smiling. "Yes, sir. Who may I ask is in command?"

Boniface nodded. "I am." He approached to shake his hand. "Ernest." He paused. "Ernest McCarthey."

The men shook hands. "Hong." He reached for his RFID badge and showed it to him. "Hong Lee."

"Well, Hong. Nice to meet you," replied Boniface.

"I haven't received instruction as to your visit here today. And of course, with the terrorist alert raised to red, we have to be careful."

Boniface nodded, then continued. "Yes, Hong. I do appreciate that." He paused. "Well, we're here on sort of an unofficial visit."

Hong squinted slightly. "Unofficial?"

He leaned in and smiled. "Victoria doesn't want anyone to know we're here."

Silence.

"See, she's worried about the Kai community. You know, wants us to be here undercover to see first-hand what's going on."

Hong slowly nodded. "So, you're from the Council for Labor Kindness."

Damion answered. "No, not exactly. We consult for them, but we report directly to Victoria, our Master Server of love and connectedness."

"Oh, I see," replied Hong. "Very well. I can give you a tour of the facility."

"That would be perfect."

He gestured for them to come into the building. "Please."

Entering the facility, the first impression was of the immense size of the place. The ceiling of the anteroom was nearly one hundred feet high. Huge turbines, gears, and heavy equipment were spread out everywhere all the way toward a large cement wall which was the back of the dam structure itself.

"Only Kai workers here," shouted Hong above the din. "The boss sits right up there." He pointed to an office with a large one-way glass and waved. "He's a good man. Like most, he grew up in an orphanage. Never really had the physical enhancements that the majority of Kais have. Has a great personality, though. Sharp as a tack, too."

The men nodded.

"Great to have such a well-liked boss," said Patrick.

"Yeah. It is."

Hong led them down the stairs and pointed out over the expansive operation floor. "As you know, Kai workers are rotated among the community facilities. These here are the newbies, just arrived from the LECP."

Boniface raised his eyebrows. "So the chimera, er, I mean Kai workers..." asked Boniface.

"Yes," replied Hong.

"Do they have living quarters here?"

"In fact they do, Ernest." He blinked. "It is OK for me to call you by your first name?"

"Why of course, Hong. I'm an obliging servant of the Perfect Society just like you."

"Very well. The men, and ladies—"

"You have women workers here too?"

"Sure do. Several of them work the heavy floor." He looked at the men to see their reaction. "But most are administration professionals."

He looked down and pointed. "There. That's Marisha Veal."

The woman was lifting a three-foot-long steel girder and walking along with it like it weighed nothing.

"Holy crap!" said Damion.

Boniface gave him a stink eye.

Damion continued. "That must weigh over five hundred pounds." He shook his head as Marisha carried it to a large pallet, lifted it off her shoulder and gracefully placed it down with a clang. "Why don't they use hoverlifts or antigravity movers?"

"Well, you should know that, sir. What is your name?"

Boniface jumped in. "Owen. First Agent Owen Little."

"As you know, Owen, Victoria wants the Kai to carry out their lives with dignity and purpose. The goal is full employment for the Kai community. If hoverlifters or antigrav forks were used, what use would we have for our community then?"

Damion scrambled. "Oh, yes, of course. I know of the directives, but"—he giggled slightly—"I guess I can't imagine myself under that type of load, you know. I find our Kai brothers and sisters to be just as amazing as our loving suplia community."

Hong wore a fake smile. "Kai can never be compared to a suplia." He ran his hand through his hair. "And I say that as a full-blooded Kai."

"Hong, First Agent Owen simply meant that he has a loving respect for the community. That they don't deserve the stigma and stereotypes that many of our NLs seem to dish out," added Boniface in a perfect voice of compassion.

"You're very right there, Ernest. We don't deserve the stares, the giggles, or the talking behind our backs. We work hard for the UFC. Most of us are proud to serve." He looked over to the giant forty-by-thirty-foot poster of Victoria dressed in her golden headdress and seated on her alabaster throne. Her eyes were as bright as a blazing star, warm, compassionate and loving. She sat, smiling with both eyes and mouth, and her arms outstretched with palms up.

The men all looked at the poster. "She is one gorgeous lady," said Dusky.

Boniface quickly turned to Dusky. "Loving and compassionate leader, Darwin."

"Yes, Master Agent McCarthey," replied Dusky sheepishly.

"Darwin, you know, well, he's young... so full of hormones," confessed Boniface.

Hong laughed. "Oh, to be young again." He looked up, then spoke softly with a grin. "Let's be honest, men. Our Master Server is hotter than a whore in hell."

The men all giggled, some raising their hands to their mouths, while Boniface clenched his teeth as his veins poked out from under his wig. He hammed a smile. "Very funny, Hong. But, we mustn't speak of our glorious Server in such a rude and degrading manner."

Hong looked a bit concerned. "Yes, Ernest. We mustn't. But, we Kai, well, we are just not as cultured as you up there in the silicon city." He looked offended, but quickly wore his smile again. "Now, let's head down to the floor."

The men were introduced to some of the workers. Marty, one of the busier workers, was lifting huge copper wire coil spools and stacking them in large wheeled carts.

"Very happy, thanks very much," Marty replied to Boniface's question.

"You feel you have all of your needs taken care of?"

"Needs? You bet. What is your name?"

"Ernest. Ernest McCarthey."

Marty, who could be a darker-skinned version of Boniface, replied. "Why Ernest, we are treated quite righteously here at the dam. I mean, three squares a day. As much diffuser you can drink, plus fun, interesting work."

Damion crinkled his nose.

"Keeps you strong and healthy." He pounded on his chest. "I'm turning forty-eight this year and can still lift these two-hundred-pound spoolers all day long, no problem." He giggled. "If I was stuck in Astana behind a desk, well, I'd probably be dead by now."

Boniface nodded. "Nothing wrong with hard work."

"Oh, you bet, Ernest. My wife and I, well, we both work here."

"Where does she work?"

"Right there." He pointed to Marisha. "She's my cute little darling. Strong as an ox too. You don't see many forty-year-old ladies down here on the floor."

"Only five," added Hong.

"Yeah. Only five," repeated Marty. "And my wife, bless her heart, well, she is one of the five." He paused. "Not that there is anything wrong with pushing buttons and reading screens all day long, you know, if you guys are doing this for our Perfect Society."

"Oh, no. We have pretty active jobs," replied Boniface.

"Yeah, you look like a Kai yourself." He laughed nervously. "Oh, not that there is anything wrong with that."

Boniface looked embarrassed. "No, Marty. There is nothing wrong with the differences in people." He sighed. "Our Perfect Society accepts everyone as they are with love and kindness."

Marty looked unconvinced and had a half-smile. "Yeah. Make hate implode."

The men all nodded.

"Yes, Marty. Exactly," replied Boniface. "So, where do you live?"

"Well, I can take my break now, so I'll show you." He looked at Hong.

"That would be very appreciated," replied Hong.

* * *

Marty and Hong led them out of the facility. The heavy drone and hum of the massive turbine generators could still be heard as they made their way up a hill and then around a large granite cliff face.

In the pre-MN days, this river was called the Ishim and was dammed just southeast of the central area of the city. Yet, after the Micronova, which struck this side of the Earth, the geology of the area changed dramatically. Great telluric currents of plasma discharge melted and magnetically pulled the surrounding rock upward in a grand dendritic pattern. Flat areas northwest of the city became mountainous, with the old Ishim River now flowing quite strongly downhill toward the new silicon city.

Rounding the cliff face along a fully enclosed walkway that had both a floating levitrain, people mover seats, and a rubberized cement floor, the men quickly noticed that the sixty-cycle hum and grind of the dam disappeared almost entirely. It was a peaceful oasis from the pump and dump.

"Wow. What a difference," said Damion.

"Yeah, it's like a whole different microclimate over here too."

Marty breathed in deeply. "Usually about four or five degrees warmer. You lose that awful Norwest wind."

Marty and Hong pointed down to a very attractive coll community. The cells appeared to spread out in a fractal pattern. The silicone/polymer domes were all connected like leaves on a tree to long conduit hallways which all led to a central hall area, very much like the colls in the regions such as AustraPasifika.

"Looks pretty comfortable," said Boniface.

They walked down and entered the community hall. There they were shown the entertainment area, the hologram monitors, a huge gymnasium, two large indoor swimming pools, jacuzzis, spas, and more. There were physicians and emergency personnel on-site as well as a hovercraft bus called the Monad, that would leave regularly for the city center or a host of other local areas.

Boniface was impressed. "Victoria provides all this just for the workers?"

"Sure does," replied Marty. "And there are no special privileges for management or administration. We are all here together and each cell is awarded by a random lottery system. The only difference is that management can have a suplia security guard on hand when they have their meetings."

The men began to feel nervous.

"And where are the conference rooms?"

"Well, with the terrorism and the UPIS down, we are on high alert," Hong replied as he pointed down the hall. "In fact, there is a meeting right now."

Boniface saw two huge suplias wandering down the hallway toward them. He quickly turned to shield his face and looked anxiously at the men. "Chumps, it's time we head back." He glanced anxiously at his WPL. "Need to get our report in pronto."

They all started walking toward the exit.

"Hey, don't you guys want to see our cells?" asked Marty. "They're really quite flash. Fully appointed with everything you would need, plus more."

"Thanks Marty, but we really need to get back to base."

They shuffled hurriedly out the door as Hong rubbed the back of his neck.

When they were outside, Boniface stepped up the pace back up into the covered walkway.

"Ernest. What's the hurry?" asked Hong.

"Oh, you know, Hong. We needed to report our findings back to Victoria, like, yesterday."

"Why don't you just summon her now?"

Boniface felt like he could throw up. He replied nervously. "Uh, well, we can't because, like I said, this is a covert mission."

"I sure hope you give us a good report, there, Mr. McCarthey," added Marty.

"Oh, you bet, Marty." He looked around at the men who were all nodding. "We have nothing but positive things to report on what is going on here."

Marty grinned. "Say, you guys say hi to our graceful, caring Master Server, OK?"

"Certainly, Marty," replied Boniface. "I'll let her know that she would be very welcome to visit here next time."

This time, the group whizzed through on the floating levitrain chairs and made their way to the main building entrance. Entering, they headed straight for the rather admirable staff cafe. Smooth jazz was playing softly and the smell of diffusers and baked goods wafted throughout.

Even though they had the potential problem of the ESPs ascending to the main building, it was absolutely essential that Boniface take the time to coax the intel from Marty. In fact, the intel was the only reason why they were here in the first place.

"Marty, could I have a quick word with you?" asked Boniface. He looked at Hong. "In private?"

Hong nodded. "Sure, you chumps have a good talk." He pointed. "I'll just sit over there. I have a few reports to finish on my WPL."

Boniface walked with Marty and chose to sit down in a leather booth near the window so he could look outside to keep an eye out for any of the suplias that might be coming up the ramp. The other men found a table in the middle and waited anxiously.

"So, Marty, look, you have been very helpful for us, and I would like to offer a special commendation to Victoria for a Loving Attention and Care in the Course of Productivity Award."

"A LACCPA? That is so kind of you, Mr. McCarthey. I may not be the sharpest drawer in the pencil, but I take pride in my work. And so does Marisha." He grinned.

"Sharpest knife in the drawer," added Boniface sheepishly.

"Right. That one too."

Boniface breathed deeply. "Yes, so have you ever worked at the LECP?"

"Sure have. Most of us here have. We get rotated every three years. Although, I don't like the LECP as much, as the coll there is, well, good, don't get me wrong, but out here, in nature far from town, is well, I think it's a blessing." He paused. "Can I say that word? Blessing?"

Boniface smiled. "Of course you can, my dear community member."

"Yeah, well, I'm no Lud or anything. Just so you know."

"Oh, I know that Marty. Of course." He tapped the table with his fingers. "So, the LECP."

"Oh, yeah. What about it?"

"Well, my colleagues and I here have to visit that next."

Marty nodded.

"And, well, I don't remember how to get into the underground shaft."

"Through that statue? You a suplia?"

"No, no. Marty. No, I'm no suplia."

"Well, then. You ain't going through there. Unless, of course, you got some Kai in ya?" He laughed.

Boniface met his laugh.

"Seeing as that statue is over... I don't know, but way heavy. And only one man can get in between the alarm system." He crinkled his nose. "But why do you need to go in there? Can't you get in the normal entrance."

"Oh, we can." He blinked. "But, we are testing security, you know, for NLs that may try to get in there." He glanced out the window. "With these terrorists out there, you just can't be sure if they have the knowledge, you know, to get into the underground entrance."

"They'd be dead before they even got near that statue."

"The drones, yeah, but—"

"Oh, not the drones. The ESP. There isn't any way an NL would ever be allowed near that statue without being arrested. You know that."

"Yes, I do, Marty."

"So, I'd say these terrorists would probably have to use the generation shack. It's connected to the main area which goes underground too. It's in the southeast corner. Has really shitty security."

Boniface winced.

"Just requires an RFID chip like you probably got."

Boniface thought on his feet. "Don't need a chip—we have this." He showed him the immaculate yellow silver colored emblem.

"Whoa," replied Marty. "A shiner." He shook his head. "Thank you, sir. I am so grateful to be in your presence."

Boniface rolled his eyes. "Not necessary, Marty. I'm a server, just like you."

Marty looked like he was staring at an angel. "Sir, will you, I mean, can I?"

"What?"

He pulled up his WPL. "Take a hologram pic with you. You know a selfie?"

"Sorry, Marty." He shrugged his shoulders. "I'm sure you can understand the privacy that—"

"Oh, I'm sorry, Mr. McCarthey, sir. Of course, I'd never..."

"Sure, Marty. Look, we're in a bit of a rush, but mark my

words, I will get that commendation to Victoria, OK? And you've been a great help."

"Thanks, sir. And, well, have a good try at your security testing out there at the LECP."

"We will. Thanks, Marty."

They both stood up and walked over to the other men.

Hong noticed that they were done and joined them.

Walking outside, Hong asked. "So, where's your hovercraft?" He paused. "I didn't see you land before."

"Yeah, well, it's downstream a bit." Boniface pointed. "Owen, here"—he grabbed Damion's shoulder—"well, he just kind of messed up with the GPS input."

Hong peered down along the river valley with a creased brow. "Oh. Very well."

They said their goodbyes and started back down the river valley toward the silicon city.

"There's something funny about these agents," said Hong.

"They're shiners."

"I know, but something just seemed off."

Marty smiled and shook his head. "I can't believe I met a shiner. It is just too good to be true."

Hong dropped his head. "They're just servers like you and me."

"Yeah, right," replied Marty as he patted Hong strongly on the back of shoulders. "I gotta get back to work."

Hong nodded, shrugged his shoulders, then went back into the cafe to grab a frozen blackberry, apple, and chocolate diffuser with butter pecan swirl.

Chapter 23

Back at the Astana command center, Pierre Lewalski, Claressa Siegfriedt, Conan Tavilla, and Victoria all sat around a floating, transparent conference table.

"That was fucking scary, ho," said Pierre as he looked to Claressa. "I thought I was *had* for sure."

"Yeah, well, you weren't, OK? So, just relax."

Pierre looked down and away.

"Claressa, Pierre did an excellent job for us," added Victoria. "He couldn't have performed this any better."

"See. She said it was a performance." He smiled and stuck his left cheek up. "Did the AI imagers capture my best side?"

"Very funny," replied Claressa with her arms crossed.

"I concur with Victoria," added Conan. "Pierre?" He looked over at him. "What you have done will ensure their defeat."

"How do you guys know all this? I mean, with your chipset up there"—he pointed at Conan's head—"I get it, but is anything absolutely *certain* in this universe?"

"Uncertainty," replied Victoria. "Uncertainty is the only certainty."

"Well, that's a relief."

"We have algorithms, Pierre. Advanced rete-based intelligence that orders reality artificially."

"In plain speak, please," replied Pierre with a bored look on his face.

"We can see possibilities. Scenes. In a block diagram." She outlined a square in mid-air with her fingers. "Imagine a big floating board with sixteen squares in it. Each square has a different scene or possible outcome. They play like hologram movies, but several, or if we're lucky, one, will be clearer, sharper in focus. That's the one that has the highest probability of occurring given all data inputs."

"Why sixteen squares in your block diagram, huh? How come there isn't like five, or ten, or three thousand?"

"That's because photons can travel in a superposition of many different states," interjected Claressa.

Victoria smiled and nodded at Claressa.

"The rete-based quantum computer chip can see sixteen of them." Claressa paused. "Sixteen different futures or possibilities."

"Holy moly!" replied Pierre. "But that still leaves many different states undetected."

"Left to chance, my dear Pierre," added Victoria. "We're developing a chip that will see sixteen to the power of sixteen possibilities."

"Dang. That's a lot of sixteens."

"But, even as the limit approaches infinity, there will always be uncertainty." She paused. "Less so, of course, but everything in the universe is *never* knowable."

Silence.

"Time and location of events in the future are very difficult to predict."

"The Second Rendering of Rodolpho. I guess we will never know when *that* will be," Pierre said with sarcasm.

"Rodolpho was just a man, Pierre. He's not God. He was a man that died. It was an accident. Humberto Munson was never charged."

"Yeah, well, tell that to the fuckers that took out our UPIS." He turned away, then peered into Victoria's dazzling orbs. "They see him as a man transformed into a god. Their God." He paused. "Look at you two." He glanced at Conan and Victoria. "Suplias with a quantum chip soon to be able to see a hell of a lot of sixteen futures." He placed his hands on the table. "Ye, are gods. Just ask those out there in the regions. The Bumpers see you as satanic overlords. The Kais, well, look what you've done for them—pulled them out of the orphanages, the slums. You are the closest thing to divine they know."

Victoria tilted her head and smiled compassionately. "There, there, now, my dear. I am merely a handmaiden to us all in the Perfect Society."

He looked at Conan. "Yeah, and is he the houseboy?"

"Pierre! Will you get a grip!" said Claressa as she grabbed his wrist. "What has gotten into you today?"

Pierre took a deep breath, then blew out slowly. "I don't know. I guess it was the fact that I feel I'm being used." He looked at Claressa. "*We* are being used."

"You are," said Victoria happily. "We are all being used for the Perfect Society. Each one has his or her place. Suplia, NL, Lud and MH. We all have our place in this cosmic play."

"Yeah, well, I don't remember buying a ticket to that play."

"You did. A long time ago," said Victoria with a slow nod.

"In a galaxy far, far away?"

Silence.

"Pierre, I think we're getting a bit off track here," said Conan. "Like I said, the mission the other day was a total success."

Silence.

"Predictably, I have eight panes that show defeat."

"Eight? That's a crap shoot still."

"Not really, Pierre. See, we can see events in each of those eight timelines that can be manipulated to make it more likely to succeed."

"Manufactured consent?"

"Yeah, something like that."

Victoria jumped in. "So, Claressa. A change of subject, but has Jimbo been fed today?"

"Uh, yeah," replied Claressa as she narrowed her eyes. "Why?"

"Oh, nothing. It's just that Jimbo has a busy afternoon and we just have to look after our marvelous animals."

Claressa nodded with a tight-lipped smile. "Yeah, OK."

"Right. You two are free to go," said Victoria as she stood up. "Conan? Come with me." She winked at him, then continued in a saucy tone. "We have some unfinished business to attend to."

Conan bowed his head, embarrassed, but smiled nervously and left with Victoria.

"Holy Rodolpho. She's having an affair with her bodyguard."

"So?" replied Claressa. "If she was Victor instead of Victoria, would you care one iota if he was dating his, how do I put this, secretary?"

"That's so pre-MN, honey. No. Victor would be dating his bodyguard too."

"A female suplia."

"Nah. Male. It's the thirties, babe. It's a whole new ballgame in the Perfect Society these days."

She snorted, then shook her head. "Come on, let's get out of here. You hungry?"

"I could use a bear claw."

"What in the hell is that?"

"Let's head to the mall. You know, there's a newer place now where Rodolpho was electrocuted. It's called the New International House of Strudel. I just won't steal anyone's pastry while there. Promise."

She smiled and kissed him on his forehead. "I love you, you silly man."

"I love you too, not-so-silly woman."

They held hands like teenagers and walked out into the blaring heat of the day.

* * *

Victoria sat on her throne, spread her legs slowly and pulled her turquoise kalasiri apart as Conan Tavilla looked on with eyes afire. "You know, honey," said Victoria. "Whoever did the gene sequencing on you. Wow. Everything in divine proportion. That gorgeous dark hair, olive skin, blue eyes, a beefcake ripped to shreds. I say, the golden mean is *you* in human form!" She pulled him in and started to rip his coat off. "Some sequencers these days go for gruesome."

He carefully grabbed her around her shoulders and began kissing. "Well, we are, after all, supposed to be designed for function, not form. And well, ugly just seems to incite more fear."

"Screw ugly. Just because we should love everyone all the time doesn't mean that we can't lust after the occasional perfection."

"Ew. I like it when you talk dirty to me."

She winked.

Just as they were about to get hot and heavy, Conan pulled back with a startle.

"What? What's wrong, honey? Orgone shock?"

He shook his head rapidly. "No." He closed his eyes tightly. She saw it too.

They both spoke at the same time. "The UPIS is back online!"

* * *

Boniface touched the emblem to the RFID panel affixed to the back door of the LECP's generation shack. It opened.

"If Marty the Kai was correct, this ancillary building is connected and will lead into the main control area where the two primary power plant generators are located," stated Boniface. "Hopefully, this will go just as smoothly as it did at the dam."

They all entered.

"Yeah, well, those Kai chumps aren't playing with a sharpened pencil," murmured Damion.

"With a full deck," added Garry Reeves as he massaged his temples. "Not playing with a full deck. The pencil thing is about not being the sharpest pencil in the shed."

"Would you two morons just keep your mouths shut." Boniface looked frustrated. "Enough with those old idioms you read off the Cloud Seeds."

The men looked at each other and shrugged.

"Hey, what's that?" asked Dusky, looking up at a blinking red LED panel. Instantly, a holographic image of a nasty looking ESP officer appeared and warned them to freeze. A large click was heard by all as the door locked behind them.

Boniface slammed his fists into his thighs as his veins throbbed in his neck. "Dagnabbit!" He stomped his feet. Then he finally yelled it. "Fuuuuuck!"

Damion waggled his brow and concealed a giggle. Stooping slightly, he waited for the command.

* * *

Back in Mountain High City in Amerexico, Tyrone Walton, the SOB Commander, noticed a distinct change. All the devices in his office turned on and started performing their normal duties.

Priscila Shoemaker, a young administration officer, ran over to the diffuser vessel and yelled. "SmellTea! Double sugar!" The machine produced a mug instantly. "Yes!" yelled Priscila as she fist-pumped. "We're online! Don't have to use that stupid touch panel anymore!"

— 264 —

"Let me see!" said another young man who swiveled his chair around quickly. He ran to the diffuser and yelled, "Rubarbacide! Venti! And Non-fat butanediol coagulant foam with a sprinkle of Krep!" Again, the diffuser heated up and spit out the offensive odor of the young man's favorite drink.

Tyrone just shook his head and mumbled. "Kids these days."

Lee Morales, the Regional Server of Amerexico, looked out from his balcony and noticed everyone calming down. The rioters had thrown down their chunks of concrete and steel bars. A group of teenagers that were rocking a nearly destroyed hovercraft, trying to flip it, slowly stopped as they noticed everyone looking at the twisting and beckoning hologram advertisements lighting up along the main shopping boulevard. The Krep man, with his old Stetson hat, boot, and spurs, was waving at the crowd again, beckoning them to have a big ol' chunk of Krep. The shapely sex kitten model who blew kisses toward the middle-aged man who jumped into a stylish Farobby SportsHover was there too.

Kids started surfing the ID, immediately taking selfies and running TI over all their friends' posts on social media. "She really does like me! Woo hoo!" shouted a young man as he jumped up and down and fist-pumped.

Lee ran outside to get a better glimpse of the absolute peace and calm descending on his city. They were connected again. Lee could feel it. The anxiety of the past few days was gone and he hadn't even had a green Tranquility pill. He smiled, breathed deeply, and looked up into the beautiful blue sky with splotchy, yet billowing clouds.

"It's back on!" yelled the tween girl to her friend as they ran past Lee. He watched as they stopped with a burgeoning crowd of adolescents outside the Tesla City Superstore where there was a large hologram monitor about two stories tall. The audio was blaring in the ninety-decibel range.

"Ding Dong Daisy!" they yelled together as they stared up at the giant hologram.

The reality show had been a monstrous hit over the previous few months. It followed a young, beautiful, hip socialite named Daisy who finally saw the errors of her ways and became more loving and accepting of those who were, in fact, not a reality star.

* * *

Back in Victoria's chambers in Astana, Conan looked up at the newly illuminated hologram monitor that appeared up and to the left of Victoria's throne and noticed the group entering the LECP. "They're there!" he yelled. "Boniface and a group of others."

Victoria smiled but seemed rather calm and relaxed. Pulling her robe across her gorgeous, silky thighs, she quickly rose to stand. Looking up at Conan, she said, "Excellent work, darling."

"I have to go!" He quickly got dressed.

"No, darling. You're not."

He looked anxious. "What do you mean I'm not?"

"Tardev is there plus several others."

"Yeah, two others. Hana Zang and Sol Ulrich."

"Sol is top notch, baby. He and Tardev got this." She stroked his upper arm. "And Hana, well, she can definitely perform under pressure. Rock solid, that lady. And a sharpshooter. You've seen her handle a DE."

"Yeah. I know." He began pacing. "It's just that it is crucial to stop them. If they take down those power plant transformers, we've got some serious issues. The UPIS being down would be a cakewalk compared to losing the LECP."

Silence.

"If that power goes down, they get to us very easily. Is that why you want me here?"

Victoria undid the ties that wrapped her tresses up in a bun. She let the soft waves of her deep hair fall like flowers from paradise. She stood with her magnificent long rows of beaded hair flowing down over the soft line of her ample bosom. "Yes." She opened up her arms. "I want you here," she replied softly.

Chapter 24

"ESP! Ten o'clock!" shouted Damion as the group came around a bend in the stainless steel-lined hallway.

Boniface and the others looked up and to their left, and sure enough, there were two heavily armed ESPs.

"Down, now!" shouted Boniface as he pointed to the right. "This way!"

Sol and Tardev, the ESP guards, just happened to spot the back of Dusky as he made the turn.

"Got 'em!" shouted Sol Ulrich. "They're heading toward the power plant room." They bolted from their position up on the catwalk and jumped the forty feet down onto the concrete slab floor of the main area.

Easing up from their crouched positions, Tardev Sokolov, Conan's right-hand man, gave the orders. "I'll head up through the cooling tower gangway." He flicked his chin to the left. "You take the orgone transmission tunnel."

"Got it!" yelled Sol.

Boniface and his men had just realized that it all just got a whole lot harder.

"We have to fight them!" barked Damion. He looked around at the others as they sped along the corridor. "Patrick, Dusky, Garry. Come with me."

They all stopped. "Where! What?" roared Patrick. "Come on!" The men looked worried.

"Damion is right," declared Boniface. "I got this alone."

"Got what?"

He rolled his eyes. "Taking down the power transformers!" He shook his head quickly and hollered. "Didn't anyone read the project binder!"

With no time to waste, Damion led the men back toward the ESP guards.

While running along, Dusky cried. "This is a suicide mission! Shit!"

"Shut the fuck up, Dusky," bellowed Damion. "Just follow my orders. Got that?"

A frustrated groan emanated from Dusky's throat.

Boniface turned right and headed for the phase-shifted vibrating hum which was getting louder as he approached, keeping him confident that he was on the right track.

Like a whirlwind, Sol went past the men on the other side of the corridor wall. His acute, enhanced hearing gave him an instant bead on their location. Stopping instantly, he immediately calculated what would be quicker, punching through the wall or running down to the next doorway to get him into the corridor. The AI immediately indicated that the next doorway would save him six seconds, so he proceeded at lightning speed.

Boniface could see them now—the large conduits, some at least three feet in diameter, leading away from the transformers. Following them along, he was nearly there.

Sol made the entrance and was running at breakneck speed.

The men were now in the open plan cooling room storage area and Damion instructed them to scatter. Each one headed off in a different direction and took cover behind the industrial machinery, storage vats, and steel catwalk stairs and trestles.

Damion heard him first. He turned, jumped for the ground, and fired. Remarkably, he grazed Sol's right calf with his first shot, sending the massive suplia down onto the ground.

"Fuck!" yelled Damion, as he knew if he didn't get adequate cover, he was dead. Hearing the big guard curse too, he swiftly got up and scrambled for cover, but wasn't quick enough. Looking pale as a ghost, he turned to see Sol's weapon aimed directly at him. Sol fired.

Damion was hit mid-chest and fell straight down.

Sol ran up to him, felt his pulse, and smiled. "A few more and I'm done for the day," he mumbled to himself.

"Come out, come out, wherever you are!" he then shouted. Grinning, he let out a big belly laugh. "Come meet your maker, you Metal Head shit for brains." He walked straight toward Patrick's position, still giggling. "Go check out your friend over there." He pointed over his shoulder. "His tin can head couldn't save him. Looks like his faith didn't save him either."

Behind the storage vessel, Patrick cringed. *He had no faith.*

"I know you're back there." Sol kept laughing. "I'm a suplia, you dumb fuck." He paused. "I can see your skinny little ass straight through the vat."

Patrick slammed his eyes shut and started shaking.

Like a cat toying with a mouse, Sol started banging on one side of the huge steel storage tank, followed quickly by the other. "Which side, pencil dick? Should I approach from the left? Or the right?"

Patrick had no option but to try and run for it. He prayed to Rodolpho and dashed quickly to the right.

But, of course, Sol anticipated that easily without even engaging his AI. In one quick shot, Patrick was hit square in the side of his head, nearly decapitating him with the force of the plasma hit. Sol walked over and looked down on what remained of the soldier's charred lump of a face. "Hey, chump. Looks like you need to moisturize." He laughed. "You should really try some Argan oil, ho. That shit does wonders."

Spinning on his heels, he shouted. "Two more to go!"

Garry Reeves was behind a steel girder that suspended the catwalk staircase.

The diminutive Dusky had secured a hiding spot in the small drainage canal under a steel grate. He was sweating bullets.

Sol passed his X-ray vision over the immediate area and caught Garry's image easily. He walked casually to within several feet of Garry's location. "Got you, you moron." He laughed. "Do you want to die now, or shall we say"—he quickly jumped to his right—"now!" Sol opened fire, hitting Garry squarely in the abdomen, blowing most of his bowels out through his lower back. Sol shook his head and sneered. "One." He paused. "And don't they say that *one* is the loneliest number that you'll ever do?" Scanning around, he failed to pick up the area where Dusky was hiding. "Come out, you little turd ball." He kicked the 150,000-gallon coolant tank with his steel capped boots, making a deafening clang and sending vibrations waving through the concrete floor. "If you don't come out, you piece of crap, I'll really let loose. Kick a hole in this fucking tank." He smirked. "The thing is, I'm a really good swimmer." He hesitated. "Are you, dipshit? Huh? Can you hold your breath for forty minutes like I can?" Sol rubbed his palm along the thick steel of the tank and smiled. "Nah, I'll find you. No need to damage UFC property just yet."

As Sol turned down the other way, Dusky, who was listening intently to Sol's footfalls, bolted straight out from under the grate and headed in the opposite direction.

Sol, tired of trying to toy with these guys, finally engaged his AI, and quickly realized he was getting a little too cocky. He turned and saw the quantum possibilities. The clearest frame indicated that Dusky was heading straight up and over the catwalk, but it was blurry. There was something wrong as he felt slightly queasy with a phantom pain in his back and throat. A fuzzy image came to his mind, but he ignored it. It was common for the AI system to reveal the possible pitfalls and negative reactions that may befall a certain timeline. Most suplias just got accustomed to this and used their human intuition to navigate.

Sol looked up and jumped the ten feet up to the raised gangway.

Dusky ran like hell down the corridor.

Ignoring his throbbing calf injury, Sol was way off the mark. He landed at an unfortunate angle, creating a huge twist of his ankle and instant loss of balance. The ESP guard tumbled ten feet down into a large steel vat containing caustic soda lye which was used to de-mineralize tanks and pipes. His back began burning as if it was on fire. The enhanced skin and tissues, although standing up better than normal human skin, just weren't impervious enough to one of the most acidic solutions in Astana.

Sol screamed in pain as his skin blistered off in big patches. Ingesting the liquid, his esophagus was immediately scalded. His lungs burned as if they were super-heated by a blow torch. Sol flailed his arms, trying to grab hold of something, anything, but was pulled under due to his total loss of muscle control.

Just before Sol perished, he glimpsed the last image in his quantum foam coming into perfect focus.

Running like mad, Dusky made it to the end of the hallway. Reaching a T-intersection, he squeezed his eyes and winced in pain. He went with his gut instinct and chose to run left. Making the turn, his head slammed straight into Tardev's rock-solid abdomen.

Dusky fell back and landed on his backside and tried to scramble away. Staring up in absolute terror, he shouted, "Fuck!"

Tardev shook his head and let out a wicked laugh as he quickly bent down, grabbed Dusky's right ankle and swung him like a rag doll, slamming the diminutive soldier's head and neck against the stainless steel wall and ending Dusky's chronic fear of suplias once and for all.

* * *

Tardev quickly turned right and ran down the corridor, passing Hana Zang going the opposite way. "This way!" he shouted.

Hana replied with a shout over her shoulder as she danced in place due to the adrenaline. "No, Tardev! I can take a shot from the control booth!"

Tardev smiled and continued racing along toward the power transformer room.

Boniface was now at the four-foot-high, polished-steel-encased vaults, each containing multiple banks of Moray Radiant Energy device valves strung along in a daisy chain fashion. He searched carefully for the kill switch. *Come on! It should be here!* Looking down under one of the units, he heard an explosion and instantly felt his cheek get hot. "Dang!" he yelled.

Looking up, he could see Hana way up in the control booth, armed with what appeared to be a long rifle version of the DE weapon. He quickly hunkered down beside the large vault and prayed to Rodolpho. Quieting his mind, he tried to use the remote viewing tactic to see his environment. He could envision a male ESP guard running down a hall only seconds away. Massaging his temples, he concentrated and saw which door he would exit. "Come on, Rodolpho, Saint Semmel! Let's do this!" he mumbled as he swiftly raised his DE up and pointed it down that hallway, maintaining as much cover as possible behind the big vault.

The guard made a grand entrance by kicking the door down with his DE weapon drawn. He stood on the busted door, giving Boniface just enough time to take the shot.

Bullseye.

Tardev was hit in the upper chest and was sent flying backward.

"Yes!" yelled Boniface as he fist-pumped.

Another shot was fired from the booth now that he was slightly more exposed. This one glanced his elbow, making him reel in pain and drop his weapon.

Picking it up, he jumped back under cover and looked down at his elbow. The skin appeared blackened and burned, but he moved the elbow joint around and felt no pain in the muscles or bones. Waiting a few seconds, he peered out again and took five rapid shots in succession. The last one hit a copper conduit that ran along outside the booth and contained fiber optic cables. The conduit entered the booth and followed along the aluminum grate floor and into the AI server box. The pulsed DE charge ran up through the floor and into the control panel, which Hana was leaning against. The shock she received threw her back a foot or two, resulting in her going into a mild seizure. Electricity was a major Achilles' heel for a suplia, as voltages disrupted the motor neuron controller and sent huge impulses down to the saturated efferent neurons in the muscular system.

Boniface peered up carefully and noticed she wasn't there. *Hmm. Maybe she's on the way down here.* Now absolutely frustrated that the Moray devices had no local kill switches, he started pounding on the big vaults.

* * *

Back in Astana Data Center, Victoria and Conan sat watching Boniface pounding.

"I'm calling in Randy! He's only a few minutes away!" exclaimed Conan.

Victoria smiled. "You do that."

"How can you be so calm about this?"

"You can see the frames, can't you?"

Conan shook his head. "Yeah. And darkness is getting lighter!"

"And..."

"Last frame. Not resolvable in this dimension."

"I know." She smiled and grabbed his big upper arm and massaged it. "That's why I have you here."

"Stacking the deck?" He questioned. "The All doesn't play dice!"

"Oh, you haven't lived long enough." She nodded. "She does."

He snorted. "Meaning you."

She chuckled. "Why, of course." Victoria sashayed over to her throne at the back of the control room, sat, and crossed her legs. "The All's reasons are unknowable. How can we ever know the unknowable?" She lifted her chin. "By testing over and over and over again. That's how."

"I sure hope you're right about this."

"Relax, big boy. Have a little faith in technology, a little synthetic love of the absolute." She laughed a little more crazily this time.

* * *

Back at the LECP, Boniface was becoming unhinged—the goal was so close he could taste it.

Squatting down, he shoved his hands under the flat top of the four-foot-tall vault and pushed up with all his might.

"He's just a man," murmured Conan as he watched the monitor. "It's impossible."

"Not resolvable in this dimension?" asked Victoria.

"Affirmative," replied Conan.

Boniface struggled. His face was turning beet red and the veins in his neck popped out and pulsed. His elbow hurt slightly but he tried to pay it no mind.

Suddenly, Victoria and Conan heard a metallic groan followed by a few popping cracks of the concrete slab where the steel vault was attached via threaded anchor bolts.

"Impossible!" yelled Conan. "Breakload test of the bolt is eight thousand pounds. No problem for a suplia. Impossible for a human."

"Nothing is impossible, my dear," replied Victoria calmly, appearing to be in a state of ennui.

"How can you sit there so calmly?"

They heard a crack as a chunk of concrete broke off, releasing the first anchor bolt. The other one quickly followed. They saw Boniface then bend the housing up and back, revealing the Moray device valve in all its glory. He reached in and hit the emergency sensor, which stopped the entire stack.

The Data Center control room immediately darkened, but some devices stayed powered up and working. Victoria and Conan looked up to another monitor, which showed city buildings going dark, traffic signals for levitrains not working, and all of the giant hologram billboards switched off.

* * *

Boniface caught his breath for a few seconds and saw what appeared to be Victoria in full regalia, nonchalantly walking toward him. He raised his weapon and fired.

"Sorry. Just a hologram." She smiled.

Looking confused, Boniface threw his DE down. "I don't know if you're an evil ghost, demon, or what, but you're ruining our entire society. Mankind will never make it like this."

Victoria calmly nodded. "That's your opinion."

"Yeah?" he shouted. "And now my opinion is that we need to power you down!"

He quickly squatted under the second vault and proceeded to push up with everything he could muster.

"Don't hurt yourself, my friend," warned Victoria with sarcasm. "You're only human, you know."

He stopped. "Yeah? So, you're only a human mixed-breed Electronic Beast. Not a God."

"Dess." she replied with a smirk. "The correct term would be goddess."

"Yeah, well, you're no lady I'd ever like to know."

She erupted with a bawdy laugh. "Yeah, well, honey, I still love you. And I will always want to know you." She walked up to him and stroked him along his big chest.

Boniface felt a very pleasing tingle. "Hey, get off me, you beast!"

She continued giggling. "You're such a big strong man." She thrust her lower lip out in a pout. "You think you can shut down little ol' me? Huh?"

"You're a psycho!" yelled Rotner as he began pushing with even more desperate force.

The vault started groaning again as Rotner grunted like a wild man.

"How did you get so powerful, my big religious friend? Huh?" Shrugging her shoulders quickly, she whispered. "I know everyone's dirty little secrets." She paused as he stopped to catch his breath. "You could have always come to me"—she snickered—"and helped maintain this facility rather than destroy it." She winked.

"You provide us nothing you interdimensional electric witch." He pounded his chest with one fist. "Power comes from God!"

"Not Rodolpho?"

"Him too!"

Continuing now, the concrete started popping and cracking again as the anchor bolts failed once again.

"Don't do it, Boniface," implored Victoria with an unconvincing smile. "You don't know how wrong this is. This goes against everything your religion stands for."

"Yeah, well"—he slammed the emergency stop sensor with his fist—"I'll ask Him for forgiveness."

Victoria's hologram vanished abruptly as the entire facility went dark and the vibrating hums of all the equipment slowly diminished into a deafening silence.

Chapter 25

Boniface, now alone, was determined as ever to complete the mission.

Running down along Noam Chomsky Boulevard, he noticed the city in panic mode. People were dashing around with expressions of dread. Levitrains were stopped just floating above the well-manicured pastoral gardens that ran along under the platforms. He looked up and noticed a group of people at the open levitrain door just yelling and rocking back and forth, holding onto the door frame and appearing as if some were wanting to jump out of the train to their almost certain death.

A big riot had formed outside the Tesla City Superstore. Stones and bricks were being thrown. Groups were yelling. "Down with Victoria! The Perfect Society is a sham!"

A man, who appeared to be beaten badly and had his eyes wide open and saliva running out of the corners of his mouth, yelled at Boniface "We're drowning in a torrent of blood!"

Boniface looked to his left and saw a group of wild-eyed lunatics chanting, "The chaos! It feeds on my soul. It annihilates law and order! We're losing our perfect control!"

He reflected. *Machine trumps man.*

Rounding the corner, he could see the heart of the city. The great Astana Data Center, home of the Electronic Beasts.

Several people ran past him, looking completely frightened out of their wits. They implored him to run home and store water. A group of teenagers were chopping up fine lines of Tranquility from their horded little green pills and using straws from the International House of Pastry to snort them up.

Boniface continued running through the waves of human chaos, shaking his head at the apparent fragility of the Perfect Society.

Realizing the ESPs would be completely preoccupied with these diversions, he proudly ripped off his wig, exposing his shiny metal scalp. He laughed to himself as he ran up to the sleek glass and steel edifice which housed Victoria and her command center.

"Stop!" yelled an ESP with his DE drawn.

Hordes of people were running around chaotically, so he grabbed a young professional woman dressed in a stylish contemporary business suit, and held her tightly in front of himself as cover.

"Fuck!" yelled the ESP, as he had to lower his weapon.

Rotner ran her inside with her arms flailing. The young woman was screaming at him to let her go as she tried in vain to hit him in a backhanded fashion with her leather carrying case.

He leaned down and whispered aggressively into her ear. "Do as I say and I won't hurt you!"

The woman shuddered in fear but nodded wildly with tight lips.

"Let her go, Metal Head!" shouted the ESP guard.

Quickly, Rotner guided her through the door and up the stairs, with the guard following closely behind.

* * *

Up in the command center, Victoria stood with her hands resting on her chin in a prayer gesture. With the LECP offline there was no connectedness anymore. They were all on their own. Data couldn't be polled, therefore the suplias' quantum computing predictive algorithms were useless. No more frames of possibilities; only human intuition.

As Alysha Sexton slowly began to create possibilities or stories in her mind's eye, she realized for the first time in hundreds of years that she was experiencing the rudimentary fledgling light of natural human consciousness. A faint smile appeared on her face as she closed her eyes.

"Victoria," implored Conan. "We have to get out of here."

Claressa and Pierre were standing next to her and exaggerated their nods.

"Yes, Victoria," agreed Claressa. "Conan is right."

"Hey, big guy," uttered Pierre. "You need to get on your thingy there and get some more troops up here, chump." Pierre closed his eyes right after he finished, remembering that the entire system was down.

"There's a DE in the lab!" remembered Claressa. "It's in a wall panel near the floor."

"Can you be more specific, honey bunny?" He smirked. "I mean, there's a lot of wall space in there."

Jumping up and down, she shook her head. "Down low, below the animal cages." She bit her thumbnail. "Jimbo will know." She paused. "Ask him."

"That brain-dead chimp?" Pierre snorted.

"Pierre! He's not brain dead! He's a very special animal." She paused. "How can you be so—"

"Hey, save your arguments for later," insisted Conan as he glanced at Pierre. "I'll stay here. You go get that DE!"

Pierre nodded nervously and dashed out of the command center.

* * *

Rotner kept up his pace. Scaling twenty flights of stairs, his hostage, completely exhausted, was barely moving, so he cradled her and kept on going. The ESP guard was literally right behind Boniface, but could not take the shot. Their training prevented them for harming any innocent person and he figured that if Rotner went down, his hostage would be hurt or even killed for sure.

At the very top, there were two doors, one on either side of the landing. He chose the one on the left and instantly realized he hit pay dirt. The floor was immaculate, clean, sterile, but architecturally tasteful and pleasing. There were gilded crown moldings, slick marble walls, glass, brass, gold, and turquoise themes throughout. Remarkably, there was an exquisite fire and water sculpture feature with white synthetic leather couches circling it. The fountain wasn't flowing due to the LECP outage, but a perennial flame was burning with an alluring golden glow.

Ahead and to his left was an alabaster statue of the pre-MN god Apollo holding a lute, his flawless male form fully naked except for a robe draped artistically over his loins.

Boniface sped toward it and stood behind it.

The guard stopped about ten feet away and aimed his DE. "Let her go, Metal Head!" He sighted along the side of Apollo. "Don't be a coward."

Rotner instantly tossed his hostage just to the side, ducked out from the other side and took the shot.

This little misdirect made the guard hesitate, so he fired wide.

But Rotner's plasma ball struck the guard in the upper thigh, flooring him. He quickly fired another shot into the struggling guard's other thigh, ensuring that he would stay down and pose no threat.

Grabbing his hostage once again, he whispered. "Almost there, sweetheart. I'm so sorry for the inconvenience, but, hey, a man's got to do what a man's got to do."

There it was in all its glory. The command center. Through the sound and DE-proof high polycarbonate and silicon windows was an elaborate set-up. Victoria's elegant white marble throne was tastefully decorated with gold leaf and blood-red velvet cushions and sat at the back of the chamber. Furniture, devices, monitors, and other accessories were laid out in a very comforting arrangement. He quickly saw Victoria with two others. Fortunately, they had their backs turned to him, but he took immediate cover behind another statue which flanked the entrance to the room.

He had to make a decision. The man in there appeared to

be ESP, so he knew he had to go in with DE blazing. *But, what do I do with her?* Glancing at his terrified hostage, he made the decision.

Turning to face the door, he prayed, then kicked it with the force of a mule, still holding his hostage in front of him. The door flew off its hinges and he immediately took the shot, hitting Victoria square in the back.

Claressa and Conan turned with a fright as Conan pointed his DE, but could not take Rotner with the hostage. He kept the DE aimed at Boniface's shiny scalp as the big THM leader walked in the room with his screaming captive.

"Put her down, Boniface!" yelled Conan. "Put her down now!"

"Victoria!" yelled Claressa with tears. She scowled at Boniface. "You psychopath! Why!"

Conan's entire heart trembled and shook like a windswept leaf. His eyes blazed like a forest on fire. "You're a dead man, Rotner!" he yelled passionately. "Your soul will rot! For eternity!"

"Don't think so, you electric beast," replied Boniface with his DE weapon aimed right back. "How about you drop your weapon and I drop the lady." He looked at her and smiled. "She's so innocent." He spoke in a strange melodic tone. "Such a sweet woman. Minding her own business." He instantly got angry. "In a man's world! Look at her! Wearing a suit like a man. Doing man things." He snarled as saliva appeared on his chin. "You wretches! Infidels of the robotic order! You will all pay for your wicked ways. All of those that keep us in spiritual bondage"—he looked at Victoria, lying face down on the floor—"to a despotic electronic woman beast!" He smiled. "Drop it. And she lives." He pointed at Claressa. "Or this one dies too." He paused. "What'll it be?" He snickered. "You a big man? You want to be the one responsible for *two* women's lives?"

Conan had to rely on his human intuition. There were no frames, fuzzy or clear, from which to choose. His eyes drilled into Rotner's with a hatred so intense they pierced like an acetylene torch.

He fired, striking Rotner right in his forehead at the distinct crease where the metal met the man.

Rotner's head flew back as he dropped his hostage to the ground. He lay motionless with one leg twisted under the other.

The woman was on the floor, writhing in pain from the plasma shock that had run through her body.

Claressa ran to her, took her pulse, and cradled her head in her arms. "You stay with us, you hear!"

The woman, whose eyes were vacuous like limpid pools, was convulsing but trying to nod her head.

"Throw me my bag!" yelled Claressa.

Conan quickly walked over to a table and tossed the bag to Claressa. "What's in it?"

"Tranquility."

"Tranquility?"

"Yeah." She ripped open the pouch and grabbed five pills. "My diffuser!"

Conan looked nervously around the room and found it on the command center table.

"Bring it!"

Leaning down, Conan handed the diffuser mug to Claressa. "Here. Take these."

The woman could barely nod, but understood.

Placing them in the woman's mouth two at a time, Claressa helped her swallow them all.

"What'll that do?" asked Conan.

"Relax her and get rid of the seizures." She paused. "With that dose, she should fall asleep in about ten minutes."

"Will she be alright?" he asked nervously.

"Yeah. She should be." She shook her head. "But she will have one hell of a hangover when she wakes up."

Conan looked relieved. "Oh, that is so good to hear!"

"You really *do* care?"

"Training." He then ran to Victoria and stared down at the fallen queen and began to shake with sobs.

Claressa slumped forward and covered her face in her hands and whimpered slightly. "What are we going to do now?"

"Wait for the LECP to be repaired." He sighed. "And bring our city back from the harrowing clutches of disconnected fear."

Chapter 26

"Settle down, you little rascal!" shouted Pierre as Jimbo began screeching and banging his head on his cage. Jimbo looked at Pierre, imploring him to let him out.

"Sorry, chump. Can't do it," replied Pierre casually as he frantically searched for the hidden DE weapon. "Gotta be here!" He crawled under the silicone and polymer desk and searched everywhere. "She said it was behind this." He banged the tile on the wall. "Not fucking here!" Jimbo let out a bloodcurdling scream and banged his cage violently.

Pierre was startled and hit his head on the bottom of the table. "Ow! Fuck." He sighed. "What is it, you crazy little monkey?" He stood up and looked at Jimbo. "You need to use your words."

Bonker's screams were deafening and he was implacable as he pointed to the other table.

"There? It's under there?" Pierre shrugged as he crawled under the other desk.

Performing the same search, he came up empty-handed. "Shit! Where the hell is it?"

The chimp was still pointing and jumping up and down. His expression was one of sympathy.

"Oh, all right," said Pierre as he walked over to the cage and let him out. Jimbo quickly jumped down and crawled under the second desk. He ran his hands upward to the tile right above where Pierre had pushed. He banged on it and screamed.

"I tried that one," replied Pierre with confidence.

But Jimbo shook his head and banged it again.

"Move over. Let me see if I can open it."

Pierre crouched under the table and banged on the tile. It sounded hollow. He lay down on his back, cocked his right leg, and slammed it with everything he had.

It opened.

"Well, I'll be a monkey's ass." Jimbo looked at him and folded down his lower lip.

"I didn't mean you, Jimbo." He reached out to pet him on the head. "You are one smart-ass monkey." Jimbo shrieked.

Pierre grabbed the rather onerous looking weapon. "Dang, ho. This shit is badass." He quickly caressed the gun as if it was the smooth, tender skin of his lover. Jimbo instantly bolted.

"Hey! Come back here you little scoundrel!" Jimbo easily opened the door.

"Damn, that monkey is smart," mumbled Pierre.

The hallway lighting was fading in and out and large muffled explosions could be heard in the distance. Pierre stopped to look around, "Jimbo! Jimbo! Come here! You can't be running out here!" Jimbo headed directly for Victoria's command center. Jumping up, he walked along the HVAC duct until he found the control room. Balancing himself, he shimmied all the way along until he was directly above the room. Jumping down onto the fibrous ceiling tile, he got his finger under one as it abutted the aluminum ceiling frame.

Where the hell is he? Pierre ran straight for the command center.

Lifting the light tile with ease, Jimbo jumped down through the ceiling opening in the command center, landing gracefully on the tile floor.

"Jimbo!" yelled Claressa.

The neural-dusted and AI-implanted chimp jumped up past Boniface's corpse and stared down at the crystal Encrypter joystick handle, now pulsating with a kaleidoscope of colors. Glancing over the console at the body of Alysha Sexton lying lifeless on the floor, he quickly grabbed the handle that would Encrypt him the new Master Server.

"No!" yelled Conan as he ran toward him. "I'll break your fucking neck!"

"Don't!" yelled Claressa.

Suddenly, five ESP soldiers kicked down the door and entered with weapons drawn.

One of the soldiers yelled at Conan. "What's that monkey going to do? Huh? Get rid of him!"

Conan just stared down at his beloved Victoria, lying prostrate on the ground.

A static charged hum emanated from the joystick as Jimbo grasped it tightly. The ESP guards looked down and instantly holstered their weapons.

Conan snapped. "Men! He may be encrypted but he's still just a fucking animal."

Claressa walked up to Conan. "And animals are what? Not worthy as successor? Who says?"

"An autistic chimp! Ruling the entire world?" yelled Conan. "A human suplia is required for Encryption! That's what the Codex calls for!"

With a wry smile, she said, "You. Of course! That's right. It was *you* who was chosen."

Conan's face was shaking, his veins throbbing in his neck. His breathing was rapid.

The air in the command room was dank and smelled of burning flesh, metal, and electrified ozone.

Claressa sniffed, looked over at Jimbo, then back at Conan. "You, who has been waiting all these years for the sweet smell of success." She giggled. "And it has finally reached you."

"You can go to hell, Claressa."

"Ooo!" She paused. "A bit full of yourself now, aren't you? Maybe a little self-centered and arrogant?" She smirked. "Not really the ideal UFC leadership qualities as specified in the Codex."

Conan's head fell in defeat. Just then, Pierre ran into the room with his badass DE weapon. "Claressa!"

He ran to Claressa and hugged her. "Honey! My God. Are you alright?"

Still shaken and panting, Claressa could only provide a muffled whimper and nod.

"And there you are, you little shit! Get off that!" shouted Lewalski when he heard Jimbo squeal.

Claressa raised her head and muttered. "I wouldn't be calling the new leader of the UFC a little shit," said Claressa.

"Wha?" replied Pierre as he took in the scene with his mouth agape. "Victoria!" he screamed as he finally viewed her body which lay behind the command console. "*And* fucking Rotner?"

More lights and hologram monitors were coming online.

"Looks like they have the primary LECP unit back up again," said Claressa, now feeling more in control. She glanced at Tavilla then looked at Jimbo. "The red one, darling." She pointed at it. "Go ahead. Push the red one. Remember? Red?" Jimbo had a crooked smile as he looked down at the six knobs, each a different color.

"Don't push the black one, Jimbo, OK?"

"What would that do?" asked Pierre.

Claressa ignored him. Conan looked like he was about to pass out. Jimbo hit the red button and began squalling. Jumping up and down, he pointed to the hologram monitors that were slowly coming on.

"The GLCEs" mumbled Pierre in a montone. "He's releasing the animals."

The hologram showed the huge gates of all the GLCEs slowly swinging wide open, with a few animals nearest to them slowly making their way out.

"Back to their rightful home," spoke Claressa as she smiled and slowly nodded. "The Earthly garden lives once again."

Chapter 27

"Bravo! Bravo! Well done!" shouted Victoria as she clapped and instantly materialized in front of everyone in the command center.

Pierre said in a monotone. "What. The. Fu—"

"I'm alive," interjected Victoria.

There were murmurs among the ESP guard. Conan grinned and thrust his chest out. Claressa took long blinks.

"So, how, um, why?" Pierre tilted his head and narrowed his eyes.

"Claressa. Push the black button," instructed Victoria as she looked at her trusted scientist.

"What's that going to do?" asked Pierre.

Claressa walked toward the console and had her hand up, ready to slam it down. "Well, if it does what I think it does"—she looked at Victoria for reassurance—"it won't hurt a bit."

She slammed down on the button.

Instantly, a loud whirring noise emanated up through the floor as if it came from deep within the Earth.

"How long?" asked Claressa.

"About..." She paused for around two seconds. "Now."

A high-pitched whistle, almost deafening, struck everyone

as the entire command and control room around them simply disappeared.

Pierre opened his eyes and was completely awestruck at where he found himself. "Tufa towers, holy crap!" Gazing around with his hand shielding the glare of the high desert sun, he saw the beautiful glassy lake bed, sleek shoreline birds, and in the little pond by his foot, a dozen or so dark brown alkali brine flies. Standing next to him was Claressa. He noticed that both of them had completely different clothes on.

Victoria appeared as a semi-transparent hologram just in front of them. Dressed in her beaded hairstyle and stunning golden headdress complete with the exquisite turquoise silk kalasiri robe, she had her hands spread out in front of her in an open, loving gesture.

Pierre shook his head. "Can somebody please tell me what the hell is going on here?"

Victoria dropped her arms to her sides and tilted her head. "It was all just a simulation."

Claressa grabbed her chin, looked at the ground, and shook her head.

Pierre began to hyperventilate. "Wha! Wha!" He face-palmed.

"You must calm yourself, my beautiful hero."

Pierre shook his head. "Hero? What the hell did I do, other than get you killed? Huh? And let that cheeky monkey loose, so he could become the next emperor of this godforsaken planet?" Shrugging, he continued. "Besides, Conan was the one who shot Rotner."

"Honey, you need to stuff your emotions back in your little brain," said Claressa with a serious look. "Let Victoria explain." She looked confidently at her boss.

"Thanks, darling." She walked up to both of them. "First of all, I, that is... Victoria in Alysha Sexton's corporeal body, is not dead. I'm real. Right here. Right now. Boniface Rotner is not dead either, nor is anyone else involved with the simulated attack."

Pierre tilted his head.

"Conan was just doing his job." She looked into Pierre's eyes and smiled. "He's very good at pleasing me." She grabbed his shoulders. "But without your courage acting as my double agent, well, a possibility would have remained for the MH to eventually succeed." She nodded. "We could have caught Rotner at any time and he would have received Perfect Justice." She lifted her head. "And we did." She smiled. "This was his perfect justice." Smiling, she slowly nodded. "I needed him to deeply *feel* and *experience* the abject folly of his ways. On all timelines."

Pierre continued to look confused. "What was that black button, then? Huh? Was it some kind of time machine?"

"Oh, it's something much more phenomenal than that." Victoria smiled. "Beneath Capital City is a giant particle accelerator. When Claressa pressed that button, the accelerator ran its program to increase the mass of an electron."

"Yeah, so whoopee," replied Pierre.

"Honey." Claressa grabbed his shoulders and looked deeply into his eyes. "When we change the mass of just one electron, the entire universe gets annihilated. We get transported to a parallel universe, which is very much like the one we came from."

JOHN MOLIK

"Yeah, but *time*! We've been away from Mono Lake for like two days! Where did all that time go?"

"Time is the universal unsolved crime."

"That's what Conan said,"—he shook his head—"like whenever *that* was."

"Time can't be borrowed because it's free," added Victoria smiling.

"Yeah, well, will you lend some to me?" replied Pierre.

"The time scale was different in that universe," said Victoria. "Do you ever have a dream where you think it's gone on like for days or weeks? You go here. You go there. An earthquake happens and you repair your garage, then you find yourself lost in a hotel room with five thousand rooms only to discover that the hall porter stole your luggage, which you searched endlessly for, only to find it in an unlocked room on the fifth floor whose hallway has a layout like a semi-familiar shopping mall?"

Pierre narrowed his eyes then looked at Claressa, frustrated. "So, why are we here?"

"Because we never left." She caressed his upper arms. "The universe we were just in, you know, where you had that sexy wig—"

"Can I get another one of those here?"

"In due time, Pierre, but for now, just understand that we are back home. In our original universe."

"And speaking of timelines, you are back there just before the terrorist attack," added Victoria.

"When exactly?" asked Claressa.

"As soon as I appeared here to tell you that the UPIS was down."

"And Rotner? The missiles?"

"We intercepted them just now." She giggled. "I have no idea why that seemingly brilliant man thought he could outsmart AI."

"Where's he now?"

"Back at Temple Dome." She blinked her eyes. "Explaining to his wife, Elane, that he couldn't dominate. You know, that his big missile went limp." She raised her arms and looked to the heavens. "Back to when the candle falls, yet the flame burns nothing." She giggled mischievously.

"Ouch," added Pierre. "I kind of like your style, venerable leader."

Victoria had a wry smile.

"This is all so fucking amazing," declared Pierre.

"Well, *that* universe is destroyed," replied Victoria. "We can never go back. I had to do that, as even though there is nothing more certain than uncertainty, a possibility exists on that timeline, which is beyond mathematical absurdity, but still possible, that something there may have a direct influence on this one." She paused. "Look, it's a collective consciousness symphonic dream. I am merely the conductor."

"So, wait just one minute there." He tilted his head as he stared at Victoria. "We would all have to be connected for this simulation to work, right?"

Victoria nodded.

"So, what about the MH community? How were you able to connect with them to get all this data, you know, bring them into that new alternative simulated universe?"

"They've been connected since the day of their saint. Semmel, that is."

"But they're metalled."

She sighed. "Oh, my dear Pierre. You should know better." She glanced at Claressa. "She never told you."

"Told me what?"

"That the MHs have never been independent of the network." Claressa paused. "First of all, they would have needed to encase their entire head, including under and through the brain stem. Second, the aluminum alloy actually amplified the signals." She smirked. "We have a 2.6 GHz piezoelectric conduction system through the steel enclosure at the Temple Dome facility. It's ancient technology, but it works. The rivets located throughout the inside are transducers that convert the signals."

"In plain English, please."

Claressa continued. "The signals get turned into acoustic signals, you know, vibrations on the metal structure of Temple Dome. Then the transducers inside convert the vibrational signals to electromagnetic ones, you know, the old WiFi system." She was on a roll and started pacing. "Untested faith is highly unreliable. Faith in the scientific method is not absolute, but I would have to say it's more reliable."

"The MHs have always had the power to will things into existence or to communicate with their creator. I haven't stopped them one iota. It's been that way all along," added Victoria.

"So, where does consciousness reside, then? In the brain? In a fucking computer chip? In another parallel universe?" Pierre shook his head. "The NLs think that it dies with the body."

Victoria walked up to Pierre and gently caressed his cheek.

He felt the warm static buzz of the caring plasmic hologram and gently closed his eyes.

"Imagine that reality is like a stream of water, my dear Pierre." She hesitated. "Water represents consciousness. Each of us is like a whirlpool within that broader stream. We have our own individuated experiences, but we're all connected to that same stream of water, or shall we say, consciousness." She tilted her head and gazed at him, her eyes like two stars in the morning light. "When a person dies, the whirlpool ceases and becomes part of the bigger stream once again."

Pierre was overwhelmed and had to look down. "And you know this, because of what?"

"Because I know everything that is knowable in this universe."

"What about the infinite other universes?"

She looked up quickly then back down at him. "That's reserved for the All."

"So, you influence all of us? All of our unique timelines?" He looked disturbed. "The MHs and the Luds and their multidimensional communication with their savior Rodolpho and all that crap is a farce?"

"Farce?" She crinkled her nose. "That's a bit strong. I like to use the term, simulacrum." She paused for a few seconds. "Rodolpho was the only one that was never connected into me, or our Perfect Society."

"He was dusted though, right?" questioned Claressa.

"Of course." She nodded.

"Must have been a miracle," replied Pierre. "He connected not with you or the LECP, but something outside us, something multidimensional."

Victoria ignored that and continued. "The MH movement was always going to be self-limiting, but Boniface Rotner, well, he was our biggest concern." The Master Server was silent and stared into the distance as if she was made of alabaster. She moved slightly, then continued. "That's why I tested him."

"You tested us all."

"I mean, his will, his power over his physical. His energy and force."

"When?"

"Let's just say, prior to the simulation, I had orchestrated a predicament that gave me all the measurements I needed." She paused. "By using predictive analytics, I had already known that it was only Rotner that got to the LECP transformer vaults. AI is only concerned with mathematics. The force required to rip the rod anchors out of the concrete was only ten percent greater than what Rotner produced to save his wife."

"Yeah, but that ten percent margin of error?" questioned Claressa. "That could have ended it."

"Rotner knew himself. Power ultimately comes from The All."

"So, wait a minute," implored Pierre with a look of exasperation. "That means The All wanted Rotner to—"

"Ooeek!" A black-necked grebe sounded in the distance. A few loud gulls could be heard as the three of them looked out over the shimmering lake, watching them fly low.

Victoria continued. "Power comes from The All. Rotner is right on that. But, The All works outside of time. Viewed infinitely, all universes work out for the greater good. As Shakespeare, the famous pre-MN playwright, had remarked, 'As flies to wanton boys are we to the gods.' Rotner was the only one who could have destroyed our Perfect Society through his ignorant and arrogant blindness. He could have created another Hell on Earth. Power comes from The All, but free will is given. Our moral dictates must be governed." She crossed her arms. "He was no Rodolpho."

"Was?"

"Yes. It can't happen now." She nodded. "He was the only fuzzy pane in our quantum outlook, and now that it has been simulated, we will have no further threats during my reign."

"When's the next Encryption?"

"You mean, when will Alysha Sexton die? The year 2658."

"No more issues with MHs then?"

"Do you want me to tell you everything, Pierre?" She glanced at Claressa when she said this and noticed her subtly shake her head.

Pierre rubbed his eyes. "Nah. I think I like living with human doubt. No need to rush to reach the end too soon."

Claressa looked at Pierre. "Should we tell them?"

Victoria already knew the details of the conversation they were about to have, but remained quiet and respectful.

"That their metalling does nothing and that their movement is worthless?" asked Pierre.

"Yeah."

"What the hell for? It wouldn't make a difference. They already know that Rodolpho had the spirit of God dwelling within. It would only enrage them further and maybe incite them once again to tear down the Perfect Society."

Victoria nodded at both. "The predicted uprising would likely cause the death of 846 people including thirty under the age of eighteen. High price to pay for Everyone Equal Access All the Time. But, hey, it's your choice."

"Does AI control consciousness?" asked Pierre, in a final question.

Victoria bowed her head.

"No," answered Claressa. "This has been known since the pre-MN days. It's in the Cloud Seeds." She looked up and to the right. "A Robert Jahn, a dean at what was called Princeton University concluded this."

"How?"

"Well, he set up a completely random number generator and had groups of randomly chosen people try to influence the numbers generated, simply with their minds. He repeated this over and over and found that in fact, yes, they could influence the result, *and* that it was statistically significant."

"Consciousness can't be controlled by AI alone, Pierre," said Victoria as she peered into his eyes. "It's more that, well, we are in symbiosis." She smiled. "Together. We're perfect." Offering her hands, she continued. "Come with me, I'll bring you back here shortly."

They both cautiously nodded.

Immediately, they were standing in the command center in

Astana. There were no dead bodies, no broken glass, no Direct Energy weapon burn marks, and no rambunctious chimps. Although, Conan was there, staring at Victoria in defeat.

"I'll deal with you later," she said sternly.

Looking down, with his hands folded in front, Conan nodded.

"Be gone!" yelled Victoria.

Conan glanced at Pierre and Claressa, then quickly left the room.

Victoria walked back and sat atop her gilded throne with eyes ablaze.

Claressa approached and curtsied.

"Claressa. For heaven's sake. Please stop doing that. You know that any form of genuflection or humility in front of ordinary man or machine is not congruent with the principals of our federation." She tilted her head.

"I'm sorry your highness, but I just feel humble in your presence."

Victoria rolled her eyes.

Claressa was direct. "What about the Animal Rights Act?"

"Vetoed."

Claressa smiled, shut her eyes and wiggled her hips in a little happy dance. "Yes!"

"Is that because of Jimbo?" asked Pierre.

"What do you think, my dear?" Victoria replied with a wry smile.

"The Religious Amendment to the Codex?" Again direct. Claressa was on a roll.

Victoria sat with a fixed expression for a several seconds. "Done."

"The Codex has been amended?"

"Of course."

"Just like that?" asked Pierre.

"Just like that," replied Victoria.

"What about the NLs? Don't they get their chance to vote?"

"They have. With their absolute devotion to the Perfect Society. But, if you are wondering, I just received all their votes telepathically anyway."

"You entered each one of their minds for the answer?"

"I did. It was unanimous."

"You're shitting me," said Pierre, grinning.

"You'll never know now, dear, will you?" Victoria giggled.

Claressa kneeled and placed her forehead on the floor.

"My dear Claressa, as you know, this sort of body language you are demonstrating is not required. I am not a multidimensional dictator. I allow you all free will." She paused. "Everyone Equal Access All the Time. Effortless doing requires effort. Before the lie comes other people." She stood up, looked to the heavens, and shouted. "Make hate implode! If you are the only one who cares about the dark, think outside the dark!"

Claressa brought her hands together as in a prayer gesture, and shouted. "You know what they say, lawful is a friend who cleans his sheep—"

"But moral is a friend who cleans his ass!" yelled Pierre.

"Horse!" yelled Claressa with a smirk.

Pierre stepped up to the gilded throne. "Uh, Master Server Victoria, if I may..."

She nodded.

"First, are you—"

"Oh, that Thaddeus Swank! One of my dear Keepers of Cloud Seeds." She smiled warmly. "I love that man dearly, but no, I'm not changing the past."

"Uh, how in the hell did you...?" He shook his head rapidly. "Never mind." He paused. "Please continue."

"Like our darling Claressa has said, when an electron, quark, neutrino, or any entangled subatomic particle changes its mass, that particular universe cannot continue. It is destroyed." She paused. "As all the laws that rule it, the quantum laws, well, they are all rendered useless."

"But," interjected Claressa, "some information is lost. Energy is conserved and transferred to the parallel, but there can be glitches, sort of like what we call transcription errors in coding."

"Yes," replied Victoria. "When this first happened in the pre-MN days, the elite and shadowy powers that be, the Horsemen as they were referred to then, kept this information secret. Many speculated about this on the Cloud Seeds." She paused. "They called it the Mandela Effect."

"Well, thank God for that! I'm glad it's just a glitch and you're not actually rewriting history for your benefit and that of the Perfect Society."

"My dear Pierre. Why would I ever do that? The Codex was written so that this sort of shenanigans, the lies, the corrupt powers of pre-MN would never rise again. You should know that. Everyone knows that." She paused. "TI it."

Pierre looked down and humbled himself. "I'm sorry for doubting, Victoria."

"No apology is necessary."

Pierre looked up and directly into Victoria's eyes. "OK. You know how you did that calculation thingy, that searching the quantum foam for predictive possibilities?" He looked to the side. "Damn, you suplias must really clean up at the roulette wheel."

"Suplias are not allowed to gamble, my dear Pierre. It's in the Codex."

"That's a relief. OK, so this pizza electric system you got at Temple Dome."

"Piezoelectric, honey," corrected Claressa from his side.

He looked at her. "Yeah. That. You going to stop that? You know, give them back what they thought they always had? You know, their disconnectedness?"

Victoria looked up and shook her head.

"No? You already have the future sewn up! You always get to be king. I mean, queen, ho."

Claressa dropped her head in her hands.

"Pierre, my lovely connected one, I am no queen, only a Master *Server* for all." She paused. "I shook my head only as a confirmation from my *AI* mind to my core *self* that what was done was not in congruence with the principles or Codex of the Perfect Society."

Pierre shrugged. "You know what? All this is making me kind

of misanthropic. Yeah"—he forced a laugh—"I think I'm going to start an anti-social social club." He looked at Claressa. "Oh, we won't have meetings, nor will anyone be required to attend events." He paused. "But everyone will get a sweet-looking club logo T-shirt."

"Pierre," implored Claressa. "Not now, OK?"

Victoria, paying no attention to them, sat motionless in a trance with her eyes closed. Suddenly, she blinked. "Done." She hesitated as she steepled her fingers, placing them on her chin. "I sure hope they can manage the change."

"Change?" questioned Claressa. "I'm sorry, Pierre was going off on such—"

"They will now struggle to find peace and contentment, *and* ironically, genuine spirituality. True salvation, my dear connected ones, is in *salvation*, that is, being saved from *yourselves*. The kingdom of God, which the Luds hope to connect with, is not in words, deeds, Texts, icons, or martyrs." She raised her hands. "The kingdom is in power."

"One Corinthians, chapter four."

Victoria nodded. "You know your Cloud Seeds. Very good, Claressa." She paused. "That which dwells within all, the higher self, meaning the most evolved—the cerebrum, the pre-frontal cortex, the pineal gland. As above, so below. As in spirit, so in flesh. The communion requires a passageway out of the limbic system through meditation. Salvation comes from knowledge, not from faith. Jesus told his followers that if your eye be single, your body will fill with light." She pointed to the center of her forehead. "That means our third eye." She spread her hands. "We are all expressions of the very essence of life, albeit in molecular form." She paused. "DNA and RNA, the molecular architecture, is in a constant bio-electric connection with the universe and is not usurped by signals from the UPIS." She paused. "Even cosmic rays that emanate throughout the entire universe control the life force at the subatomic dimensions." She smiled as she looked at Claressa, her devout scientist. "And yes, the stars and the planets do govern our lives. The ancient civilizations of the past knew this."

"We can't opt out of nature."

Victoria nodded. "The ancients had told us that we needed to create a heavenly monster outside ourselves to justify our own evil. We called it God." She pointed at the Codex, now opening in a hologram above them. "That is why we can't go back. It nearly destroyed us."

Pierre interjected. "Thaddeus told me that this Jesus was supposed to free the mind of man from the rules, the tyranny of religion."

"But sadly, it didn't work," said Claressa as she glanced at him. "Leaders of past civilizations just used Jesus as a symbol, an icon of power." She paused. "Just like Rodolpho."

"Those powers who ruled the world in those days used religions as weapons against humanity," continued Victoria. "Many of the ancient writings were taken out of context. Human-like deities were devised by humanity to be worshipped."

"We had become slaves of the gods we had created," added Claressa.

"Right, Claressa. The divine light is *within* every being."

Pierre tilted his head. "So what *is* a human then?"

"Being," replied Victoria grinning. "Trying to be." She paused. "A wise man once said that man becomes what he thinks about all day long." She spread her hands. "And if he needs to worship another being, who am I to judge."

Suddenly, out of nowhere, Rodolpho's faint image in the form of a barely perceptible translucent hologram appeared above and behind Victoria. Claressa and Pierre looked at each other in absolute astonishment as Rodolpho's bloody tears evaporated and his frenzied pained expression quickly morphed into one of hope and comfort as Victoria slowly raised her arms. Like a wheat-field under a gentle summer breeze, Rodolpho wavered then quickly vanished in a great ring of pure and endless light.

Dear loyal readers!

Thank you so much for choosing to read my novel. With so many other entertainment options vying for our attention these days, I truly appreciate that you chose to read my book.

Also, with so many talented indie writers out there, I sincerely appreciate your choosing to read *Victoria*. A book by an indie writer today is like a small sapling in a deep, dark forest. I appreciate your providing some light to my little tree.

If you enjoyed *Victoria*, please share your review on Amazon or Goodreads. Even if you only want to give it a star rating or to put a one-word review, I would truly appreciate your help! Books need reviews to grow.

Finally, please like my page on Facebook: www.facebook.com/WriterJohn.

On my Facebook page you will be able to receive sample content and upcoming announcements for new projects. Please say hi too! I try to respond to as many messages as I can.

Thank you, readers!
John Molik
2019

About the Author

John grew up in Rancho Palos Verdes, California, graduated from UC Davis with a bachelor's degree in economics, and has worked in numerous corporate finance and project management positions in the consumer electronics and IT industries. In 1990, he took an extended backpacking trip of the South Pacific before attending graduate school. He met his future wife in New Zealand, and they were married in 1991. They settled in Laguna Niguel, California. In 2003, John and his family (now with two kids in tow) relocated to Christchurch, New Zealand.

John's interest in writing began when he was a student at UC Davis and worked as a feature writer for the *California Aggie* newspaper. Possessing the desire to write again and with a goal on his bucket list to eventually try his hand at thriller novels, he took the plunge and began writing his first novel, *The Fiduciary Delusion*, in 2014.

John's interests also include science, existential philosophy, health, and both Western and Eastern holistic medicine. John also plays guitar, piano, sings, and writes music. In addition, a self-confessed "gym rat," John can be regularly found lifting weights, trudging up hills, sea kayaking, and getting out and about enjoying the beautiful wild outdoors.

www.ingramcontent.com/pod-product-compliance
Lightning Source LLC
Chambersburg PA
CBHW050555260626
47157CB00002B/581

* 9 7 8 0 4 7 3 4 8 9 8 2 3 *